"Are You a Rake, Sir?"

Lord St. John eyed her and grinned. "Assuredly, I am, miss!"

Miss Beaumaris flashed him a brilliant smile and seemed not a whit put out. "Excellent! I have been on pins, you know, to meet one."

He raised his eyebrows. "I trust your governess and guardians are aware of this particular ambition?"

She tilted her nose loftily and actually winked. "Devil a bit!"

My lord, finally intrigued, almost choked on the last of his orange. "Setting aside your execrable language, young lady, am I to assume you actually enjoy the company of a dangerous gentleman like myself?"

Her response was quick. "Am I to assume that a hardened rake would actually represent himself as such to me? I have to suspect, dear sir, that you are an impostor."

He viewed her with a sudden dangerous and calculating air that made Cassandra's delectable bodice seem uncustomarily tight against her ribs and the soft, rounded flesh that it encased. For an instant she feared he might take her carelessly spoken words as a challenge. She shivered, and he seemed satisfied by her sudden response, for he permitted the tension to ease and grinned lopsidedly at her as though he'd scored a silent but indefinable point.

BOOK YOUR PLACE ON OUR WEBSITE AND MAKE THE READING CONNECTION!

We've created a customized website just for our very special readers, where you can get the inside scoop on everything that's going on with Zebra, Pinnacle and Kensington books.

When you come online, you'll have the exciting opportunity to:

- View covers of upcoming books

- Read sample chapters

- Learn about our future publishing schedule (listed by publication month *and author*)

- Find out when your favorite authors will be visiting a city near you

- Search for and order backlist books from our online catalog

- Check out author bios and background information

- Send e-mail to your favorite authors

- Meet the Kensington staff online

- Join us in weekly chats with authors, readers and other guests

- Get writing guidelines

- AND MUCH MORE!

**Visit our website at
http://www.zebrabooks.com**

BY WAY OF A WAGER

HAYLEY ANN SOLOMON

ZEBRA BOOKS
Kensington Publishing Corp.
http://www.zebrabooks.com

ONE

The penny blinked in the sunlight, causing Miss Cassandra Beaumaris to cease her humming and squint momentarily against the glare. The lilting notes faded into a crisp silence as she shaded her eyes and reached among the jumble for her fringed parasol. Sad to say, it was lying in a most lamentable heap together with her discarded gloves and the delightful confection of chip straw created personally for her by Miss Peeples of Bond Street.

Curiously, she plucked the coin carefully from its hiding place in the sand. She tilted it in her palm, quite oblivious to its mostly sandy state. It glinted in the mild sun and felt disappointingly light across her palm. It was not an ancient Roman artifact, then, despite her rather ridiculous hopes. Still, one never could tell with such things.

It was only last year, after all, that the Marquis of Rensford's eccentric mistress had blithely taken a pickax to a very fine Roman mosaic. She'd been digging the foundation of a new hothouse at the time, and the damage to the mosaic was said to be irreparable. The laughingstock of the ton it had been, and the marquis was reported to be furious. Cassandra chuckled naughtily as she imagined his face. Of course, a gently bred young lady such as herself should not have known—let alone reflected—upon such matters. Cassandra did not care a whistle. How thankful she was to have servants who gossiped!

She sighed. The day was conspiring against her. Even her line, dangling artfully into the crystal water, refused to yield an obliging catch. She reeled in the rod and threw it carelessly on the pile with her bonnet. Then she tipped back her head and squinted at the sky.

It was later than she'd first calculated, for the sun was casting telltale shadows, and the afternoon's warmth was rapidly fading to a gentle chill. Natty should have been back long since. A small smile of tolerant vexation crossed Miss Beaumaris's deliciously curved lips. Scatty Natty, she'd scold, to strand her mistress without a suitable companion. Still, she did not care over much, for she knew the maid was enjoying her half day off. The Greensides' stable boy no doubt offered a powerful reason for permitting time to elapse so unpardonably.

Cassandra sighed again as a sudden fit of the dismals threatened to descend upon her normally light-spirited person. It was unlike her to grow mopish, though the strange pang for a romantic encounter of her own took her by surprise. Nonsense! Hoydenish nonsense! She grimaced and retrieved her feet from the sparkling, cool water in which they dangled. No one could deny that they were extremely dainty little feet, nor yet that she presented the most charming picture of unruffled innocence. Miss Beaumaris, however, was oblivious to these interesting facts. If truth be told, she was more concerned with the delicate task of emptying sand from her new kid slippers than in cutting any sort of dash. She laid her souvenir down and shook out each damp shoe with vigor.

She missed the long, tall shadow that fell across the rows of ripened cornfields and onto the bramble bush close to her side. Her lips parted merrily as she idly resumed her tuneful warbling of the sun-dappled day. Natty would not, she hoped, be too much longer.

Her basket was quite filled with blackberries, and the ripening fruit seemed suddenly inviting to a young lady who'd eaten only a very light luncheon some hours before. She bent over her basket and tucked in with appetite. Delicious! She licked her lips blithely at the first satisfying sweetness and bent once more for her coin.

"Will you have good luck, my pretty?"

She startled and swung around to face quite the most devastating gentleman she had yet encountered. Not that her experience at the tender age of seventeen had been all that vast, but only the veriest nodcock would not take this paragon to be a lord of the first stare. His beaver was set rakishly at an angle, and his buckskins were a perfect match to his well-toned thighs and crisp, starched shirt. He held the reins lightly, and from the corner of her discerning eye, she noticed that his beast was an Arabian stallion, deep chestnut, and at least seventeen hands high.

"Beg pardon?"

The vision looked amused. He pointed to her hand, which was tightly closed around the half-forgotten coin.

"See a penny, pick it up; all day long, you'll have good luck."

Enlightenment dawned, and she emitted a gurgle of laughter. "Oh, this, sir?" She unclutched her fist. "I had hopes of it being an ancient Roman relic, but I rather fear it is more like to be nothing at all out of the common way."

"Unlike it's finder."

Cassandra did not pretend to misunderstand. Instead, she blushed delightfully and scolded the gentleman for his forward ways.

He nodded in agreement, but his eyes twinkled unrepentantly.

"Forward? Very likely! Nonetheless, I retain hopes that your little penny will bring you luck."

For no particular reason, she felt herself coloring under the stranger's steady regard. Her hair was tumbling down her face in the most unruly mop, and her bonnet was too far under the pile for her to surreptitiously retrieve it. Further, the half-eaten berry was staining her fingers with its juices, and she had nowhere but the sides of her gown to wipe the sticky mess. She popped the remainder into her mouth and swallowed hard.

The gentleman coughed, and she had the most lowering suspicion that he was smothering a laugh. She glared up at him. The tips of his boots gleamed in perfect order, and there was not a hint of the disarray in his dress that was so apparent in her own. She became suddenly aware of the absence of her slippers as she felt a small pebble dig into her toe. She blushed crimson and tucked her feet firmly under the folds of her gayest morning gown. To her annoyance, she was perfectly certain the nonpareil understood her dilemma and was most intolerably amused.

"Over there, I fancy." He pointed to the rock where she had lain the offending footwear out to dry. She was not impressed.

"I am aware of that, sir!" She felt indignation rising and added a rider for good measure. "I must say, I think it perfectly horrid of you to point them out!"

The stranger threw back his head and laughed. The sound was deep and brimful with enjoyment.

"Shall I get them for you?"

"At once!" His amusement deepened, and Cassandra realized she had fallen into his trap.

"You horrid man! No! Best leave them there. I shall rely on your chivalry not to so much as peek at my toes!"

Despite the severity of her tone, Cassandra felt herself unbend. A tiny, traitorous smile found its way to the edges of her cherry-red lips.

There was an answering gleam in the gentleman's eye as he took one foot out of the stirrups and leaped effortlessly to the ground. His generous mouth curved as he made her a bow with mock elegance. Miss Beaumaris affected a decorous curtsy, then dimpled at him.

"What a fine looking animal, sir."

She patted the horse, then drew out a lump of sugar from the folds of her modish dress. The offering was well received.

Pleased, she turned to her unexpected companion. He seemed bent on removing his riding gloves and divesting himself of his whip. They joined the pile of her haphazard assortments, and though she raised her eyebrows somewhat inquiringly, she made no demur.

He shook his head. "You are far too beautiful, you know."

Cassandra blushed and wondered rather guiltily why ever she had allowed her maid to stray so far.

"Too beautiful, sir? You tease! I know I am not at all the thing! Miss Hillsborough says . . ." She found herself drawn to answer, but thought, rather fleetingly, of his strong masculine scent and his deep, dark eyes of velvet. They were compelling, and she felt herself shamefully captivated.

"Miss Hillsborough says what?"

Her eyes faltered. She suddenly reflected on the propriety of discoursing on Miss Hillsborough's views on the preferences of the gentleman sex. Her companion noticed the confusion with some amusement, but his brows took on a forbidding aspect.

"Do you always wander footloose and unaccompanied across private domain?"

The dreamy look deserted her, and her eyes flashed. The man was insulting with his innuendoes.

"I'll have you know, sir, that I am not alone! I'm sure I know well enough what behooves a lady! Natty, my maid, accompanies me and will, I am perfectly certain, arrive shortly." She crossed her fingers as she made this last dubious announcement and hoped fervently that it was true.

The gentleman let this certainty pass but was not altogether deceived. Before he had a chance to ask her, rather reasonably, where this absentee young servant was hiding, he was faced with yet another attack.

"And, I'll have you know, if I am on private property, it is at least my own! The land marches close to that of the Earl of Greensides, but this side of the hedgerow is definitely Surrey property." The gentleman seemed maddeningly unimpressed, so she continued. "Which means that you, sir, are trespassing!" Her voice sounded wickedly triumphant as she made this pronouncement.

The gentleman seemed quite untroubled. He shook his head and led Jess gently down to the water. When he was certain that the stallion was happy to drink quietly without tethering, he turned his attention once more to the appealing damsel before him. She was too young for his tastes, but he did find her diverting!

He pointed south. "See those conifers close to that stone bench?"

Cassandra squinted and did see. She nodded.

"That, my dear, is the border." His eyes gleamed. "I fancy I should know, for I've just taken over the lease."

Cassandra gasped. "Is that so, sir?" The implication struck. "Then it is I . . ."

He finished her sentence. "Yes. If we are going to quibble about it, the trespasser is you!"

For the second time that day, the Honorable Miss Beaumaris felt a revealing blush stain her cheeks. She put her hands up to them and felt they were hot. The gentleman thought they were adorable, but he had the good sense not to say as much. Instead, he sat down at the water's edge and helped himself to some of the fruit that was spilling with tempting abundance from the wicker basket.

He patted the ground and obligingly laid out his many-caped greatcoat for her comfort. "Call a truce." His smile was disarming.

Cassandra was shocked to find herself raising no objections as she carefully arranged the folds of her skirt and sat down. "Nurse's veal pasties are held to be the best in the county," she offered, as she indicated the basket. The stranger forswore the pie, but cheerfully handed her one before selecting an orange. She noticed with interest that he was able slice his way around the fruit and leave a rind that was as narrow as it was winding. She wished she had the knack of it and was just about to inquire into the skill when he tumbled once more from her good graces.

"That maid of yours ought to be whipped." He said it in a conversational tone, but she did not miss the dark note behind the utterance.

Cassandra felt herself grow indignant. She drew herself up as loftily as she could, given the half-eaten pie. "And why may that be, pray?"

He discarded the peel with satisfaction and carefully edged out a wedge of succulent fruit. When he looked up, his eyes were unreadable. "For leaving you at the mercy of a rake like myself."

Cassandra, far from looking shocked, looked flatteringly interested instead. "Are you a rake, sir?"

The gentleman eyed her and grinned. "Assuredly, I am, miss!"

Miss Beaumaris flashed him a brilliant smile and seemed not a whit put out. "Excellent! I have been on pins, you know, to meet one."

He raised his eyebrows. "I trust your governess and guardians are aware of this particular ambition?"

She tilted her nose loftily and actually winked. "Devil a bit!"

My lord, finally intrigued, almost choked on the last of his orange. "Setting aside your execrable language, young lady, am I to assume you actually enjoy the company of a dangerous gentleman like myself?"

Her response was quick. "Am I to assume that a hardened rake would actually represent himself as such to me? I have to suspect, dear sir, that you are an impostor."

He viewed her with a sudden dangerous and calculating air that made Cassandra's delectable bodice seem uncustomarily tight against her ribs and the soft, rounded flesh that it encased. For an instant she feared he might take her carelessly spoken words as a challenge. She shivered, and he seemed satisfied by her sudden response, for he permitted the tension to ease and grinned lopsidedly at her as though he'd scored a silent but indefinable point.

Cassandra allowed herself to breathe once more, and tea was savored in a companionable though slightly intimate silence. The sun was now sinking low in the skies, and the sight, though spectacular, brought a worried crease to Cassandra's brow. She stood up and reached for her bonnet. The ribbons were all in a tangle, and the stranger resignedly took the offending garment from her. She watched impatiently as he slowly restored order to chaos, threading each ribbon through the confusion of knots with suspiciously practiced ease.

At last the task was complete, and she carelessly bunched up her hair and tied a quick bow under her chin. Her dresser would have the vapors, no doubt, but the amused gentleman suspected she did not much care. She took up her basket and her line and her gloves, parasol and slippers and made to walk across the fields that stretched long and far ahead.

"And where do you think you are going, young lady?"

She raised her eyes haughtily. "Home, of course! Just over yonder." She pointed as far as the eye could see, but it must be said that the gentleman saw precious little.

"You don't propose to *walk?*" His voice was incredulous.

"Why not? I don't propose to sit here forever, and no doubt Natty has forgotten me entirely!"

The stranger's jaw tightened, and he swore silently under his breath.

"What was that?" Miss Beaumaris had missed a few of his well-chosen epithets. He did not enlighten her, but instead came to a swift decision.

"That maid has more to answer for than I had first thought! She should count herself lucky she is not of my household!" His tone was ominous and for some reason, Cassandra was silenced. Not for long, though. She peeped at him from under her lashes.

"Why, sir? Are you such a tyrant?" He stared at her uncomprehending for a moment, then shrugged with a wry smile.

"Try me and see! Up you go, baggage!"

Before she knew what he was about, Cassandra felt herself swung high up on to Jess's fine, well-proportioned back, tumbling bonnet and berries, bits and pieces.

In less than the blink of an eyelash, the stranger had gathered them all and alighted with quicksilver swiftness. Brooking no nonsense, he asked her to hold tight to the saddle and relax in his encompassing arms. Then he gripped the reins and set off at a sedate trot before she could think of a protest. Cassandra had never ridden without the benefit of a sidesaddle, much less in the arms of a gentleman as personable as the one she found herself clutching at that moment. She felt a curious mixture of panic and content well up in her being.

Essaying a few meaningless commonplaces, she felt her words swallowed up in the wind. Soon her heart was beating in a slow, constant rhythm that mimicked that of the stallion's hoofs steadily drumming across the pastures.

The familiar, welcoming lines of Surrey Manor slowly emerged in the dim dusk light. Not without a small pang of regret, Cassandra found herself set down and dusted firmly. The gentleman grinned at her with an endearing, delightfully conspiratorial twinkle and reminded her that her gown was somewhat disheveled, and she would do well to creep in through the servants' entrance.

On her dignity, Miss Beaumaris afforded him a superlative society curtsy and extended her hand. His eyes gleamed in amusement as he kissed her palm, then, of an impulse, each little finger, until she felt quite intoxicated with the sensation. Too late she recalled her dignity and retrieved her gloves from the berry basket.

He bowed. "It was a pleasure, my dear!"

She dimpled mischievously. "I think maybe you are, after all, what you say!"

He looked at her, and his expression was hooded. "A rake? Perhaps. I trust, though, that I am not so much at my last prayer that I need dangle after innocent maidens!"

She colored deeply and dropped her eyes.

"On second thought . . ." He placed his arm about her waist, and she caught the faint hint of musk and something infinitely, undefinably masculine. Before she could protest, she found him surveying her lips with a quirkish expression that made her knees tremble and her lips go suddenly dry.

"On second thought, I might just take what is my due."

"Your due, sir?" Cassandra's tone was deceptively submissive.

He smiled. "Yes, my due. The right of a rake! Do you read Herrick?"

"Herrick?" Cassandra looked puzzled, until enlightenment dawned, and she fussed with the basket in confusion. "Oh! You mean . . ."

"Yes! Your gorgeous lips, innocent one! Cherry ripe, cherry ripe they cry!" He was very close to her, his tone caressing. His hand brushed against her lightly. "Full and fair ones they are indeed!"

"You insult me again, sir!"

"No, I think I will just teach you the folly of wandering so disarmingly about without benefit of a maid!" His tone was teasing. He bent and kissed her, his lips as firm and generous as in her wildest moments she'd suspected they would be. Cassandra felt a number of unfamiliar sensations beset her before she struggled free and delivered a most resounding slap to the stranger's face.

He released her in amused surprise. A bright red mark formed at the side of his left cheek, but he managed an aghast chuckle at the lady's resolve.

Cassandra seemed more shocked at her actions than himself. "Have I hurt you, sir?"

His eyes were tender. "No, baggage! My pride perhaps! I'll have you know I am not in the habit of having my suit rejected!"

She folded her arms and giggled. "I warrant not, sir!"

She paused and a cheeky glint entered the corners of her

deep, indigo eyes. "It is Thomas Campion I recalled! Do you know it?"

"Know it?"

"Yes! 'There cherries grow that none may buy until cherry ripe themselves do cry.' "

The gentleman doffed his cap in recognition of the apt verse. His eyes gleamed at her quick wit in coining the rejoinder.

"I stand corrected, then!"

She curtsied and steadied the impatient colt.

He opened his fingers and pressed the grubby coin into the palm of her hand. "Perhaps it will bring good luck! Keep it as a talisman until we can further our delightful acquaintance upon more legitimate terms!" He shook his head in distraction. "I look forward to your presentation, ma'am. Perhaps I shall leave a card. Mayhap, after all, I shall make your lips resoundingly cry cherry ripe."

His eyes burned into hers, and she felt the sensual tremblings of longing she had experienced earlier when waiting for Natty. Only this time, they were so unexpectedly intense that for an instant her eyes closed. When she opened them, he'd swung around and was gone.

Cassandra gazed with unseeing eyes as she recalled the incident, still vivid in her memory after such a very long time. She sighed and turned from the diamond-latticed windows that looked out onto the cornfields. Far beyond that, the river streamed prettily past the Surrey estate and edged precariously on those of the absent Earl of Greensides. So much had happened since that chance encounter with the unknown stranger. She hadn't even asked his name! Perhaps if she had been presented in the fall of that year, things might have been otherwise.

As it was, she found herself on the verge of tears, her world a tumult of conflicting feelings and bitter emotions.

Who would have thought that she would come to such a pass? Her grandfather dead in a hunting accident and her brother lost in one of the bloodiest battles across the seas. Even now, the odious Harringtons were settling their vulgar belongings into her family home.

With a sigh, she kicked the tassels of her Aubusson carpet. It was useless to speculate, yet again, on how the earldom was to pass to her minor relations. She did not think she'd met the Harringtons above twice in her lifetime, but now it seemed they were to invade every private corner of her life.

The thought was bitter. Doubly so, for while Surrey land had been entailed to the earldom, the accompanying fortune had not. The Harringtons had shrieked in ill-bred fury when they'd discovered this eccentric codicil of the fifth earl. Since her brother Frances was missing, presumed dead, the fortune defaulted not to the earldom, but to her.

It seemed inevitable that Cassandra should be hounded night and day to rectify this fault. Through marriage, she had it in her power to unite fortune with title once more. She bit her lip. Nothing, *nothing,* was going to induce her to wed Sir Robert Harrington. The very thought of him repelled her. With a shiver of distaste, Cassandra jumped down from the window seat with sudden decision and tidied her skirts. She was in the devil of a coil. Unless she took steps to help herself, she would be undone. Much as she detested airing her dirty linen in public, she would have to. Tonight at the ball she would enlist the advice of some of the earl's staunchest friends. She sighed and placed the penny back in the furthest recess of her ribbon drawer. A talisman, her handsome stranger had said. If ever she needed its luck, she needed it now.

TWO

The Honorable Miss Elise Harrington clicked the jewel box shut with a little moue of distaste. Her cheeks were alarmingly flushed and held all the signs of an impending rage. Her unfortunate lady's maid, taking note, excused herself with a curtsy and fled the chamber.

The lady seethed with ill-concealed outrage and turned on her dresser. "However I came by such a nip-farthing, penny-pinching great skinflint as my brother I shall never know!" She tossed the offending trinket box to one side and preened herself. "Why, I have it on the best authority that he gave Miss Amazonia Brown a bracelet of rubies but a fortnight ago!" Her lips were petulant as she uttered this indignant, if far from genteel, observation.

Symmonds took up the silver-handled brush and vouchsafed not a word. Instead, she began the merciless strokes she deemed necessary for any young lady venturing out to her first ball. Miss Harrington did not look suitably gratified. Quite the contrary. She threw the retainer a venomous glance before continuing with her tirade. "Oh, don't, I beg you, look so odiously disapproving! I am not some milk and water miss that I do not know very well the kind of flirts he's taken up with."

Amelia Symmonds opened her mouth to remonstrate, then snapped it tightly shut. She knew her mistress better than to offer worldly advice, no matter how well warranted.

Let her burn her bridges if she chose. It was no concern of hers.

"Stop hurting so!" The reproof came just as the maid was putting the finishing touches to a particularly recalcitrant lock of sadly lackluster hair. Symmonds said nothing, but set down the brush with her lips firmly pursed. She'd become accustomed enough to her mistress's outbursts to take no more notice than to mutter disapprovingly and push a filigree pin firmly in place.

"If you press so hard you will pierce me!" The Honorable Elise glared at her, then turned back to the glass. Her thoughts flitted, not for the first time, to the coveted Surrey diamonds she knew to be stowed safely in the library below stairs. Perhaps if she broached the subject with her mama . . . but no! That lady was still out of temper with her for needing the seamstress in again.

She failed to see that it could matter that her new jonquil muslin was a tad tight. After all, she still had the whitest skin and the softest hands of all her acquaintances in Harrow. Mr. Thomas Pultney had told her so only the other day, and heavens, he was a one to know! Besides, her consequence had vastly improved since Robert had come into his expectations.

Somewhat mollified by this reflection, she paused to select from the tray an invitingly rich strawberry confection that was glazed with sugar and filled with a delectable quantity of whipped cream. She bit into it thoughtfully, conveniently ignoring Symmonds's admonishing sniff.

"Amethysts indeed! I suppose he'll save all the really good stuff for his countess! Well, I won't have it! And if Mama thinks she can contrive to make him marry that odious Cassandra just because she has forty thousand pounds coming to her, well let her think again! I'll not have her decked out in the Surrey gems! What is more, I reckon it is a guinea to a groat that Robert will run shy of the notion, too!"

Her eyes drooped slyly as she patted down the folds of her voluminous ball gown. Its startling shade was perhaps an unfortunate choice for one of her coloring and years, but if she found the gilded trim and lacy embellishments excessive, she showed no sign. She pouted over her choice of the formal hot house roses or the nosegay of early spring dewdrops and carelessly chose the former.

"On second thought, Symmonds, I'll take the trinket back myself. I think it is high time Robert and I had a little talk." Her expression appeared suddenly smug as she grasped for the offending box. "My nonsensical brother's been a bit high in the instep lately, and I know just how to take him down a peg or two! You see if I don't return with the sapphire drops at the very least!"

Her step was brisk as she strode down the long gallery that led to the atrium on the west wing. As she passed the portraits of the first Earl Surrey and his progeny, she reflected that it would not be long before her mother bestirred herself to have them removed to the basement.

No doubt the action would cause them all be treated to yet another impudent display from the lower staff, but no matter. If their sullens continued they'd be given their marching papers. Of course, their loyalties still lay with the late Earl Surrey, but they'd change their tune soon enough when the papers came through.

For the thousandth time that day she bewailed the fact that communication was still so bad across the channel. The process of confirming the death of Lord Frances Beaumaris was both tedious and irritating. She was heartily sick of looking in on the fringes of the beau monde and dancing attendance on the likes of Eleanor Peabody-Frampton.

It was especially galling to have to look to Miss Cassandra Beaumaris for entrée to the soirees and balls she should have be invited to by right. That the boot would soon be on the other foot was her only conceivable consolation.

This salve to her rapidly mounting temper was offset by the sudden rip she noted in her hem. It must have been caught on the landing stairs and would no doubt take her maid an age to mend. Scowling crossly, she realized there would be little time to interview her brother before the coach arrived for the evening's entertainment. She turned on her heel and made for her chamber.

"Oh, double hell and damnation!"

Mr. James Everett gave a small start as he completed his inscription. Though softly uttered, the expletive was sufficiently audible to alert him to the fact of his employer's return.

He could, perhaps, be forgiven for not hearing His Grace's advent sooner. That gentleman had chosen to enter from the terrace rather than the long gallery, a circumstance that the more formal Mr. Everett still found strangely bewildering. With painstaking care, he blotted the excess from his missive before rising from behind the neatly piled stacks before him.

"What is it, Your Grace?"

The frown that marred the eighth duke of Wyndham's really indecently handsome features was disturbing to one used more to a friendly nod than to unexpected outbursts of temperament. He need not have worried. The inquiry was met with a distinct lightening of the brow and an airy gesture that belied any real cause for concern.

"Be seated, James! I cannot conceive how many times I've told you not to stand on ceremony with me!"

The indubitable Mr. Everett found himself waved inexorably into a chair. The severity of His Grace's words was belied by the distinct twinkle lurking at the corners of unusually enigmatic dark eyes.

Relieved, His Grace's secretary took the small Queen Anne closest to the window. He settled himself attentively into the deep velvet and reflected, not for the first time, how refreshing it was that Duke Wyndham set comfort and a quite impeccable taste above current fashionable modes.

It could not be denied that the duke's own person offered

a pleasing prospect as he eased his hands out of an exquisitely edged pair of Sevres gloves. That he thrust them down with such uncommon force upon the table before him was proof positive of his natural vexation.

Eyeing the negligent gesture, Mr. Everett thought with fleeting pity of His Grace's valet, who'd no doubt spent many a morning searching for just such a pair.

No matter! His attention turned to the probable cause of the duke's displeasure. "Not the Greensides' lease I take it? I spoke to his lordship's man of business myself, but I misliked his manner. Like as not he'll renege and sell to Lord Abbington given half a chance. . . ." He trailed off uncertainly.

The duke looked speculative. "Will he, do you think?" His voice had acquired a low, silken edge that boded no good for the agent. He clicked open his drawer and reached for an elegant but slender snuffbox of the finest rose gold. Extending his hand carelessly, he offered his secretary a pinch before helping himself to the exotic, Mediterranean blend.

"I think I'll need to have a word with—what was his name? Ah, Abney if I do recall. A vulgar little man! I hear tell that he is overreaching himself with my tenants at Roscow. He'll have to have a care." There was menace in the duke's tone, and Mr. Everett shivered slightly.

"If it is indeed the Greensides' lease that worries you . . ."

The duke interrupted him. "Not, I'm sorry to say, anything so mundane as the Greensides' lease!" Suddenly, unexpectedly, his mind reverted to an image of a young maiden with tip-tilted nose, speaking blue eyes, and bright tumbling hair.

He had not thought of her since their encounter amid the berry bushes, and he fleetingly wondered whyever not. He shook his head and returned to the present, his tone assuming an unexpectedly teasing quality.

"The Greensides' lease, I'm aware, I could fob off on you with the most unconscionable of ease!" The words were accompanied by the wide smile so typical of the man who had become known to the monde as "the inimitable."

Despite his customarily serious manner, Mr. Everett was drawn to conclude that His Grace the Eighth Duke Wyndham, Earl Roscow, and Baron of the Isles was quite the most charming peer of his acquaintance. This was not to say, of course, that His Grace was incapable of offering a crushing set down when the occasion arose. Mr. Everett could cast his mind back to several occasions where the duke's notoriously wry consequence had been invoked. He did not gladly suffer fools or sycophants.

The duke now cast his eyes heavenward in picturesque exasperation. "I'm rather afraid it is nothing that need concern you, my dear James! This is a personal affair entirely."

At this, Mr. Everett coughed apologetically and uncrossed his legs. The duke's personal affairs were notorious among his set, but that, James knew, was none of his business. In spite of himself, his mind conjured up a long-remembered image of his employer in nothing but a hip-hugging pair of buckskins buttoned carelessly and without benefit of a shirt.

Not that he'd needed one. The shadows of the long pines had offered more than sufficient succor as his long fingers had rested lingeringly on the invitingly soft lips of his bonny *cher d'amour.* James could well remember the crimson laces of her tight-fitting bodice as she bestowed a slow, sensuous smile on the young heir to Wyndham.

Too late, he'd reined in his stallion. Before he could make good his escape, however, he'd been confronted by the impishly mocking gaze of Miles St. John, then the Marquis of Wade. His Grace had been impossibly young at the time, but the vision remained etched in his memory. Flushing with embarrassment, Mr. Everett now found himself plucking an imaginary hair from his morning coat and making to withdraw.

His employer, correctly divining the direction of his thoughts, looked mildly amused. "Oh, don't be so stuffy, James! No need to get up on my account! When I said personal

I did not—on this occasion at least—mean improper!" His eyes sparkled as the aging Mr. Everett declaimed. The duke was convinced that if the man could blush, he would have. Instead, he shuffled his white-tipped Hessians and muttered something vaguely intelligible. "If it is personal . . ."

"No, nothing of such great moment after all." His Grace looked rueful. "It is just that my great aunt, Elthea—the dowager marchioness of Langford, you know—has become relentless in her quest to get me leg-shackled this season. As if she hasn't already done enough—presenting me to every new chit out from the schoolroom!"

"But I thought you liked the young Miss Yarborough?"

"Liked her? No, my dear Mr. Everett, I pitied her! With an encroaching mama like that what else could I do? It is fortunate, indeed, that young Battingham came up to scratch before I was obliged to sadly depress the pretension!"

Mr. Everett, though somewhat disapproving of the duke's dismissive tone, nevertheless found himself repressing a smile at the display of righteous indignation.

His Grace expanded on his theme. "Anyone would imagine that fiasco would have been enough to dampen Aunt Elthea's all too transparent zeal, but *no!* I am now to escort her to her country manor in Shropshire, there to be introduced to some mysterious young protégée she has apparently conjured from abroad."

Mr. Everett looked nonplussed. "You cannot think of obliging, Your Grace? The London season has scarcely started, and I know you are anxious to put in a bid for the Arlington stallions. Tattersall's simply cannot be given the go by this time of year! Besides, your man of business sent in his card only the other day. You'll want to be consulting him of course. . . ."

The duke put up his hand, a single ruby momentarily flashing as it caught the dappling midmorning rays. "Stop, Everett, you are making my head spin maddeningly!" He grinned disarmingly. "That is, quite apart from making the whole ridiculous notion sound suddenly attractive!"

Mr. Everett did not seem unduly put out by the teasing. "No really, that's doing it too brown, Your Grace! Nobody can accuse you of shirking your responsibilities!"

He was rewarded by a slight ironic bow. "Maybe, Everett, maybe! I'll set your mind at ease though! My departure appears to hinge on the social calendar my aunt sets such store by." He looked up from the paper he was holding with no small degree of humorous distaste.

"To be sure, she is a regular gadabout is my aunt! It seems I am to wait until after the Debinham soiree, which she is apparently at great pains to attend." He squinted doubtfully at the heavily underscored letter he'd produced from his unimpeachable morning coat of deep maroon superfine. "At least, that is what I think she writes. I find her scrawl, as always, frustratingly illegible." He shook his head and with a wry shrug abandoned all further attempt to decipher the closely crossed wafers.

"I gather at all event that the Lady Suzannah remains in France until next fortnight's packet, so I shall be well clear of my most pressing business before making the journey. She, I expect, will need some time to recover before making her debut, as she crosses with no more than an abigail and a chaperone of sorts."

The duke grimaced, his eyes suddenly twinkling. "Poor girl! If I know anything of my great aunt, Elthea, she will not be deemed suitable for presentation until she has worn out her slippers, purchasing all the necessary frills and furbelows. I warrant there'll not be a Bond Street milliner, mantua maker, or ribbon bazaar that will remain unexplored before my exacting aunt is satisfied."

He paused, his voice softening subtly. "It keeps her young, you know. Short of marriage—and I really do feel I must make that exception—I find I simply can't resist humoring the old dear!"

Mr. Everett allowed himself a chuckle before resuming his customary air of common sense.

"Is the crossing safe, Your Grace? With the fighting ended I realize that traffic must be much easier, but I'd not have thought the arrangement particularly *epris* for gently bred young ladies."

A thousand thoughts flitted through the duke's unusually expressive face. The horrors of a war-ravaged Europe may be lightly dismissed by the ton, but they were raw enough in his mind not to be so easily set aside. He shook himself mentally and shuttered the unwelcome memories. No doubt the Lady Suzannah would have nothing more to concern her than the sad crush of her traveling dress.

"She'll make do, James. I'm certain of that." A hint of cynicism crept into his world-weary voice. It was not the first time a young lady was to be presented for his inspection. He supposed, with a small sigh, that it was time he seriously set about the business of finding himself a duchess. He owed it to his position if not to his inclination.

"Shall I send a reply, then?"

"No, James, this one I'd better take care of myself." He grimaced, his tall frame offering a pleasing prospect to anyone inclined to take note of the circumstance.

"When I'm done I'll frank it for you, and you may see that it is delivered. Also, if you can cast your mind back to a decent hostelry I'd be much obliged. I rather think that a coach and four will be sufficient to my needs, though the horses will no doubt need a change somewhere along the route." He granted his secretary a magnificent smile.

"I'll leave these details in your capable hands, James. That way I'll be assured of superlative service along the way."

Mr. Everett swelled with modest pleasure. To be sure, his master was very obliging.

St. John tapped at his shirtsleeves. "I know you. You will be puffing off my consequence long before I take to the road. If there is not a hot brick and tolerable repast awaiting me at every minor way station from London to the full extent of Shropshire I misread my guess. Yes, I know! You'll have my crested linen out and the ducal ostlers awaiting my pleasure at every godforsaken watering house this side of Faveringham."

"It is only fitting, Your Grace."

The duke sighed. "Fitting, James, but nonetheless a sore trial. I find I tire of all the pomp!" He brought himself up sternly. "And now, my friend, I must make short shrift of that wretched letter. I fear if I do not hurry, I'll have my young nephew down in a trice. We're to attend Countess Petruschca's masquerade in"—he consulted his delicately wrought timepiece—"less than an hour, by heavens!"

THREE

"I hope you're satisfied, my dear Rupert!" St. John said, throwing a querulous look at his young nephew. The evening was stiflingly hot and the entertainments sadly lacking in any novelty. Not that he had anticipated much better, but the thought of the fine port and quiet newspaper awaiting him at Wyndham Terrace acted as an uncommon irritant to his already jangled nerves.

Stifling a long and very weary yawn, the duke found he could think only of making good his escape. His own eyes certainly did not reflect the excited anticipation so palpable in those of the young man beside him.

He glanced now at his companion, his eyes holding the steely yet enigmatic smile that was regarded by some as his habitual demeanor. "You must know that I find these masquerades an absolute abomination," he said to his nephew. Achieving no answer, he tossed his head in mock despair. "I do trust that we may soon leave?"

The severity of his words was lightened by the good-natured smile he cast on his young relative.

"You may, Miles! I will see my way home with Lamberton over there. But Miles?" His Grace raised an eyebrow. "Be a sport and stay awhile?"

Imperceptibly, the duke's eyes softened. "Cawker! All right, another hour perhaps. I take leave to inform you, however, that I find the night insufferably humid. Not to mention the affectation of a loo mask! What a ridiculous trial!"

Second Viscount Lyndale seemed not a whit put out by this rather dampening comment. Instead, he saw fit to grin engagingly at his elder, remarking that he was a great gun and not at all the toplofty maw worm he was so often taken for. Before his guardian could think up a suitably biting retort, the young viscount's attention was distracted by the caviar and fresh salmon patties that were being replenished in abundance on the trestles outside.

"I say, Miles, I vow I am starved! Can I get you a plate?"

"*May* I get you a plate?" His Grace corrected with precision. "And no, Rupert, you may not! I am heartily sick of these vile concoctions we are always being fed. Run along, though, I can see we do not offer a sufficient enough table at Wyndham Terrace." His tone was ironic, but entirely missed on the young viscount, who disappeared into the fray with a vague promise of a speedy return.

St. John sighed and returned to his musing. The air of languorous fatigue emanating from his person was not lost on the dowagers who eyed him avidly from beneath their dusky turbans. Some of the more spiteful could be heard tittering behind their fans, noting that the gentleman in the sea green cape was far from amused. The evening would be declared a failure, a shocking squeeze. After all, if the duke found it lacking, there was nothing more to be said.

Rather to his despair, Miles St. John found himself the undisputed catch of the season. If he felt himself hunted, it was with good cause. Society was too eager by far to captivate the attentions of His Grace the eighth duke of Wyndham. Without doubt, his rank, his lineage, and his fortune made him fair game to every watchful parent and debutante from far and wide. Word was about that he was on the catch. Very proper, too, if one took into consideration his two and thirty years. More than high time he be setting up a nursery.

The chaperones dotted about the great hall could hardly be blamed for reflecting on the prospects of such a connection.

As wave after wave of young dancers took up the set, they glittered like the flash of crystal caught by sun. The duke remained a central figure, dark amid the color. Only the occasional gleam of emerald relieved the starkness of his aspect. For those who watched, his cropped black curls offered a tantalizing prospect.

"Admit it, Miles. You must be just a trifle curious as to the identity of that beauty."

The duke startled. His ward had returned faster than he'd expected, his gloved hand clutching a plate of delectable-looking truffles. It must be said that while the irrepressible viscount did not actually point, his interest in no way went unremarked. St. John cursed silently under his breath. His displeasure was blithely ignored by his recalcitrant ward, who was outfitted to the nines in a cape of russet merino with shirt points starched stiff to the cleft of his chin. His eyeshade was quite remarkably studded with rivulets of amber crystal.

"Do you see the one I mean? The lady in the scarlet domino. The one dancing, if I guess it right, with Portland. Dashed if I don't have a mind to cut him out!"

The duke smiled indulgently at this youthful high-handedness. The Marquis of Portland was hardly likely to be bested by the sprig beside him, but he said nothing to shatter the young cub's illusions. Instead, he gently reminded his charge that pointing was not *comme il faut* in the polite circles in which they moved.

Rupert remained undeterred. "I know, Miles. But she is a diamond of the first water!" He grinned at his guardian. "Come, now, not even a little interested?"

The duke put his hand to his throat, where a cascade of lace glittered with the small scatter of emeralds he'd chosen to affect. The dark, woven superfine hugged his shoulders neatly, the effect enhanced by a tightly nipped-in waist, satin edged and of a complementary deep green hue. Over this

ensemble fell the sea green cape, clasped with the slightest
hint of gold. His thoughts, however, lay not with Weston, his
tailor, but with the question so innocently put to him by the
young man at his side.

Miles found himself shaking his head with a world-
weariness that saddened him. "To say the truth, my dear
Rupert, her identity is not of the smallest interest to me. For
all I care, she could be yet another of those exiled Russian
princesses we all hear interminably about." His voice held a
note of contemptuous dismissal that was not missed on the
impressionable young sprig at his side.

"But Miles . . ."

"No buts about it, Rupert! Devastated though I am to dis-
illusion you, from my experience of the world, you will
scarcely find much difference between your delicious piece
of feminine charm over there and that brazen doxy standing
under the pergola." He lifted his quizzing glass.

"My God! Just look at the way she flutters her fan. If she
blinks her eyelashes any faster she's like to have an apoplexy!
And as for her mama . . . well, I wonder however she got
through the gates? The Countess Petruschca was wont to be
more discerning."

It must not be thought that the young viscount was left in
any doubt as to his mentor's meaning. Both ladies in question
were displaying a distressing lack of decorum, even in a situation so lax as a masquerade ball. The older, evidently the
chaperone, presented to the discerning viewer a hideous vision
of emerald ostrich feathers atop an orange bejeweled turban.

What made the scenario slightly more piquant was that
they were accompanied by a young lady of quite unimpeach-
ably good ton. That this lady was acutely embarrassed and
suffering greatly from the ordeal was obvious. Without
knowing it, she presented such a forlorn picture of quiet
dignity that both men's hearts were moved to pity.

Miles regarded her closely, his curiosity piqued. In spite
of himself, the duke felt his attention arrested. "Who is that

chit? Not a fitting companion, surely, for that garish set of pretenders?" He looked again.

Her eyeshade hid much of her fine bone structure but did not conceal the fresh beauty of her youthful complexion or the gleaming auburn locks that were firmly pinned in a tight coil around the nape of her neck. Something of the color struck dim chords in the duke's memory, but the thought was elusive.

There was something in the way she glanced at him, something in the quiet grace of her hands that arrested his attention, tugging at some deep, disquieting aspect of his psyche hitherto remained untouched. It seemed strange indeed that a single gaze should so affect him, that he should be more deeply aware of her than ever he had been of a woman before. She was definitely not in the mold to which he felt himself inclined. Nevertheless, his attention was fixed. The gnawing memory flickered into sudden recognition.

He had encountered a carefree maiden of impudent aspect and innocent ways. What he now beheld was that vision transformed into quiet dignity and unwarrantable sadness. His interest deepened. She was far removed from the little tumbleweed miss with her delicious bright lips and impudent outlook of long ago.

Her demeanor in fact appeared as well-bred as it was restrained. For an instant the duke regretted the maiden. Then his pulse quickened, and he knew he'd good reason to prefer the lady that she'd become.

St. John felt uncharacteristically dazed. While it might not be love—for had he not been in and out of love a dozen times or more?—his feelings could be described, perhaps, as an awareness of her being, an amused sympathy with the tilt of her chin and the lift of her shoulders as she sought vainly to hush her two companions. It was obvious that she wanted to disappear circumspectly into one of the less-frequented side rooms. Her lack of success in this enterprise was as annoying to Miles as it was to her.

Her urgent appeals were wholly disregarded by her consorts. They, it may be said, were displaying a most alarming tendency to make their unctuous way toward him. Torn between the sudden and unexpected desire to deliver them a sharp set down or to beat a hasty retreat, the Eighth Duke Wyndham decided on the latter.

"Rupert!"

The viscount turned toward him with a start. He'd been pondering with delightful equanimity the identity of Miss Red Domino.

"I say, Miles, you did make me startle!"

The duke sighed and patiently repeated his earlier question. "Do you know anything of the young lady dressed in gossamer white? The one attending those wretchedly out-of-place countrified chits?" His tone was so vicious that Rupert was startled to attention.

"I can't say, Miles. She looks awfully out of place, doesn't she? Perhaps Sally will know."

The duke nodded resignedly. He knew all too well his chances of private discussion with the famous countess.

As it happened, it was quite some time before the Lady Jersey was close enough for conversation. Indeed, it was only between the end of the fourth minuet and the beginning of the new quadrille that the duke had been able to hail her.

"Sally!"

"Your Grace!" Lady Jersey's face diffused in a wreath of smiles as she responded to the duke's handsome bow with a slight curtsy of her own.

"And Rupert! How delightful to make your acquaintance once more! Glad you could tear yourself away from Oxford." Rupert grinned merrily. His eyes, though, wandered wistfully to the vision in the scarlet domino.

Miles exchanged a speaking glance with the countess, then relented. "Go on then! Off you go, scamp!"

The viscount grinned as he made his excuses. She waved him away with her fan and turned on Miles with a throaty chuckle.

"Not a bad match, there, Miles! Lady Cordelia Marville." When St. John looked bemused, she elaborated. "The Countess of Bingham's daughter, you know! A trifle flighty, but I put that down to high spirits rather than want of conduct." She smiled indulgently. "She should never have worn a scarlet domino, of course, but she has tolerable manners and a pleasing countenance. . . ." Her voice trailed off. "But that was not why you hailed me, I dare swear."

His Grace threw her an amused glance. "Astute as ever, my dear. And no, my lady, it was not why I hailed you." He waited for the set to resume before drawing her aside.

"Well, Miles?" Her face dimpled prettily, despite her years. "I know that look in your eye! What is it that you want?"

Miles responded in kind. "A kiss, my pretty."

It ought at this time to be reported that Lady Jersey, that awesome patroness, that fearsome guardian of the portals of Almack's, positively laughed in delight. The cheek of the man! No other, save perhaps Prinny himself, dared address her in that fashion.

"Touché!" She tapped him playfully with the stem of her fan.

The new set was commencing, the musicians tuning up in fine style. Across the room, there was a great flickering of light as the candles burned down merrily, their glow reflected in incandescent mirrors erected on all sides of the hall. The tallows were replaced at regular intervals by great numbers of attendant footmen, so the flames were ever bright, yielding luminescence unfaltering in intensity. The effect was breathtaking. The chatter continued ceaselessly, as did the ebb and flow of hundreds of the jeweled and sequined debutantes known to an envious world as "the monde." The sultry night positively lent itself to the mingling that was occurring, both in and out of the great chambers and gardens of Countess Petruschca's large estate.

Sally Jersey dimpled at the duke. "You cannot imagine the stir you have aroused tonight, Wyndham."

The eighth inheritor of Wyndham raised his brows.

"Oh, don't get on your high ropes with me, I beg. You must be aware of the talk! What I cannot understand is why you choose to be here at all. I must say, I find it really a most dreadful squeeze myself."

"Indeed it is, ma'am. I'm only here under the strongest of coercion, I assure you! But you see for yourself my young ward's winning ways!" His eyes twinkled momentarily as he gestured in Rupert's direction.

Lady Jersey found herself smiling in response. "Mmmm . . . I do, indeed! But I'd cast my eye on him, Miles. This is a very mixed set. Rather let him loose in Almack's, where he can't get up to too much mischief. I wouldn't myself vouch for the company this evening, you know."

The duke emitted an imperceptible sigh. "Which brings me to why I wanted to talk with you."

"Aha! I knew there was an ulterior motive!"

Miles smiled patiently. "Who is the young lady standing with those utterly repulsive specimens? She looks decidedly out of keeping with them. Unless I mistake?" The subject of his interest inclined her head to the Honorable Sir Robert Harrington. A puzzled frown momentarily shadowed the duke's urbane features. Sir Robert was as unsuitable a companion for the young woman as the ladies.

What could her chaperone be thinking of? Every wary dowager knew Sir Robert to be a rake, a gambler, and patently unfit for the company of ladies of quality.

Lady Jersey started talking, but his attention lamentably strayed. His eyes followed the unlikely duo out the stuffy interior, past the hedgerow, and through the long lines of chestnuts that grew in columns along the path. As he watched them disappear into the night, he thought he caught a murmured plea, then shrugged at his mistake. Unlike him to grow whimsical!

Shaking himself from his reverie, he turned back to Sally.

"It's a damnable scenario, Miles! Miss Beaumaris's

brother, the current earl of Surrey, is on the war lists, pre-sumed dead. Sir Robert, as next male kin, stands as heir. I believe he and his delightful family are making life ex-tremely uncomfortable for Miss Cassandra Beaumaris. She is the lady you are gazing after with such open astonishment. Hello?" Lady Jersey recalled his attention with a sharp tap of her elegant fan. At his blank look, her ladyship's mouth pouted in exasperation. "Your Grace, I vow you have not heard one word I've been saying."

The duke blessed Sally with one of the comical grimaces that so endeared him to womenfolk.

"I am sorry, my dear! Continue, please!"

"I will if you favor me with your attention! Miss Beau-maris has a tidy sum coming to her on her marriage and charm to boot. An unusual combination and one Sir Robert is only too well aware of, I'll warrant." She glanced at St. John assessingly. Sally was a veritable goldmine of useful social anecdotes, but he felt she needed prompting.

"The brother? Dead, I assume?"

"Well, that is the problem, Miles. We just do not know! The war lists have the current earl down as missing, although all the world knows his chance of survival is set at practically naught."

"Poor girl! A tragedy."

"Yes. But what is worse is that the Harringtons, being a distant connection, lay claim to the earldom. They've been denied vouchers, of course."

There was a smug smirk at this last, for without the sanction of the said Countess Lieven, Princess Esterhazy, and a small but select group of patronesses—of which she was one—the Harringtons, title or not, were as nothing, doomed forever to the lower ranks of gentility. It said much that for once all the illustrious ladies had been in agreement: Robert Harrington, earl or no, was simply not Almack's material. To admit him or his singularly vulgar family through the sanctified portals of the club would be a desecration in the extreme.

"A charming revenge, my dear"—Miles's dry retort brought her back to the discussion on hand—"but what of the sister?"

"Miss Beaumaris? It has placed her in a terrible position, of course. She cannot bring herself to accept the reality of the situation. Instead, she clings with touching—if misguided—eloquence to the belief that her brother will return. I spoke with her only the other day and was quite moved to pity. Of course, his being gazetted missing, not dead, adds fuel to the hope and only prolongs the agony."

"What of the Harringtons? Surely they cannot lay claim on the estate until the matter is settled?"

"Not legally, no. But from what I gather, they've moved into Surrey Manor, lock, stock, and barrel. There is some small dispute over the legality of Harrington acting as guardian to her, as she is not yet of age. At all events, while he has not been invested with the title, he seems to be making ample use of its privileges. Rumor has it that the duns have only held off because of his expectations."

Her lips curled at the thought. "By all accounts a debtor prison is too good for him, Miles! And there is little that we can do, save offer Miss Beaumaris our support and patronage. She's not been seen at Almack's since all this has happened. I'm surprised she's here tonight. And in such company!"

"Perhaps she had no choice." The duke's voice took on an unexpectedly grim tone. His valet, sensing his mood, would have taken good care not to anger him. My lord St. John was devilishly good to his servants, but there were times where it was wise to steer good and clear. By the set of his mouth, this was one of those times. Lady Jersey looked up and sensed rather than saw the rigid tightening of his muscles and the almost involuntary twitch of his left cheek.

The eighth duke of Wyndham, she knew, was very much like his father. Not the type to be easily aroused to momentary passion and transient adoration. He would like as not sneer at sentiment and label romance a fool's pleasure. It was a notable contradiction, then, that when he did feel deeply about something, he became wholly absorbed. She watched his eyes flicker in thought then move back to her face. She guessed that he wanted to be alone. Alone to absorb the information imparted to him and to ponder truly on the circumstances of so striking a young lady being vulnerable to such manifest coercion.

When he misheard her for the second time, she permitted herself a tiny sigh before nodding to a gentleman of her acquaintance and allowing him to lead her in, once more, to the swirl of skirts and the delicious world of the *beau monde*.

FOUR

In the gardens, the rain had not yet turned to showers, but the misty haze did not portend well. A cluster of gray clouds lingered low in the sky, showing every sign of fulfilling the duke's prediction of a stormy road home. Young ladies, lightly clad in ball gowns of sheer merino, muslin, and diaphanous patterned silks, took themselves off for the shelter of pavilions and the great hall. Tinkling laughter followed in their wake, the querulous tones of dowagers quite lost in the magic of the evening.

The duke found himself walking against the throng of people. Had his mind been less occupied, he might have been surprised at the number of men and women out in the gardens that night. As it was, his tread was firm and a little on the brisk side as he walked over to the hedgerow and down toward the long line of towering green chestnuts on the far end.

The Honorable Sir Robert Harrington was not known among his contemporaries for chivalry. On the contrary, the man had been dubbed an outright cad, although to Miles's knowledge he had in the past dabbled more with the opera-singer set than with ladies of quality. All the same, it would not do to be complacent. The sooner he satisfied himself to the fact of the young lady's well-being, the better pleased he'd be.

He did not like to dwell on the faint plea he had earlier dismissed as imagination's fancy. Miss Beaumaris's background coupled with what he knew of Harrington added up to an uneasy alliance that did not bode well for the unfortunate lady. He knew it was not his place, but in the absence of a close male relative he felt it his duty to intervene. The duke's steps hastened to a run as he rounded on the far pavilion.

What he saw there stopped him short in shock. It was worse than his hazily foreboding instinct had envisaged. Harrington had the girl's arm pinned behind her back. Sheltered from passing eyes by the contours of the folly, he was forcing himself upon her with a laugh that held no mirth at all. His voice indeed, was sibilant with an anger that raised prickles down His Grace's spine.

"You will pay for that, you termagant!" Sir Robert rubbed his cheek dismissively then edged his face closer to her own. "Lay hand to me once more and I warn you, you will find yourself regretting it!"

Cassandra turned her head away, her cheeks high with color and revulsion. Pinned as she was, she could not move, but her expressive face said much

Harrington released his grip, amused at her open terror. "I hope you understand that, my sweet. We needed to come to a more conformable arrangement." His mouth moved to close on hers, an ugly leer transforming his features.

"For now, I will merely satisfy myself with a little light punishment. You may consider it the discerning taste of a treat in store." The threat was palpable as his dank breath closed in on her lips. His eyes lit with a strange sort of amusement as he gave her a brief respite. Then he began his advance once more. Miles realized that Sir Robert was enjoying a little cat and mouse game at Cassandra's expense and he shivered. As Sir Robert drew closer, she wrenched her hand from his grip and gasped in an involuntary combination of anguish and anger.

This was silenced on the instant. The detestable Sir Robert quelled her protest with a deft twist of his arms, his head bending toward her with a sudden savagery that shocked Miles from his momentary paralysis.

With a murmur of stony rage, he took the steps of the pavilion two at a time and caught the Honorable Harrington in a steely vice that left him rasping for breath. Surprised into releasing his grip, Cassandra's captor fell back. She found herself stepping clear, nursing her arm, and suffused with a sudden shame for what had just occurred. While she knew herself to be utterly indebted to the mysterious gentleman in green, she knew, too, that she was compromised beyond all hope of redemption.

Recognizing in her savior the man who had so boldly locked eyes with her earlier in the evening, she felt a hot blush suffuse her being. That he should see her thus! In her weakened state, she could only reflect remorsefully on what he would think. The Honorable Miss Beaumaris knew well that she would be judged by the company she kept. First her encroaching female relations and now the odious Sir Robert Harrington. As she caught her breath, she reflected—not without a measure of bitterness—that she was fair game now in the eyes of society. It could not be hoped that her shimmering cream redingote would obscure her identity for long. The incident would ruin her, as no doubt Harrington had intended.

The thought was so lowering to her self-esteem that it was some moments before she allowed herself to heed the tableau unfolding before her eyes. Harrington was seeing fit to spew obscenities fit only for a bawdy house. He had released himself from the duke's grip and was now facing him, anger blazing from every pore.

What license had this unknown gentleman—duke or not— to interfere with something that was rightfully his? With an obtuseness shocking in its candor, he failed to see that Cassandra's revulsion of him bore on the matter at hand. To a man of his twisted perspective, she was all but his, no person having the mandate to overset his well-laid plans. Forty thousand pounds was not anything to sneeze at, certainly, and an heiress within his grasp was as good as money in the bank. In a moment of frenzied outrage, he challenged his opponent.

"Name your men!"

The duke demonstrated a masterful control. When angered, his movements became deceptive in their simplicity, lethal in their conclusion. Like Harrington, he was at the pinnacle of an exquisite rage. He did not, however, expend one ounce of surfeit force. His methods tended to be as vigorous as they were nice, perfection in their simplicity of motion and accuracy of intent. Not for him were the coarse epithets and the brazen appeals to a greater audience. He needed not the stimulus of applause to rouse himself to dizzying heights.

Though Miles's fingers fairly itched to run the villain through, his face remained impassive, silent. Those who knew him would have cringed in awe. The duke in a mood like this was a man dangerous in the extreme. His voice had deepened, deceptively soft. "A duel is too good for you, Harrington. I'd not sully my name by having it linked with yours."

The insult came as a sharp blow. Puffed up as he was in his own consequence, Sir Robert nonetheless knew all too well that his situation in society was precarious to say the least. In far too many circles he found himself a persona non grata and the circumstance rankled. The outright implication that he was no gentleman was the perfect stimulus to further fuel his rage. It was perhaps fortunate for the duke that Harrington's sidesword was presently on the mantelpiece at Surrey Manor.

Sir Robert lunged, his fists poised to strike an earnest blow at the interloper's temple. His breathing was ragged, perspiration oozing from every pore. As his arm lunged forward, it was caught in an unstoppable grip. A split second later he was doubled over, groaning audibly and hanging from the balcony in an attempt to retch. My lord St. John, satisfied that a flush hit had been delivered, turned his back in contempt.

"Miss Beaumaris, you are unharmed?"

Cassandra turned to him wonderingly. A flash of memory shook her, but she quelled the thought.

"You know my name, sir?"

The duke's eyes softened for a fleeting moment, then regained their habitual gallantry. "Indeed I do, fair creature! May I lead you in?"

Miles had resumed his veneer of quiet banter, secure in the knowledge that Harrington would present no further menace for that evening. The light drizzle was changing to heavy droplets and his suggestion was opportune.

As Cassandra presented her hand, stammering her thanks, he hushed her with a smile so dazzling she was enchanted.

"Don't thank me, my dear. The man is a villain, and the less said the better." He bowed formally. "I claim the next dance, however!"

"It's a waltz sir." Cassandra's half-coy protest amused the world-weary duke. A far cry from the simpering young ladies within. They, he was sure, would be only too happy to oblige him in the execution of a dance still considered "fast" in the more fastidious circles.

"I know." Miles's eyes twinkled as he let the implication of his words set in. He realized with a great deal of irony that he longed to have his arms encircle this delicate yet strangely self-possessed young woman. He hadn't felt that way since his salad days. What an enigma she was, so fragile, yet exuding such an immensely firm inner strength. The red streak blighting Harrington's cheek had not escaped his all-encompassing attention. Clearly, she had courage. His mind flitted back to the only slap he had ever received from the gentler sex, and he grinned. She hadn't changed that much, after all. "Never say you're afraid of a waltz?" Miles's eyes challenged her, teasing.

Cassandra could feel her heart beat just a little faster under his unerring gaze. That sort of behavior was strictly reserved for storybook heroines. She could hardly credit that she was responding in such a gauche and missish manner. Annoyed, half shy, half bold, she took up the challenge. "Not of the waltz! The partner, perhaps?" Cassandra amazed herself by her audacity.

"Afraid of me?" Miles feigned astonishment. "How can that be so, fair creature? Have I not already demonstrated a willingness to fight for your honor? And shall I not continue to do so if need be?"

His tone had been bantering, but the last sentence was uttered with so much quiet force that Cassandra looked up, startled.

What she saw in his eyes made her recalcitrant pulse race once more in that unaccountable, yet rather wondrous manner. "Here," her heart cried out, "is a man!"

"Your name, sir? I rather think we've not been introduced."

Her voice held an interrogative. The duke, like herself, was still sporting an eyeshade. Though she must have been one of the very few that evening to be ignorant of his person, there could be little doubt that she was, indeed, so ignorant. His face, like his motive, remained a mystery.

For an instant Miles looked skeptical, but the moment passed.

"You'll have to stay for the unmasking. Until then, dearest, my identity shall remain a secret! So much more edifying, do you not think?"

Cassandra's eyes were reproachful. The man was playing games with her. And yet . . . why not? How long had it been since she'd put away her cares and just danced without worry? A very long time, she reckoned.

Lady Sefton had indicated strongly that she might dance if she wished. She could not be expected to remain in mourning for her grandfather and now her brother forever. That she had chosen not to dance was a decision entirely of her own making. Tonight, for this one waltz, she would rescind the ban and enjoy herself. If only for the sake of one new and pleasurable memory amidst her daily sorrows.

The music was striking up and before she knew it, she

found herself heading for the great dance hall, her handsome protector's elbow just a fraction away from her own. She was curiously aware of this fact as their steps hastened to avoid the pelter of rain now descending earthward. Harrington not quite forgotten but no doubt still retching in the far off arbor, she took her place, the duke's arm gently circling her waist.

His touch was as light as gossamer yet it burned into her senses like nothing had ever done before. Acutely aware of his closeness, she allowed herself to be guided around the room, reveling in the sensation that for these few moments, at least, she need not be in control. Quietly, unconsciously, she yielded to him. He, sensing this, tightened his grip over her person, his very being caught up in the singularly unusual sensation of closeness, of oneness.

He had danced the waltz thousands of times before, with women far, far more beautiful than the little mite in his arms at that moment. What he'd never before felt, however, was this strange sense of union, of bonding. He felt her trust and instinctively responded to it.

His mouth drew down close to hers, and he could feel her warm breath on his neck, tantalizing. Feeling for all the world like a callow halfling smitten with unbridled passion, the duke of Wyndham, Earl Roscow, and Baron of the Isles found himself yearning for the music to stop, for time to stop, and for the two of them to stand together and become one, his mouth on hers, her hands in his.

Perhaps she sensed this longing, for her eyes looked up at his, searching. For a moment her body became so still that she forgot her steps and stumbled. He reached out to catch her and smiled. It was a moment that would stay with them always.

Cassandra conjured up the picture of the dark young rider on his stallion, and she knew of a certainty it was he.

"Tell me," Cassandra urged. "Who are you?"

"Miles. Miles St. John. The duke of Wyndham." The

words were out before he could stop them. What he felt was no longer an idle game.

For an instant Cassandra was struck dumb. Then she laughed. "You can't fool me sir! Play the masquerade if you will, but you'll not deceive me in so witless a manner!"

"No?"

"No! You're no more the duke than I am the Duke of Cumberland's duchess!"

A smile hovered around His Grace's mouth.

"You seem very sure, my dear."

Miss Beaumaris laughed shyly. "I am. Forgive me for noticing, sir, but you're hardly what might be called a dandied fop."

St. John's eyes turned to steel. "And the duke is a dandified fop?"

"Why, yes. Everything I've seen and heard of the man indicates he is merely a gilded lily. A shallow social butterfly so steeped in his own self-confidence that he dares defy all convention."

"Is that so very terrible? I can think of worse sins than that of defying convention."

"Not if overweening pride is at the base of it, my lord!"

The duke missed a step. "Perhaps you think too much!" His tone held a fleeting note of bitterness unlost on Cassandra.

"Why sir, do not take me amiss! Perhaps I'm being presumptive. . . ."

Her voice faltered as she watched him, his eyes shuttered once more. His Grace, the Duke of Wyndham felt suddenly cold. Years of unquestioning adulation had blinded him to the fact that he could be viewed in less than an admirable light. Coming from whom it did, the revelation was no pleasant shock.

He broke the silence, steering her expertly clear of the couple in front.

"Not presumptive, no. Misinformed, perhaps?"

Cassandra tossed her head doubtfully.

"I doubt it, sir! The man is a warrantable rake! I have it on the best authority that his boots are shone with champagne and his silk stockings are all clocked!"

The duke relaxed, remembering her innocence. She did, after all, have a penchant for rakes, as he well remembered. "And that makes him a rake?"

Cassandra smiled. "Not just that, no . . . I've heard tell that he's had a dozen or so flirtations over the years and not one of them serious. When one thinks of how mamas have pushed to catch him and to no avail, it fair makes one weep!"

Her tone had lost its severity, indicating that she was aware that the mamas, too, were ridiculous. Miles laughed.

"Surely your sense of justice admits that his flirtations have never extended to the young and innocent? Life is dull. Sometimes, my dear, deadly dull." His voice assumed a fleeting and uncharacteristic inflection of grimness before changing once more to its intonation of amused tolerance.

Cassandra smiled in delight. "See, sir? You are speaking of him in the third person. I knew you were not he!"

The duke inclined his head and continued with his theme.

"Surely you'll allow us fellows a little light relief? Fun at the expense of those ever-present mothers?" Cassandra's eyes danced as he continued. "A dandy, maybe, but a fop? That's a bit too strong!"

She allowed a small giggle to escape her otherwise very proper countenance.

"You still don't fool me, you know, sir! But I grant you have a point. We ladies tend not to think of the gentleman's point of view. It must be rather tiresome trying to avoid entrapment and other such hazards." Her partner looked quizzical but bowed in assent. Feeling she had made a significant concession, she once more took up the offensive. "But champagne? Come, sir, how do you explain that?"

"Why easily, my dear. If he's the type who delights in the groveling sycophant, what better way to get him to lick his boots?"

The repartee was taking its course, allowing Cassandra to relax into an easy familiarity that stripped away her reserve. Never before had she felt this at ease with a gentleman. Never before, that is, except with the gentleman of her dreams. Too much to hope and believe, perhaps, that they were one.

Common sense, certainly, refused to allow her to believe that this comforting, laughing savior was the notorious Duke of Wyndham as he proclaimed. She imagined the duke to be positively in his dotage, fat and languorous from all the years of surfeit and pampering.

Nevertheless, despite her accusations, she allowed that it was a long time—a very long time—since the duke had been known to have anything to do with females of her class. Whispers abounded of his associations with the demimonde and with women who were safely wedded, but she could not recall a time in the recent past that he had actually distinguished any young eligible with a dance.

As she whirled around the room, her partner guiding her with an expertness hitherto undreamed of, she could scarcely be blamed for not taking in the poisonous glances cast her way. Were she to notice the attention she was attracting, she might well have set it down to the circumstance of her dancing at all than to the identity of her mysterious consort.

All too soon, the tumultuous strains of violin and harpsichord died away, leaving Cassandra looking through the mask and into the devastating eyes of her protector. His eyebrows were cocked in such a delicious mixture of tenderness and amusement that Cassandra quite trembled with the newness of her feelings. His arms had dropped to his sides, but the warmth of his touch stayed with her, lingering like the scent of jasmine long after it is picked.

"My turn, my dear."

The earl of Glenby cast an impudent look at Cassandra's partner before cutting him out and demanding the forthcoming dance with her. It was on the tip of her lips to rebut him, but a warning glance from her comely partner reminded her of her social duties. It would not do to make a dramatic emergence from full mourning, then dance only with an unknown.

Accepting the unspoken communication with a smile of gratitude, she clasped the earl's hand with a pretty acquiescence and permitted herself to be led into the newly forming set. The obliging Glenby set her at ease with a great deal of chatter and an idle attempt at flirtation, but her thoughts were not to be engaged.

Images of high-arched brows, a mocking smile, and snowy sarcenet edged with lace crowded her mind, superseded only by thoughts of piercing dark eyes and the twinkling lights of tenderness. Twice she missed her step and twice the earl set her right, laughing at her discomfiture. She could not, she knew, be making the very best of company. She pulled herself together with an effort. Out of deference to her partner she owed it to him to show a little interest.

He was talking now, his words seeming to Cassandra to take an interminable time to reach her ears. Not for the first time she sighed at being so small. The earl was looking down at her with such saucy mischief that she was startled.

All at once, the words "St. John" and "Wyndham" rolled into her ears like echoes of her own consciousness. What could the man be saying? Paying closer attention, Cassandra realized at last, that he was gently teasing her. Teasing her because she had snared the unsnarable St. John!

With dawning comprehension, Cassandra began to understand the gist of the man's talk and with it the implication that she had in fact been dancing with Wyndham. The unmasking would surely verify this, but the thought came as a shock. He had not seemed not to mind her remarks, but how could she tell? How had she come to be so addle-brained as to talk of the duke in that spirited vein? What, again, must he think of her?

So occupied was she with these disturbing thoughts that she failed to notice the gentleman's departure as the set drew to its inevitable close.

FIVE

"Well young lady, you've got a lot of explaining to do!"

Violet Harrington positively hissed as she spat out the words, heaving herself onto the great white cushions of the baronial chaise. Her feathers were limp, having spent half the evening in a state of unseasonable humidity. Without so much as a backward glance at the two outriders who'd so sturdily helped her into the equipage, she tucked at the folds of her voluminous dress and admonished her daughter to do the same.

Squashed in the corner seat of the chaise, Cassandra closed her eyes. She had no wish to face her irate relative, nor yet for a further distasteful scene. The strange enchantment she felt hung about her like a mantle and refused to be shaken off so soon.

It had been a long and emotional evening. There was, too, the problem of Harrington to contemplate. For all her patience, the situation was now untenable. She would have to make some decisions in that regard and soon. Cassandra reflected with resignation that the time had come for her to make arrangements to leave the protection of the manor that had once been her home.

"Well? I am waiting!"

Cassandra remembered that she was the granddaughter of an earl and drew herself up in uncustomary haughtiness. "My dear Mrs. Harrington, if you're referring, as I think you are, to that disgraceful scene Sir Robert felt impelled to enact, I can only say I have nothing to explain. An apology from that quarter might be pleasing, too!"

Cassandra was in no mood to be toyed with, and the defiance that sprung so readily from her lips was antagonism born of long days of mourning and numerous heartrending attempts to be conciliatory. She felt compelled, all at once, to release the rage that had been welling up inside her like an ugly, festering wound. Since the moment of the Harringtons' arrival on the scene, she'd imposed a rigid regime of self-control upon her being.

Fighting the urge to have the insinuating people bodily removed from her home, she had turned a blind eye to the desecration of her grandfather's dream. Most of all, she had kept the silent pain of Frances's death or imprisonment locked in her soul, unable to share the misery or even express her doubts. The Countess Jersey had noted how passionately Cassandra defended the belief that he still lived. What she did not adequately perceive was the agony of uncertainty that daily racked her being.

"Don't be impertinent, girl!" Violet Harrington's voice grew shrill with anger. The night had not been a success for her. First, her son had made the most dismal mull over winning Cassandra to his side, a circumstance that was imperative if they were to maintain their newfound standard of living. Second, London's most eligible party had been witness to the whole affair. Third—most calamitous of all—he had looked, to all the world, like a man in love. Nothing could more have overset her plans for Cassandra.

"Sir Robert is your guardian, my dear. Like it or not, you had best come around to that notion and fast. If you act like a fast woman and allow yourself to be whisked around the ballroom in a shameless waltz, you cannot expect him to be pleased. Elise, don't slouch against the cushions. It does not become a lady!"

Cassandra ignored the ugly pout of protest from the young

Miss Harrington's painted lips. She was finally outraged beyond belief. "Sir Robert's pleasure has little to do with me! I hesitate to tell you this, dear aunt—no you're not that, are you?—but I will not and cannot tolerate his treatment of me. To say the least, his behavior more befits a cad than a gentleman! Had I anywhere to stay tonight short of causing a scandal, believe me I would not be sitting here right now. Tomorrow, just as soon as I have made arrangements, I shall leave."

Her chin tilted in a way that spelled danger to those of her intimate acquaintance. Normally her nature was even-keeled, but the auburn lights of her hair were an apt reminder that beneath the sunny countenance lay a streak of untamed demon. She would not and could not be abused. She had reached her stormy limits and her soul cried out for a fight. Tonight, she'd see to it that her room was kept locked and an abigail slept on a pallet beside her bed. There had been something not quite sane in the way Sir Robert had stared at her earlier that evening. Something she did not like at all. She shivered.

"Get out!" Violet's face was suffused with puce as she spat out the words. "Stop the coach, you fool!" She rapped on the windowpane with the stem of her fan, but to no avail. The torrents of rain were remorseless, making it impossible for the groom or outriders to hear anything of what was said inside the barouche. Turning angrily, she put her head out the window, only to see the last of her hat whisked away in the raging skies.

"I said halt! Can't you stop, you goddamn idiot?" She was bellowing now, in a manner most unbecoming to a lady.

Cassandra's irrepressible sense of humor began getting the better of her. "Stop it, Aunt! If you expect me to dismount here, you've got another think coming! You'll just have to bear my company for the next twelve hours, I'm afraid. After that I can only hasten to assure you the less we see of one another, the better happy I will be!"

This strident appeal was lost on the Harringtons. Mother and daughter alike had taken up shrieking, much to the acute embarrassment of the groom and outriders stationed but a few feet down the path.

For the first time, Cassandra realized just what sort of a predicament she was in. Clearly, both Violet and Elise were serious in their intention of throwing her out of the barouche. Struck dumb by the enormity of what was happening, she scarcely knew how to respond. One thing she was certain of, though. An abject apology would not be wrested from her lips whatever the provocation. Rightly or wrongly, she'd rather die than yield to their vulgar and insidious pressure.

"Try for a little decorum, Mrs. Harrington! I have said I will leave tomorrow and that I will. There is simply no need for this undignified display."

"Undignified!" Violet Harrington fairly blustered with annoyance. "Who do you think you are, Miss High and Mighty, to treat me thus? Oh yes, I've seen the stare of your friends and the way they turn their noses up at dear Elise and me! Why, I daresay if Robert didn't hold the vowels of any number of the young men about this town, he too, would be treated thus! Your father may have been a viscount and your grandfather an earl, but just remember one thing, my girl, they are long gone and Robert is the earl now!"

She lurched forward as the chaise at last came to its grinding halt. "Now get out! If you're going to leave tomorrow, I'd as lief as have the pleasure of evicting you!" She spat in fury. "Hussy! I wonder what the great almighty duke would think of you now? You and your missish, prim gowns and your silly cameo necklaces! Who do you think you are kidding? I just wish he could see it!" She laughed a mirthless laugh and literally thrust Cassandra from the barouche. "Walk home, if you can, my fair lady. I daresay, after all, that the new earl might be delighted to let you in."

Cassandra would stand the treatment no more. This last sally revolted her to the core, and she found she was rather more reconciled to the idea of dismounting. A few more minutes in their company may well have sullied her very being.

Without a further word—what, after all, could she say?—she opened the carriage and began to dismount. The thunderbolts, she found, had progressed to a deluge from the heavens, rain pouring unstintingly in sheets. Steadfastly ignoring the craven desire to climb precipitously back into the chaise and shut the door, she jumped neatly out. By dint of great care, she avoided an enormous mud puddle to the right of her foot.

It was to her credit, indeed, that she summoned sufficient strength of will to neither cry nor beg sympathy from the two ladies seated with so much ceremony and so very little dignity inside the waterlogged conveyance. Rain was trickling down the misted windowpanes, leaving a faint impression of two darkly shadowed figures within. The Gothic image was marred somewhat by the flapping of gilded ribbons against the carriage side. Elise was forced to open the door to retrieve the offending lace and so spoiled the otherwise high drama of the event.

Despite her predicament, Cassandra could not help but see the funny side of this scenario, likening herself to the proverbial damsel in distress. Only, she chided herself, it was not so funny and there was no handsome prince hovering somewhere appropriately nearby. When her mind started playing games, featuring a certain enigmatic gentleman with hair black with curls and steely eyes that softened in turns to liquid gold, she drew herself up sharply.

With a defiant lift to the shoulders, she stood back to let the carriage continue along its distant way. In this kind of darkness and inclement weather it was an arduous ride from Curzon Street to the more ponderous address at Kensington. *Perhaps better,* she thought with a wry attempt at humor, *to be spared the trial of such a journey.*

Her brief reverie was interrupted by the sound of a gruff farewell and a murmured apology. The groom, it seemed, was loath to leave her out there in the bitterly cold, wet dark. It was strange how fast the humidity of earlier had changed to a whipping cold. It was more than his job was worth, though, to disobey his madame. Not when she was in one of her moods. Nevertheless, he was bound to recognize quality when he saw it, and this lady was undoubtedly that.

Responding to his mute appeal, Cassandra found herself shouting reassurance out into the night air. It was all she could do to make herself heard over the blistering wind and pelting rain. "Never fear, Adams," she yelled. "I'll make do. Be off!"

Doffing his cap in silent obeisance, he picked up the reins and coaxed the horses forward. Thus it was that some time before the crier called the hours of morn, Miss Cassandra Beaumaris, erstwhile granddaughter to the fifth earl of Surrey, found herself alone, homeless, and soaking wet.

Covering her thin muslin gown with the velvet folds of her cloak, she dubiously tested the ground with the tips of her toes. As she suspected, the soil was rapidly turning into liquid mud. Not an auspicious start to a tramp that might lead anywhere. Where was she to go, after all? If she tarried on this road much longer, she might be taken for a serving wench and whipped for her trouble.

Anyone looking at her now could be forgiven the mistake. It would be hard to believe that she was not some brazen hussy out on a lover's tryst. Without benefit of maid and presenting the type of bedraggled appearance she did, she looked quite wanton. While it was true that some ladies of fashion had taken to dampening their undergarments to affect a "clinging" appearance, this was going too far.

The weather was offering no respite. Indeed, by the sound of the thunder, it was worsening. Cassandra shivered, casting aside the protection of the cloak. It was no longer any use to her, waterlogged as it was. Laden with frosty icicles, it had been sitting heavy, wet, and cold on her shoulders. Just a burden. She needed to be light on her feet if she were to run in this rain for shelter. A tree, perhaps? A cottage? She judged by the distance they had traversed that she must be but a few steps from Grosvenor Square.

Grosvenor Square? Impossible to think of. The best ancestral homes were situated there. Not a fit place for one such as she, alone and destitute. She grimaced as she realized she would have trouble getting through even the servant entrance. Knowing this, she looked around wildly for a tree. Clearly, it was her only hope. She tried not to think that lightning might strike at any moment.

The clamor of horses impinged on her consciousness. A carriage? She must get out of the way. Her feet slipped deeper into the mud. With a determined air she extricated them, and lifting her skirts, made to run. Hands outstretched to steady herself, she teetered, trying desperately to gain a foothold. The mud was more treacherous than she had imagined. The coach was drawing nearer. The occupants had not seen her, of this she was certain. If she tried to scream, the words would be lost on the wind. She had to move.

Just as the chaise drew parallel, she stumbled on a gnarled tree stump that providence had set in her way. With a shriek, she went down, face first, into the pooling mud. At the same moment, lightning lit the night sky, fierce in its intensity and serving to make her appear more wretched and pathetic than ever she was. What a sight for the driver! As for the occupant, he called a halt immediately. The sight was intriguing.

Cassandra desperately wrenched herself from the thorny, pooling mess of mud. She was oblivious now to the sounds of whinnying and footsteps filtering through the windy night air. She was beyond looking for shelter and almost beyond hoping for help. This was a nightmare, and she gave herself up to it totally and without reservation. The morning would take care of itself.

She longed only for the dark to end and for the oblivion of sweet sleep. When she felt the weight of strong arms enveloping her, lifting her as if she were of no more consequence than a bundle of straw or a light feathered muff, she was too swamped with exhaustion to make any demur.

It seemed like no time at all before she had been deposited

among the soft velvet cushions of the chaise, a warm kerseymere blanket straddled across her shoulders and onto her lap.
In the far recesses of her mind she was aware of a certain
warmth beside her, but she was too caught up in her fright and
misery to take much stock of the changed circumstances.

Had she but noticed it, she was seated beside a man quite
dazzling in the simplicity of his finery and in the cut of his
evening coat. When lightning flashed once more, it was to
be observed that a fleeting smile was hovering at the corners
of his upturned mouth, leaving a momentary impression of
something very warm and infinitely gentle beneath the hard
and uncommonly dark visage.

Cassandra could be forgiven for not seeing it, however. In
the past few hours, she had experienced exhilaration, humiliation, defiance, and overwhelming despair. Never one to suc-
cumb to the temptations of swooning, she proceeded to defy
her own rigid principles in this matter by doing just that. Before
she knew what was happening or she could make sense of the
imperious commands shouted to the driver, her head had
slumped against the great red velvet seat cushions and her
wish for oblivion had, temporarily at least, been granted.

When she came to, she was aware of voices and a jolting,
and most astonishing of all, the human warmth of a body in
close proximity with her own. More to the point, she was suffused with an irrepressible sense of well-being and comfort.
Feeling safe and uncommonly satisfied, she snuggled deeper
in the arms of the mystical rescuer, and thought no more.

It was only when she became aware of a certain fumbling
that she began to take stock of the situation. Opening one
eye resignedly, she began idly to take in her new surround-
ings. Through her lashes she saw hands gently reaching out
for a white silk kerchief. A shock of warmth as fingers
brushed firmly across her face, removing streaks of mud,
soiling the brightness of the soft cloth as it floated before
her dazed countenance.

Then realization. A cry of alarm. Both eyes flashed open,

focusing with clarity on the man seated so boldly next to her. The tremor that flooded through her being as their eyes locked was indescribable. Fully conscious, she sat up, pulling at her straggling hair as she did so.

"It is you!"

The man nodded, a wide grin lightening his frowning features.

"From the river and the blackberries and the . . ."

"Ancient Roman good-luck penny. Yes." He finished her sentence and his smile was tender. She sat up as she remembered all and it came to her of a sudden that the man of her summer's idyll was one and the same with Wyndham, the duke of her careless disparagement. She blushed and the blush warmed his being. She did not notice, too shocked and confused and curiously out of kilter was she with the beating of her own heart. All she knew was that once again, she was compromised.

"Your Grace!" she expostulated wildly. "I know not rightly how I came to be in this chaise, but I beg you, set me down at once!"

For moment her head reeled with the enormity of the situation. How could she, Miss Cassandra Emily Marianne Beaumaris, have allowed herself to be humbugged into entering a man's carriage? More specifically, this man's carriage? She was no fool, and mask or no mask she knew no man but one to invoke such a response in her.

Without benefit of the eyeshade, he looked as dangerous and as devastatingly handsome as when she had first seen him. The duke of Wyndham! The very person she had so idly insulted but a few hours before. She gasped in outrage. Muddled, her thinking was still colored by the Harringtons' treatment of her. Could this be His Grace's revenge? Something told her that this was not the case, but the lowering thought persisted. She was in the suds and well she knew it.

The glint of tenderness reflected in his eyes passed quite

unheeded. "Answer me honestly if you will, sir! Are you my lord St. John?"

His eyes gleamed. "The notorious rake you mean? The gilded lily, the dandied fop?" His voice was alight with laughter. "Why, yes, I am he! Where is your hartshorn, my love? I'm persuaded you need it!"

Cassandra's heart sank. Ignoring his last ignoble remark, she sought to make her position quite clear. "Hartshorn indeed! I'll have you know that no Beaumaris has ever had to recourse to smelling salts or medicinal powders, nor ever will! Nor I may add, are we in the habit of swooning!"

"No?"

"No!"

"I'm devastated to have to contradict you, my dear, but after your recent fine performance, I find that rather difficult to believe."

Cassandra had the grace to blush.

"As to that, I beg your pardon, sir. I had no desire to importune you in any way. It has never happened before, I assure you. I'd appreciate it, now, if you'd set me down. I'm not certain my good name will survive the night with such a notorious rake!"

While Miles appreciated the note of humor she had introduced into the situation, he would have been obtuse had he failed to detect the underlying fear and trepidation that shone from her eyes. He noted, too, that her voice had lost a good deal of its clarity. To be blunt, it was veering dangerously, now, on the side of the trembly.

He smiled as he looked down on her, swathes of unruly hair spilling out from under the pins and clasps so hopefully set in the style known to the ton as "a la Sophie." As she impatiently waved offending wisps out from under her eyes, her lips parted in as alluring a manner as any man could wish. The memory of the summer morning he'd spent baby-sitting in the absence of a suitable duenna flitted through his mind.

The chit had still been in the schoolroom then, but he

could remember her still: ebullient, brimful of laughter and light. He remembered those lips, too. . . . Silently suppressing a groan, Miles concentrated on her face as she peeped at him a touch defiantly, her chin inclined firmly upward like a knight prepared for battle.

St. John decided to oblige. If battle it was to be, then it would be he who got in the first shot. The evening looked like to take on an interesting turn. "As for unhanding you, sweeting, that will be a pleasure. Forgive my presumption, but I had thought you amenable to our . . . eh . . . delightful position."

Crimson, Cassandra recalled that it had been her hand, indeed, that had so convulsively clutched at the intricate folds of the duke's neckcloth. As if to rectify what had gone before, she impulsively thrust the offending wet, gloved hand behind her back, presenting such a charming picture of ruffled innocence that Miles had great difficulty holding back the soft little kisses that were by now yearning to envelop the adorable countenance before him.

With fastidious and quite out-of-character control, he collected himself enough to maintain his rallying tone. "Since you have recognized me, dear one, what say you we call a truce? You may consider me your humble servant, if it pleases you."

Cassandra remembered the last time they had called a truce and looked up sharply. Something in his tone made her forget, almost, that the man was a gazetted rake and no more a bulwark of comforting, stolid support than her cousin had been. Something she caught in the lilt of his voice was special, attuned to her. She shrugged it off. Such figments of unchecked imagination could bode no good. If she were to have a care to herself, she had best not be trapped by foolish flights of wishful fancy.

"I cannot permit myself to impose on you, Your Grace." Her face remained firm and uncompromising as she surveyed the duke before her. "Be so good as to set me down and let me inconvenience you no further. Already, I fear, your carriage is quite the worse for wear!"

She looked down ruefully at the splattered velvet seats that were testament to the truth of her words. In other circumstances she would have laughed out loud at the sight she presented, bedraggled and tearstained, squeezing out a cloak that was slowly dripping water all over the ornately decorated equipage.

As it was, she had never before been this close to tears. The sensation was unfamiliar to her and rather frightening. It seemed such a weird twist of fate that she should be seated now beside the very person who had caused this trouble at the outset.

There was no denying the physical strength of this man, the duke of Wyndham. The same man, she paused to reflect with brutal honesty, who had played such havoc with her heart two summers ago and again that evening in the enchantment of the ballroom.

"Never mind the carriage! I rather like the idea of having it refurbished. What say you to yellow with bright canary wheels to match? Word has it the Prince of Wales has purchased just such a one!"

Momentarily diverted, Cassandra responded with alacrity. "Perfect! If you don't watch out I'll purchase a monkey for the interior, as I believe Lady Caroline Thornby did two seasons ago. What a sight it must have been! I was rather sorry to have missed it, in fact."

"Did you?"

"Yes, I was at Tunbridge Wells, actually. It was just before my grandfather . . ."

Her voice trailed off at the memory and brought her back with a jolt to the problem on hand. "I'm obliged to you, Your Grace, truly!" The tears were welling up behind her eyes and she felt in danger of letting them drop, unbidden, on His Grace's immaculate pantaloons. If only he wouldn't smile at her so, she'd be able to summon up enough dignity to save herself the shame of spending a night alone and unattended in his company. If only he weren't so exceedingly devastating, or have such a very polished address! If only she didn't feel quite so attached to his soft dark curls or the smile behind his deep gold-brown eyes.

"It's your fault! Don't look at me so!"

"What's my fault?"

"Oh everything!" she responded crossly. "Can't you see I have no wish to be taken to your home? I assume that is to where you intend to abduct me?"

The smile vanished from his eyes, leaving at once an impression of flint mingled with steel. As if in answer to the changed mood, his eyebrows knitted together in a dark furrow that somehow infused his countenance with a hitherto unsuspected sternness.

"What do you expect me to do with you, my dear? Turn you out in this inclement weather and allow you to sleep under a tree? Only supposing you find a tree, of course! We'll discuss it tomorrow, but I assume you have no wish to return tonight to Surrey Manor? Say the word if you do, and I'll have the horses turned round at once."

Cassandra sighed. Given a choice of two evils, she knew there was no choice. Her conscious gave a definite twinge when she realized how little persuading she would need to enter this man's home. Her grandfather would like to have disowned her, were he to have known what she'd be up to. He was always quite punctilious about these things. He'd probably have forced the duke into a marriage.

Miles watched the fleeting thoughts as they danced through her mind, her face as expressive a mirror as ever he'd seen. As he watched, his own countenance lost its heavy sternness, leaving only a trace of the strength and power locked behind the gay facade.

"Well?"

"I'll come with you, of course! To be honest, I don't much relish the idea of the tree!"

The tears were banished with that decision. The duke was touched. Too many females of his acquaintance used tears to manipulate or beguile. Miss Beaumaris used none of these tactics, giving as good as she got, but playing fair. Her hair was now quite irremediably wet and wild, forcing him to display, once more, his rigid self-discipline.

It was not too long that they sat thus before the horses slowed to a mild trot and the road turned to cobble. It said much for Miss Beaumaris that by the time they veered into the tree-lined avenue that heralded the entrance of the St. John estates, she'd regained her composure and had even gone so far as to venture a tremulous smile.

As the coach halted at the steps of the great edifice that was Wyndham Terrace, her courage momentarily failed her. Sensing this, the duke lightly squeezed her hand and treated her to a smile so dazzling in its reassurance that all thoughts of fleeing were instantly dismissed. It had been said by no less a personage than Brummel himself that when my lord St. John set out to amuse, he did so in style and with unfailing aplomb. In this most extraordinary circumstance, he was proven right.

The kerseymere shawl prosaically draped over her petite little being, Cassandra allowed herself to be helped from the carriage and set down on her freezing feet. Her eyes were dancing with ill-restrained amusement at the little *on-dit* that His Grace had chosen to impart but seconds before.

Perhaps, she thought a trifle dolefully, *the Harringtons have achieved their aim and driven me quite, quite mad!*

Mad it was, indeed, to be standing, gloves in hand, on the steps of Wyndham Terrace at a quarter of two in the morning. Despite her reservations and fear for her name, Cassandra could not resist the surge of overwhelming relief that flooded through her senses. In the last few months, Surrey Manor had become a mausoleum, its inhabitants as oppressive as the general atmosphere of gloom naturally attendant on a recent death.

Sir Robert, a miser when it came to pecuniary matters relating to himself, had ordered the holland covers to be placed over most of the grand furnishings in all but the great reception salon. These small economies had paved the way to the dismissal of the core of her grandfather's staff, a circumstance that greatly distressed and discomforted the young mistress Beaumaris. Perhaps if she were to set up her own establishment? It was something to think upon.

For the moment, the great marble steps loomed large before her. What waited for her beyond those doors was unknown; she could but take the first steps and hope with a fervency born of real necessity that fate would be temperate in its dealings with her.

The great chestnut doors glowed red in the night light, open before she had reached the seventh stair. She caught a momentary glimpse of a polished brass knocker before a stream of light left a path on the steps and four liveried figures emerged with a scurrying of feet and a host of half-uttered commands.

By the time she had reached midway between the bottom stair and the grand entrance, the horses had trotted off to be stabled, leaving the sound of hooves echoing through the near-dawn air. The duke, satisfied that his bays had not been overstrained, took the stairs two at a time to join her.

The entrance smelled of pinecones and honey, chestnut and wood. It was warm and welcoming, a stark contrast to the cold marble of outside. Fires flickered in strategically positioned grates, flooding the mansion with warmth and flickering light. Chandeliers of candles hung from the ceiling, half lit with fine wax tapers.

The hallway was a mass of rich red carpet, tinged with the pale pinks, blues, and greens of the orient and fringed with thick crimson tassels. Damask curtains hung from the great windows while the winding stairways were fashioned from a dark mahogany, centuries old and preserved with shining, slightly aromatic beeswax. It was an exciting house, a home that Cassandra felt an instant affinity with, a sense of well-being.

The butler was making his stately way to greet them, his face a mask of wooden propriety. Following behind and in a far more agitated fashion rushed His Grace's valet, the incomparable Vallon.

"Vallon!"

"Oui, monseigneur?"

"Take this and destroy it!" Holding out the sodden cape, the duke could not but smile at the stricken and indignant visage presented by his valet. That the humor was not lost on Cassandra, either, did not escape his attention.

"But monseigneur . . ."

"Take it I say!"

"But yes." Gingerly, the short and immaculate Parisian reached up to take the mantle, his face a picture of complete disgust. He would not for a thousand years admit it, but he was extremely attached to his master and thus prepared to swallow the indignity thrust upon him at times. For a valet to take charge of such a thing! It was insupportable.

His expressive face said it all. The duke laughed. "Be off with you! And to bed! Have I not already said it is unnecessary for the entire household to await my return? I rather think I can do without the attendance of four lackeys, a butler, and a valet at this time of the night. To sleep, all of you!"

With a gesture of the hand, he dismissed the hovering footmen, indicating the butler to remain for a few moments.

Vallon, knowing when and when not to disturb his master, took his leave. His sharp button eyes had not missed the pretty piece beneath the soaking bonnet and kerseymere shawl.

Harboring the Frenchman's love of an intrigue and scenting the soporific smell of romance, he was quite happy to forgo the dubious pleasure of informing His Grace of his ward's latest misdoing. As he reckoned, that could wait until the morning. Allowing himself a lugubrious sigh and an impudent wink in the direction of the lady, he nimbly climbed the servant stairs and disappeared in a trice.

"Hard day, Pickering?" The duke appeared sympathetic as he handed the man his marcasite cane. It was always his wont to treat the servants with both respect and civility. He would have been astonished to know the wholehearted dedication that this approach engendered.

"Oh, no, sir!" The butler allowed himself the ghost of a smile. "Little ones up to mischief, again, of course. Had poor Vallon and the cook in a rare taking, today, they did. Something about pink frosted candy and using your venetian clocked stockings as jump ropes?"

His Grace St. John was by no means misled by the blandness of his tone. "One of these days, Pickering, I'm going to take the whip to them!"

The butler bowed, but his immobile face registered disbelief at this threatening pronouncement.

The duke turned to Cassandra, who was curiously inspecting the carved rosewood statuette that stood high off the ground, its intricate patterns casting warm shadows across the room. If she wondered who the little ones were, she made no comment, basking in the aftermath of her rescue and the warm glow of the flames. The quietude of the house pleased her, at variance with the vulgar changes that had been instituted at Surrey Manor.

"This is the Honorable Miss Beaumaris, Pickering. See to it that she's housed in the yellow chamber and that she has a lady's maid assigned to her. Also, I believe some refreshment may be in order."

As Pickering bowed, he added, as an aside, "It would please me greatly, my dear fellow, were none of the matter to leave this house. You take my meaning?"

Pickering indicated that he did indeed, and Miles led the way up the first flight of stairs to a charming but strongly masculine room.

SIX

"You are cold, my child."

Miles's eyes were warm as they rested on Cassandra, his sharp eyes noting the clinging gown, wet through and through, and the soft kerseymere shawl that clung closely to her shivering figure, as much for modesty, he guessed, as for warmth.

"It's astonishing, is it not, how such a humid night can turn cold? Don't shiver, my sweet! We'll soon have you as warm as toast. Tomorrow you will send for your clothes while we discuss what is to be done with you. Tonight I'll lend you my thick brocade dressing gown and you'll feel, if you'll excuse the humor, as right as rain!" He chuckled.

"Do not stare at me so. I'm not a monster!" Understanding the sudden apprehension in her eyes, he paused. "I am also not in the habit of keeping lady's attire in my home, so if you don't wish to catch your death, you'll do as I say."

Relieved, Cassandra smiled. "Very well, I place myself in your hands. But I warn you, sir, I expect you to behave with propriety!"

St. John smiled, his teeth gleaming white in the candle-light.

"Rest assured, madam, that so long as you remain under my roof, no harm shall come to you. On my honor as a gentleman."

His tone was so unexpectedly sincere that Cassandra bit

back the retort she had started to make. Clearly, despite his reputation as a flirt and heartbreaker, she was in no immediate danger.

Perhaps, after all, she had mistaken the looks he had cast her way all through the evening. It was possible, too, that the dance had meant nothing to him, lost already amid the haze of other dances he'd bestowed on eager young women in the past. Far from easing her mind, the thought depressed her, leaving her with a sadly flat sensation.

The timid knock on the door heralded the entrance of a nervous young maid, hat askew, who began her curtsy before Cassandra even had time to wonder at how quickly she'd been seconded. The duke nodded at her stammered attempts to introduce herself.

"It is Alice, is it not?" The maid bobbed a nervous curtsy, her eyes darting from the duke to Cassandra, who stood huddled by the hearth. "Alice, this is Miss Beaumaris. She'll be staying with us tonight, so make sure that she is comfortable, if you please. Take her up to the yellow chamber and ask Vallon to send down the striped brocade. That will be all, thank you."

For an instant Cassandra's eyes met with those of the hesitant little housemaid's and they locked in a moment of unspoken empathy. Cassandra was not to know that the reassuring smile that passed between them had secured for her a well-tended fire, a posy of violets from the garden beneath the servants' windows, and a devotion unswerving in its loyalty.

All she did know was that she was now alone with the one person in the world with whom she felt a strong affinity, and the bond was like an ache of sweet antithesis, strong, yet yielding, tempting yet frightening. She longed to smooth away the line of fatigue etched in the furrows of his brow, yet felt herself vulnerable.

She was very wary of the unspoken connection between them, the unvoiced bond. Unnerved by the unknown, by thoughts unbidden and sentiments unlooked for, she sought to introduce an element of lightness to the now electric moment.

"I'm starving. I swear I could eat a horse!"

Miles startled, his handsome features changing from concern to amusement in an instant of admiring comprehension. He looked her up and down for a moment, as one assessing the likelihood of a horse fitting into the stomach of a creature as fragile as herself.

"Not a chance, my dear! No room, I guess, unless you want to try for the little piebald pony I have but purchased?"

Cassandra laughed, her usual *je nais se quais* restored. "A pony? My dear, sir, with your lanky legs I'd not miss the spectacle for the world! When, pray, will I have the satisfaction of an exhibition?"

Miles's admiration for her spunk grew as he gave her an answering grin. "Alas, you'll just have to wait for that. Georgie, one of my little brats, has first option on that sight."

Cassandra's world dimmed. No longer could she ignore the oblique references to my lord's progeny. Misbegotten? Conceivably, but surely even he would obey the conventions? Obviously not. She felt a cold shiver cross her spine, then resolutely set aside her reverie. What mattered it if there were a whole host of misbegotten varmints? In the morning she would be gone and the events of the evening would be one more episode in a life filled with interludes and chapters. For now, she was hungry and by the smell of it, dinner would not be long off.

It was Pickering himself who delicately coughed before entering with a tray of delectables that sent Cassandra's taste buds reeling. Hot stuffed duck quenelles, florentine of veal, and thin slivers of Norfolk turkey preceded the cold sweet of pease pudding and a selection of banana and apple fritters topped with cream. For drink, a steaming cup of chocolate was set before her.

It was such an unexpectedly appetizing array that fears and confusion were duty bound to recede to the point, almost, of permanent expulsion. Miles crossed the room to stoke the fire before answering the rap on the door with a half-stifled oath. Cassandra was amused to note the sheepish look when he found it was simply Vallon with the dressing gown.

Brooking no argument, he helped her into it and tied the knot with a firmness not missed on the perceptive Miss Beaumaris. Clearly, he had no wicked designs on her this evening at least. How perverse to feel that faint twinge of disappointment! Really, the shock of the whole evening must be playing more on her shattered nerves than she'd previously imagined.

"Do you always eat like this, Your Grace?" Cassandra asked. He raised his eyebrows questioningly. "I mean at this time of night? And in this sort of quantity?"

Miles made a face. "Terrible, isn't it? It's my wretched servants, of course. They've got a greater idea of the consequence due my title than I do myself! They seem to feel that twenty-four-hour cuisine befits my station in life, and nothing I tell the housekeeper can convince her otherwise."

Cassandra bit into a hot quenelle. It was quite delicious, so subtly flavored her tongue savored it with undisguised pleasure. Truly, a taste sensation of the first order.

As she settled at the small oak table where the tray had been set down, she could not help but peek at the man who had been so good to her. What an impact he'd had on her life that evening. The candle flickered, reflecting his face in a light that was soft and warm.

Her glance was reciprocated. What Cassandra saw in his eyes made her tremble with wonderment. There was laughter and strength and a hint of sternness. There was also, she could feel, an underlying sentiment that was indescribable in its depth yet quite overwhelmingly sincere. She experienced the absolute conviction that she was safe, as close to home as ever she had been.

When his hand reached out from across the table, it seemed the most natural thing in the world that she should place her own within its warm confine. When he smiled, it was like a light that mirrored her soul, an accurate reflection of her own subdued sense of merriment and tenderness. She felt that her fears, her pain, her anguish had been lightened. Not taken away, but shared and understood.

No words, just the silent communion of two people. The sensation was magnetic, awesome in its simplicity. Cassandra had no need of reassurances, sympathy, or banal talk. Had Miles attempted any of these, the magic might well have been lost, constraining her once more to commonplaces.

In the event, such social etiquette was unnecessary and in the sheltered haven—unlikely though it was—Cassandra blossomed like a flower, rare and fresh and sweet. No words! Miles found himself with an unknown quantity. A woman who did not bore him to death, who used neither caprice nor falsity nor pretension to capture his attention. Speculatively, he gazed at Cassandra once more. The uplifted little nose looked charming on her countenance and the thick mass of rich auburn was a magnificent foil to her strong, vibrant character.

Her very petiteness served to make her more adorable. When he'd held her in his arms she'd seemed to him as light as a dewdrop on a spring morning. When she spoke, she was forced to look up and her lips were certainly seen to their best advantage—maddeningly so for one in his unenviable position.

The duke revised his original impression. In looks, she was beautiful. Not conventionally so, but beautiful, nonetheless. In character? Well, so it would seem. Time would tell. Old habits died hard, and the disdain that Miles was wont to deal with women was not easily eradicated, especially not on so short an acquaintance.

The lady in question was tucking, rather unromantically, into the plate of fritters. Fear allayed, the said damsel found that she had the most enormous appetite. The result, she succinctly informed the duke, of attempting entrechats in the quadrille after so long without practice. The duke thought back to the blackberries and smiled.

She continued impishly. "You can have no notion of how many times I missed the mark with poor Lord Glenby! Dear man, I doubt that he'll be leading me out again too soon!"

She stretched out for a little sugar, sprinkling with abandon on the last of the banana. "You're sure you don't want more?" she asked, glancing at Miles a trifle doubtfully, the fritter balancing precariously on the edge of the silver embossed fork.

Miles assured her with a gleam that he was certain he'd not be requiring the last of her treat. He moved instead to the glass cabinet, pouring himself a little of the port he'd craved so much earlier in the evening. What an interminable time ago it seemed.

The port sparkled as the light caught the crystal, sending tiny shadows across the table. Cassandra could not help but notice the duke's long, straight fingers as they twined round the stem of the glass. As he twirled the goblet, absentmindedly releasing the bouquet through force of habit rather than intention, his demeanor assumed a thoughtful appearance. A small smile lurked at the corners of his very masculine mouth.

"Is it too late to discuss your predicament, Miss Beaumaris? Would you prefer I withdraw and we address the issue in the morning?"

Thoughts of his leaving came as a shock to Cassandra, who quite enjoyed contemplating the tips of his rather well-shaped fingernails. She wouldn't allow herself to muse on the morrow or on more bitter speculations.

He seemed, however, to be more than earnest. With a sigh she realized she owed it to him to cast away the magic and herald in, once more, the light of day, the unpalatable practicality.

"It is not too late, Your Grace. I owe you an explanation. I know not how to begin, nor what you may think of me, but honesty compels me to speak the truth."

"Indeed it does, Miss Beaumaris! If I believed there to be

the faintest chance you'd tell me a whisker I'd have you over my knee in a twinkling!"

Cassandra was not fooled. The severity of his tone was unmatched by the betraying laughter of his eyes. Indeed, far from engendering alarm, he seemed instead to effect a calming influence upon her jangled nerves. His amiable banter provocatively engendered a spirited retort from the lady, making it easier by far for her to unburden herself.

For the first time in a long time Cassandra sensed a sympathetic ear. She talked freely but with a quiet restraint that said much. It was not what she said but what she left unsaid that roused the duke to passion. More than anyone he could imagine the anguish she'd been through, the humiliation she'd suffered at the hands of the Harringtons.

He vowed to avenge himself on the Harrington family. He'd set the record straight and settle the matter of Beaumaris's disappearance to his own satisfaction. If he were dead, better to know than to repine. He would buy up Harrington's gaming vowels, pay off his plethora of bills, and hold him personally accountable for the debt. He would have the new lord so hamstrung in credit he would not be able to blow his nose without first consulting the duke. Miles's eyes grew grim. If it took a debtor's prison to make the vile Sir Robert realize the error of his ways, then so be it. Earl or no, the man would be made to regret the behavior of a cad.

If Lord Frances were alive, however . . . The duke's jaw set. He would find a means to contact and repatriate him. Silently he gave up thanks for his not inconsiderable influence both inside and outside the House of Lords.

His deliberations assumed a new turn as he watched the lady before him grapple with tears and lose. He noted with pleasure that she did not heroically allow the tears to flow, unchecked. She did not assume the attitude of a forlorn Madonna and revel in the pathos of the pose as most ladies of his acquaintance would have done. Far from it! My lady, it should be reported, was blowing quite prosaically into a large and suspiciously masculine handkerchief. For an instant the duke's sympathy was with Vallon, who'd doubtless be outraged at this gross abuse of the finest cambric.

"More fool he for keeping the thing in the gown pocket," the peer reflected fleetingly. Then his thoughts were all for Cassandra, who had somehow become entangled in the ruffles of his shirt, her head snuggled deep within the recesses of his chest. How she had gotten there, he never would know. Perhaps as a result of a silent gesture on his part.

Heavens! He'd never been in so damnable a position before. So tempting to incline her head backward just slightly and shower her with wild and ardent kisses. So easy, too, to slip his hand inward into the folds of what was after all his own dressing gown. He could see the shadow of her pale, rounded flesh, and he nearly forgot his promise of only moments before.

The demon passed. What madness should seize him when he had the pick of the season's beauties! He was not vain, just prosaically truthful. He held more store by the strong attractions of his name and fortune than those of his hand and heart. He tried now to concentrate on the problems at hand, but with scant and sorry success. In the end, he gave up, stroking her gently until the sobbing subsided and she'd drawn sufficient breath to give another vigorous blow on the ill-fated handkerchief. When she withdrew from him, the sensation of her touch lingered on, teasing his senses in the most delightfully distracting manner.

"Cassandra."

She looked up, the natural use of her name offering no uncomfortable obstacles.

"We must talk of your future. Your being here with me the whole night will not do."

She grimaced deprecatingly. "I know! Admit it, Your Grace, did I not beg you to allow me dismount from your equipage? Now, I fear, I am quite ruined!" She smiled mistily. "Shocking, isn't it?" Her tone was deceptively blithe and Miles found himself admiring her all the more for her self-restraint. She may be funning, but there was nonetheless an unpalatable element of truth in what she said. Were he ever so careful of her reputation, there could be no doubt that by the morning she'd be ruined, reduced to a veritable societal *on-dit* before something juicier arose to displace her with the gossips.

As a gentleman, His Grace the duke of Wyndham had no recourse but to offer for her. Accepting the fact with an astonishing degree of equanimity for a bachelor so well-established as himself, he tossed back the drink he was holding and made a whimsical bow.

"Ruined? Come, my dear, you must by now have a better opinion of me than that!"

"What can you mean?" Cassandra was staring at him in puzzlement. She picked up a paperweight and fingered it idly as she spoke. "If you mean to quash the scandal, let me assure you it will not fadge! My dearest Robert will not let slip this opportunity to sully my name." Her voice was laden with uncharacteristic sarcasm.

"Why, I shouldn't wonder if he's not doing the rounds already!" She stopped and thought better of the statement. "No, for now at least, he is unaware of my whereabouts. But this sort of thing cannot remain under wraps forever. I reckon it is a fair bet to assume he will come by the interesting knowledge some time or another!" She stopped for breath and nearly choked as she caught sight of the tender smile hovering on His Grace's lips. Almost, she thought wistfully, as though he truly cared.

"Silly goose! Cannot you think of another way talk might be averted?"

His eyes were unwavering upon her face.

For an instant Cassandra guessed at the truth, then put the thought firmly away. The memory of his children made mockery of such a contemplation. Besides, it was only in storybooks that one married handsome dukes and lived happily ever after. Life had a rather more jarring way of dealing with its protagonists.

She hesitated for a fraction, reluctant to relinquish the dream, then sighed as her humor resurfaced. "Short of running the whole wretched lot through in their beds tonight, no."

An honest answer, free of the guile Miles was half expecting to detect. He was spurred to put the question and have done with it.

"Marry me, Cassandra."

The words were so unexpected and such a mirror of her secret yearning that it was some seconds before she made a reply. When she did, the words stuck to the roof of her mouth like dry ashes, bitter and utterly devoid of hope.

"I cannot, Your Grace. You must know that I cannot."

The words were out before she could retrieve them.

"Why not?"

How could she say what she suspected? If the little "brats" he referred to were by-blows, he insulted her grossly. Perhaps he thought she would overlook the impertinence given her situation. If she could have, she would have. But her upbringing was too strong, and the children would be proof, always, of his roving nature and infidelity.

She knew she was fooling herself. She knew that all this was as naught in comparison with her desire for him. In her heart of clamoring hearts, she knew that it was her very need that prevented her from allowing him to make this most supreme of sacrifices. Had he but loved her . . . ah, then it would be different! She had no choice but to cling on to the prosaic objections of her mind and deny the romantic yearnings of her will.

Cassandra became incoherent as the multitude of thoughts and reasons flitted through her consciousness. When she needed it most, her studied calm deserted her. "I will not think on it, Your Grace. You rescued me from certain illness and perhaps a lot worse. That should be enough. To throw away your life for the sake of some chivalrous impulse is the height of absurdity."

Her voice trembled at this last. It was a dazzling attempt at bringing the duke to a sense of reason. It failed.

The man was implacable, his white shirt stark against the dark of his lashes and close-cropped curls. Cassandra drew a sharp breath, regretting the necessity of resisting a man who could play such havoc with her sense of equilibrium. His presence made her feel that anything was possible. Everything was *impossible!*

The duke was pulling her toward him, and she was not making the least push to protect her virtue.

"Don't slap me, my pretty!" His thoughts were echoing hers as she remembered her youthful encounter with him so long ago. His voice had become rough and it was not long— perhaps two agonizing seconds—before she felt the weight of his mouth bearing down upon her, crushing the last vestiges of her unspoken protest. Two and a half seconds before she felt her body molding to his, his ardor her ardor.

If His Grace was surprised at the intimate stirring he felt awakening in the young woman his arms encircled, he seemed not to mind. In fact, the response prompted him to set aside his nobler feelings. Heathenlike, he took full advantage of the hunger he was generating, lifting Cassandra high off her feet in his exuberant passion.

When he released her, he looked shaken. The langorous boredom with which he had come to be associated was no longer in evidence. Too late did Cassandra quell the last vestiges of her madness. Marriage was out of the question. She'd not marry him for the sake of her honor, of that she was certain.

He offered marriage as a sudden caprice. If he lived to regret it she'd be mortified for the rest of her days. Better never to get involved than to live with the bitterness of entrapment and a youthful mistake. Besides, there were the children . . . The quizzical look had returned to Miles's face as he watched the inward struggle of his lady love.

How perverse life appeared to be. Had he but offered for another woman there would hardly, he was convinced, be a moment's hesitation. Certainly his affianced would scarcely be presenting the picture of misery that Cassandra was, eyes downcast, foot kicking at the tassel of his patterned rug.

"Your Grace, I'll not wed you! I appreciate the great honor you do me and can only say that I am deeply in your debt. Beyond that, I fear I cannot commit myself. In the morning, if you please, I will dispatch a letter to Miss Plum, my old governess, and make arrangements to leave with her. In all conscience I can importune you no further. Too much has already occurred between us."

She blushed at this last, willing herself not to think on what had indeed passed between them. If he thought to beget further brats he must indeed search elsewhere! Besides, as she glumly reflected, the talk of marriage could merely be a ruse to remove her guard. It seemed suddenly monstrous that he'd not sought to explain the presence of the youngsters under his roof.

The contradictory nature of her musings could largely be set down to the novel pangs of love, jealousy, and insecurity that settled like a dark cloud on the recesses of her mind, confounding her at every turn. She was angry and immensely grateful at one and the same moment. In love and afraid of love. Fear makes a mockery of the best of us, and Cassandra was no exception. Where she would have done well to hold her tongue, she taunted, perversely pleased at the ripple of annoyance she detected in the duke.

"Your children . . . misbegotten, I presume?"

Miles started. He was shocked at the turn of her thoughts but steadied himself. Deliberately and slowly he poured another drink from the decanter before answering the challenge she had thrown down. Back turned, Cassandra could not help but admire the fine fit of his coat, the broad shoulders that molded to the dark superfine in a perfect symphony of good taste.

When he turned, he was examining the fine cut of the crystal. He flicked the glass with the back of his finger to produce a sound of the purest tenor. His voice held a warning that was not lost on Cassandra. Her stubborn nature had found a kindred spirit and she was unsure of whether to be pleased or sorry.

"In the morning, Miss Beaumaris, we shall discuss your predicament. For the moment, I shall ignore your impertinence."

Cassandra made a move to respond. He held up his hand.

"Right now, I believe us both to be too fatigued to be responsible for any words or actions arising from the day's events. You will do well to rest on the problem. I don't doubt the new day will herald in its own solutions. For now, though, I suggest you sleep."

The bell was peremptorily rung before Cassandra could protest. The day had been unequaled in its demands on her and exhaustion was finally and resolutely taking its toll.

It was perhaps wistful to hope that His Grace would be sensible to the fact that it was anguish, not rudeness that impelled her to refer to the youngsters. It seemed hardly a moment before Alice was ushering her out of the room with a small backward curtsy for His Grace.

As she sank back thankfully into the well-aired sheets, she could not for the life of her remember whether the feather-light kiss he'd dropped on her forehead before she left had been real or simply a figment of her overtired imagination.

SEVEN

The day was well advanced before Cassandra was roused to the intriguing sound of a smothered giggle. Sleepily, she opened an eye to discover an impudent little face staring at her with eyes as dark as chestnut.

As the details slowly filtered to her drowsy senses, she shifted to one arm on the huge, brocaded four-poster bed in which she found herself. She peered with drowsy interest beyond the drapes in the direction of the elfinlike presence.

Blinking, bafflement changed to surprise when not one but two little beings laughingly presented themselves for inspection. Before she could muster sufficient coherence to raise a question, they had jumped up onto the bed as effortlessly and unconsciously as if it had been their life's practice.

"I'm so glad you've woken! We've waited and waited, haven't we, Gracie?"

The more exuberant of the two, if so she could be described, had stopped bouncing.

"Uncle Miles said that if we were good we could go on a picnic. I love picnics, don't you?"

The question was evidently rhetorical, for she hardly stopped for breath before rushing headlong into a new line of inquiry.

Cassandra relaxed back into the pillows, perplexity giving way to very evident amusement. What a pair they were, these lively twins! The first was now seeing fit to inspect the clasp of her tiny cameo necklace, while the latter was making tentative attempts to stroke the silky hair that flowed in abundance out from the mob cap Alice had so thoughtfully provided the night before.

"Who are you? And yes, I adore picnics." The image of one particular impromptu picnic flashed through her mind and she colored quickly. The girls, fortunately, took no note.

"I'm Grace, but I hate being called that. Georgie is Georgie, of course!"

With these rather cryptic remarks Cassandra had to be satisfied, for the housemaid had entered the chamber and was apparently highly flustered by their presence in the room.

She spoke severely. "His Grace said you were not to disturb Miss Beaumaris, you two! Where are your manners?"

Shamefacedly, they slid off the bed and made their curtsies in so quixotic a fashion that Cassandra felt her mouth twitching, a sure sign of an imminent chuckle.

"What time is it?"

"Why, just past noon, miss!" The servant had expertly pulled back the drapes, allowing a flood of sunlight to bathe the room in morning warmth.

"Noon!"

"Yes, miss. His Grace gave orders that you were not to be troubled. Scarper, you two!"

This last was to the twins, who were watching Cassandra with a degree of curiosity she found unnerving. Their bobbed black hair looked singularly in keeping with their pixielike features. Cassandra winked at them, making friends for life as they responded in kind. They scuttled off with an enjoinder not to tell Uncle Miles about their latest escapade.

Despite her curiosity, Cassandra made a practice of not gossiping with the servants. Rather, she allowed her hair to be vigorously brushed and set into a tight coil. Despite the abigail's coaxing, she somehow could not see her way clear to allowing the shiny mass to hang loose.

Such a pity it was that it had such a will of its own! How wonderful it would be to have masses of curls—no need for papers and pins, fasteners and clips. Long, straight hair without a whisper of a ringlet was her despair. The hours she had spent trying to wangle it into some kind of style! Fortunately, she was not sufficiently vain to have her spirits too long depressed by commonplaces.

It occurred to her that she had not a thing to wear besides the ball gown of the previous night. Hardly an auspicious start to a day that quite naturally held its share of terrors. Still, it was better than nothing, she supposed. No doubt it had been duly cleaned and pressed by the housekeeper earlier in the day.

It had not been. As she stood up to survey the room, she gasped at the sight of the sapphire jaconet hanging delicately over the side of the broad chaise longue. Sprigged with lemon and trimmed with tiny rosettes of satin and lace, it had appeared as if by magic.

Next to the day dress were matching slippers of venetian velvet and a trimmed bonnet that bore all the hallmarks of Miss Peeples, the Bond Street milliner of such famed repute.

The maid noted the direction of her gaze and felt compelled to enthuse over the duke's impeccable taste, throwing open overflowing wardrobes with pride and excitement. Her words were lost as the enormity of the scenario struck Cassandra for the first time that morning.

She had spent the night in a gentleman's residence. The world as she knew it would never be the same. The thought was all too much. She shocked the kindly maidservant by demonstrating a singular lack of interest in the fashionable treasures that met her eyes.

The duke had evidently been very busy. Or had he merely sent a minion out on this quest to clothe her? Cassandra could not help but wonder.

"Alice, where is my muslin?"

"I don't rightly know, miss. Like as not old Pomerey

burned it. You won't mind my saying it was hardly fit for
much after the drenching it received last night! I had it in
mind to patch the lace torn from the hem—French it was,
I'm sure—but His Grace would not hear of it."

"Who is Pomerey?"

"Why, the housekeeper, miss!" Alice looked astonished
at the question. Cassandra sighed. Nothing for it, but to be
helped into the jaconet. She was forced to ruefully acknow-
ledge the wisdom of presenting herself respectably. Heaven
only knew what notions the servants had dreamed up to account for her presence in the house!

On consideration, it might well raise a few brows if she
were to catch the mail in a very much worse for wear ball
gown. The morning dress, at least, was unobjectionable. Actually, it was rather becoming. Nevertheless, she deplored
the circumstances that made it incumbent upon her to accept
it. She'd persuade the duke to send her the reckoning. Expensive, perhaps, but worth being no further entangled in his
debt. In the light of day the extent of his kindness seemed
overwhelming.

It seemed, too, that she had done him a gross injustice.
The twins had referred to him quite naturally as "uncle."
Since she had no reason to suspect them of duplicity, she
had to assume that this was the innocent explanation for their
presence in the ancestral home.

In which event, she realized miserably, her behavior of the
night before had been inexcusable in the extreme. Her talk
of by-blows must have put her quite beyond the pale. For a
lady to disclose knowledge of such matters was inexcusable
enough—to openly taunt a man with untrue and unsubstan-
tiated guesswork was positively vulgar. The most she could
hope for was that he'd display some vestige of the humor
she'd glimpsed in him and ignore the whole dismal outburst.

It was a lowering thought, indeed, that she owed her honor
to a man gazetted as a rake. Worse, that his behavior had
been irreproachable while hers had left rather a lot to be

desired. Even the thought of his embrace excited a deep, unlooked for craving within her breast.

It was a longing that infuriated her, rousing her out of the uncharacteristic melancholy that threatened to envelop her completely.

"Alice!"

"Miss?"

"I want you to pack a portmanteau for me and see to it that you organize a ticket for the first stage—no, mail, I think—to Bath. You may charge it to the earl of Surrey's tab. My family has horses posted at the Harrowgate interchange, so if you try there I don't believe you'll have a problem."

She hesitated, then continued. "Also, a little light luncheon might be in order. Ask, if you may, that I be given a seat at the window."

Misunderstanding the maid's wide-eyed gaze, she clarified, somewhat apologetically.

"I get horribly sick, you know. Even in my grandfather's well-sprung chaise I am wont to feel ill. I rather think the rigors of this trip might call for a little fresh air."

Alice nodded uncertainly, too astonished to make demur. What the young lady wished to be jaunting about the country for, she could not conceive. Perhaps Pickering would enlighten her further in the kitchens. She'd have to seek his counsel on this strange demand. No doubt Miss Beaumaris was sickening for something.

The dress looked dazzling, complementing the purple-blue of her eyes as nothing else could have done. For an instant Cassandra was diverted. There was something so especially gratifying about a well-cut dress!

Especially, her heart betrayed her, *if the beholder is one as personable as Miles St. John!*

The very name echoed delightfully in her mind. It seemed ages ago that she'd accused him of levity. Dandied fop indeed! How could she have? She knew it was useless to pretend indifference.

All considerations had been lost the moment Wyndham had clasped her tight in his arms. That she loved him in spite of his reputation, his ironic humor, and his often steely will was beyond all question. Her task now was to hide the rather unfortuitous sensation. It would be unfair to him to let him see. The man had already offered marriage. Unsporting it would be, indeed, to take advantage.

At a signal, Alice put down the glass she'd been holding and ushered her charge from the room with feeble assurances that the portmanteau would be packed and ready for the afternoon's stagecoach.

It said much for Cassandra's peace of mind that she remained for the time being in blissful ignorance of the furor the request had made. The lower quarters of Wyndham Terrace had never known such a day for momentous excitement.

Word had it in the kitchens that His Grace had sent for Messrs. Brandon, Brandon and Longey but a few hours hence. What could His Grace be thinking of? What could he possibly be wanting of England's foremost shipbuilders? Speculation raged among the footmen and under housemaids.

It was common knowledge that the war had brought the firm unforseen profits. The merchants were in a fair way to making their fortune by ferrying human cargo across the channel. That His Grace had ordered his best team to be saddled and had given the posting stations advance warning of a journey to the coast was further cause for consideration.

The groom, an expert if ever there was any on the whims of his lord and master, saw fit to pronounce in accents of profound sagacity that "something is afoot."

Quite what this something was remained an unresolved riddle. For once Vallon, puffed up in consequence as he was, remained silent. His ignorance was a piquant spice to the mystery.

The lord himself was partaking of a leisurely breakfast, quite unruffled by the night's events. That he'd been up since dawn did not seem to weigh with him. Nor, it must be added, did it in any way detract from his enjoyment of the enormous repast of oats and ham set before him.

Messengers had been in and out since around seven, but traces of this fact were not to be detected in the immaculately high shirt points and the gilt-buttoned morning coat he'd chosen to affect.

That he was tapping idly at an antiquated snuffbox was of little interest to the stiff-backed lackeys in attendance at either end of the long, damask-clothed table.

As Cassandra entered, his eyes filled with light. The enigmatic expression that momentarily harshened his features disappeared, banished at once by the adorable picture presented by his lady.

"Good morning, my dear Miss Beaumaris! I trust you slept sufficient?"

Cassandra chose to ignore the pointed humor. At half past the hour of noon, it would have been surprising had she not slept sufficient. Even keeping town hours, waking at this time was the outside of enough!

Commenting mildly that she'd had more than her fair share of slumber, she blushed at the patent disbelief on Miles's seraphic face. Was she that transparent? She could hardly credit it.

"And what have you been doing, Your Grace?" Her tone was dryly amused. "Up none too early either, I see."

She'd promised not to engage in a battle of wits with her heart's delight that morning. How, then, came she to be the first to draw metaphorical swords? It passed all bounds, and yet she could not help herself. There was something so challenging about his indulgent gaze and his patronizing demeanor. It riled Cassandra, forcing her to respond in kind.

It would have discomforted her to know just how much Miles relished putting her out of countenance. He loved seeing the flashing quicksilver of her indigo eyes, the impatient brush of her recalcitrant auburn locks. How he longed to give them a good brushing! To feel their softness warm against his fingers. He'd buy her a brush as his wedding gift. He'd seen just the one for her only the other day. Expensive, but superb quality. He'd get Everett to see to it.

He grinned before helping himself to yet another slice of pink Westphalian ham.

"I regret to inform you, Miss Beaumaris, that you are wrong in that assumption. You have but to ask Vallon to know that I've been quite active since we last met. Arranging a special license is no easy thing, you know."

He blithely sank his teeth into the ham while watching, from the corner of his eye, the comical look of dismayed confusion he'd engendered.

"Unfair, my lord!" She leaned toward him and went a long way to knocking over the glass of Ratafia set before her. "You know I cannot quarrel in front of the servants!"

Her fierce whisper reached him just as he extended his hand for the side dish of hot potato Anna. Steadying the glass while at the same time positioning his spoon over the tempting delicacy, he found himself choking in delight.

Good for her! He'd not been wrong in thinking his betrothed a sight spirited. What a dance she'd lead him and how much fun they'd have. Not a trace of the vapid insipidity that so beset womankind could be detected in her being. Trouble, yes! Boring, no! He could rest assured.

Playing fair, he thanked the liveried figures before waving them away. Cassandra was stifling a desire to snuggle into the arms that so invitingly placed morsels upon her plate. How infuriating that he was so close and there was naught she could do save preserve a semblance of outward calm.

"You were saying?" The amused voice prompted her.

"Your Grace . . ."

"Miles," he corrected.

Cassandra ignored him. "Your Grace."

"Miles."

They'd reached an impasse. Really, he was the most infuriating of men. If she did not humor him, they'd sit there the whole day. With an exasperated laugh, she bent to his will, swearing determinedly that the honors of the next skirmish would be hers.

"Oh, all right, Miles, then!" she acceded crossly, her tongue acting traitor to her wishes by rolling with a certain pleasure over the utterance.

Her eyes dared not meet his. The session was not going at all the way she'd planned. "About this special license thing . . ."

"Yes?" Miles's tone was indulgently encouraging.

"It is not at all necessary, you know. I cannot and will not marry you. Not with all the licenses in the world!"

Miles did not seem concerned, deliberately obtuse.

"You want me to post the banns, then? A wedding befitting the future duchess of Wyndham?"

"No!" Cassandra was determined.

"If I can just get to my governess in Bath, no one at all need know of this unfortunate night. Miss Plum I know will be delighted to take me in for the moment, until I can set up a suitable establishment for myself."

"On the fringes of society? It is not at all the thing, you know, for a young lady of uncertain years to be setting up house."

"Well, that can hardly be to the purpose. After all, it is not at all the thing for her to be spending the night alone with a gentleman, either!"

He acknowledged the justice in this but stated wryly, a little under his breath, "Hardly with, my dear, hardly with!"

She chose to ignore him, although her cheeks betrayed a faint hue the duke found both becoming and charming. His sharp eyes missed nothing and he chuckled, in spite of himself. She looked at him crossly then smiled herself. "You know what I mean, Your Grace!"

"Miles!"

"Miles, then! I am grateful to you, indeed, but I find I am quite determined to set up my own establishment." She hesitated, pondering on the prospect. "I daresay I will find some genteel company if I remain a little out of the London way. No doubt Sir Robert will silence his delightful relatives. He may be the nastiest specimen I've ever had the misfortune of coming across, but that is not to say he is entirely without brains."

Cassandra helped herself to a smidgen of stuffed truffle. A man less gallant than Miles might have commented on the fact that her hands were traitorously trembling, a sure sign that outward composure was inward turmoil. His Grace noticed but said nothing. Instead, he drew closer. It was strange to him, this protective instinct. He'd only ever felt it in his dealings with his young wards and then to a less poignant degree. What he felt now was fierce and resolute and incontrovertible.

Cassandra continued, attempting not to notice the warmth of his hand as it covered hers, casting her into a confusion that delighted its beholder. "No matter how vindictive he may be, he'll realize soon enough that discrediting a Beaumaris is not likely to raise his consequence with the ton. He is, after all, my nominal guardian, although that will be over my dead body! If I go down, he sinks and I warrant he knows it."

The duke looked at her inquiringly.

"I deplore people who puff themselves off, but truly I believe society only tolerates him because of his Surrey connection."

The duke inclined his head in agreement. She retrieved her hand to take a delicate mouthful. Swallowing, she continued, "God knows I despise him, but I believe, nevertheless, he is neither clumsy nor stupid. I don't doubt he's cut out for a spot of blackmail, but he'll be sorry he even contemplated such a course if he tries it with me!"

Brave words. His Grace smiled to himself at this further evidence of the treasure he'd so unexpectedly stumbled upon. "I don't doubt you're right, Miss Beaumaris, but do me one favor, I beg of you. Humor me at least."

The seriousness of his manner struck Cassandra, who left the ironic rejoinder she'd formulated dangling at the tip of her tongue. What harm could it do, after all, to hear the man out?

"Last night's business was both ill-timed and unplanned. As a gentleman, the fact that you spent the night under this roof must weigh with me. Wait"—Miles held up an imperious hand as Cassandra began her protest—"don't interrupt! You shall have your say later." His brows lightened as she sank back into her chair.

"Now, Miss Beaumaris, I beg you to pity me." His eyes twinkled irrepressibly. "I'm not in the habit of making young ladies proposals. I have no doubt I'm making the most dismal mull of it, but just so that I need not repeat the process with some equally hard-hearted young female at some other date, will you not have me? I promise to make you the best of husbands and not beat you more than you deserve!"

Humor gleamed in his eyes. He dodged as Cassandra made to pour a glass of negus down his shirt front. "Termagant! Is this not proof enough of the sacrifice I make? When I think of those happy bachelor days . . . but no! I cannot go through the torment of making another offer. You'll have to have me, I'm afraid."

The temptation was almost too much for Cassandra. What trick of fate sent her way the man of her dreams and refused to allow her to yield to him in the way she wanted? She'd be but a burden to him, an odious reminder of one mad moment of chivalry. She, a duchess! It was beyond all bounds. Gently she shook her head, playing now with the clasp of her reticule. Her eyes were flashing violet, regretful, and his mood at once altered in sympathy with her.

He wanted to throw all caution to the winds and carry her off then and there. The tilt of her lovely chin dictated otherwise. Instinctively, he knew that to marry her—and he realized with sudden, fierce clarity that this is what he wanted most truly—he must prove to her that she had no need of him. Ironic, but true. While she was dependent on his generosity she would not countenance wedlock as a convenient measure, of that he was rapidly becoming more and more certain. He loved her the more for it.

After? The duke allowed himself a small smile. After was perhaps another matter. The memory of their encounters was still sharp in his mind. Her lips tasting of ripened blackberries, her eyes merry, changing to sadness, changing again to warmth and—yes, he was certain of it—changing yet again to passion. He had reason to believe the Honorable Miss Beaumaris, despite her protestations, was not entirely impervious to his suit. It was up to him, then, to secure her freedom and to ensure that she would be importuned no more by the likes of Sir Robert Harrington and his ilk.

The key to this task lay in the missive in his pocket. The means in a certain yacht held at anchor for him by the Messrs. Brandon, Brandon and Longey, shipbuilders to the king. Large bundles of auburn strands escaped Cassandra's chignon as she regretfully shook her head. The duke could not help but smile. When she was his he'd insist she wear it loose, exposing the full glory of her shining mane. The well-meaning abigail who'd tried to school it into the present fashions had undoubtedly done her a disservice. The glory of her hair was to be seen, not hidden in coils of primly pinned plaits!

He tried once more to assure her that matrimony was the proper course.

"Don't shake your head at me, my sweet!"

Cassandra blushed crimson. Miles grinned, pleased at this effect.

"Hear me out. What I wanted to say was that I have reason to believe you are in danger. If you were to marry me I'd protect you in a way I cannot as the situation stands right now. Will you not trust me?"

Cassandra was overwhelmed. Never had she encountered such selfless concern for her well-being, and the sensation quite shook her. She was almost inclined to wish that His

Grace had indeed tried to take advantage of her. At least then she could be self-composed and resolute.

She could not much longer stand the unspoken communication that flowed between them. His Grace was so near it seemed a sin not to place her fingers on the broad expanse of his chest. She needed something, she knew, to keep her mind off temptation. Temptation was no easy foe to grapple with.

Whist? Dice perhaps? She was surprisingly good at games of hazard. The late earl had been an inveterate player, insisting that Cassandra be the same. Many was the time she'd beguiled away his crotchets with some spark of sporting brilliance. Indeed, when he'd fallen ill she'd been only too glad of the skill, concocting all manner of diversions for his benefit.

Cassandra was certain that if she could lose herself in play, she'd like as not be less inclined to twirl her fingers through his pitch curls. The soft fluff emanating from the nape of his neck was just too tantalizing. Shocking, was it not?

A speculative twinkle appeared in her eyes. Impetuously, she threw down the gauntlet. She could see her words stunned but intrigued him. She laughed. Once uttered, it was impossible to retract. "I'll marry you, Your Grace, for a wager."

Miles's arm was arrested in midair, his coffee receiving more milk than originally had been intended. He looked at her assessingly, his eyes never leaving the loveliness of her person. "A wager?"

Cassandra licked her lips. For a second her heart failed her. What had possessed her? The instant passed. "Yes, Your Grace."

Miles looked down, scrutinizing for an instant, the large emerald at his cuff. He folded his arms deliberately, then looked directly into the indigo-blue of her eyes. What mischief could she possibly be up to?

"What kind of a wager?" he asked cautiously.

Cassandra's head reeled. What could she say? The die had been cast. "A round of dice, a hand of cards, a game of chess. Best of three." The words came unbidden as his eyes fastened onto hers. Her heart beat in heady excitement that was not entirely due to the prospect of play.

"And the prize, my dear?"

Miles's eyes gleamed as he watched her, his fingers arrested round the delicate venetian drinking cup. His gaze was intent as he scrutinized her, fascination etched on every pore. Cassandra gulped, her lashes faltering under his steady scrutiny. How traitorous of her heart to flutter with such abandon! What she had started, however, she could not stop.

"The winner decides what is to become of my honor. If I win, I will almost certainly make for Bath."

The words were little more than a whisper. Miles's eyes softened infinitely.

"Marriage is honorable, Cassandra. It is not as if I'm offering you a carte blanche." His voice was velvety, so endearingly gentle. Cassandra averted her eyes.

"I realize that." What right had the man to be so maddeningly desirable? "I just don't think it fitting that I entrap you, that is all." She ignored his slightly raised brows. "My honor will be as nothing to my shame if I force you into a loveless union. It would be so much easier if I could just contact my governess. Between the two of us, we should make some story stick."

Miles relaxed, his thoughts veering between a not unnatural sense of exasperation and an infinite tenderness. Loveless indeed! He shook his head and smiled. He had no compunction in agreeing to the contract. He just might enjoy himself after all. "Done! Gentleman's agreement!" With a mocking grin, he held out his hand and took Cassandra's in his, shaking it as he would a peer. If he retained the small, warm palm a fraction longer than perhaps he ought, none was around to gainsay.

He had just released it, in fact, when Rupert entered the breakfast room with all the energy of a robust lad who'd not seen food for a week. St. John must have apprised him of the night's events, for he evinced no surprise at seeing Cassandra at the duke's table. Instead, he greeted her with an engaging grin and how do ye do before tucking into a plate of hot croquettes and eggs with relish. Between mouthfuls of his favorite treat he managed to smile benignly at Cassandra and impishly at his guardian.

His advent put an end to more private discussion, much to Miles's whimsical frustration. Breakfast—or lunch to the viscount—proved to be a lively affair, the young Lyndale seeing fit to regale his elders with gossip gleaned from the previous night, including the latest odds at Brooks. It seemed, although Cassandra was not perfectly clear on this point, that Brummel had bet Bollinger an egg-sized ruby that the regent would appear in blue for the fireworks display the following week.

The finishing touch to this little impromptu gathering was the zany entrance of the twins. They'd decided, quite naturally, that a second breakfast would be most satisfactory. Miles's voice was lost to their chatter. He gave it up. There'd be time enough shortly.

EIGHT

The duke had not minced his words the previous night. Harrington winced at the thought and unconsciously rubbed his swelling jaw. His eyes narrowed as he recalled St. John's insulting words and the blow with which they were delivered. So! His Grace did not consider him enough of a gentleman to accord him the dignity of a duel. Well, he would live to eat those words! Sir Robert inwardly seethed, his body still bearing the humiliating marks of his evening's encounter. His face was tender, his cheeks puffy, and the bridge of his nose alarmingly sensitive to the touch. A suspicious patch of yellowy-blue was beginning to form on the underside of his right eye, a circumstance not unreasonably giving rise to a certain degree of wrath.

The damnable fact was that the incumbent earl of Surrey simply could not be certain of his man. The duke might well prove too haughty a fellow to roll up his sleeves and involve himself in a sordid kind of wrangle. Jackson's Boxing Saloon was simply not his style. Harrington's brows knitted together at the thought of the double humiliation he'd suffered the night before. He'd get even if it was the last thing he did. And that fool of a girl, Cassandra? He'd find her and make her sorry, no idle boast!

Her whereabouts still remained an unresolved mystery. Despite the fact that he'd sent his groom, the Surrey chaise, and a number of footmen he considered relatively loyal servants to locate her, they had yet returned empty-handed. Notwithstanding the hours of impatient pacing, the search had proved mysteriously fruitless. The problem, however, was of no great moment, since she was bound to return at some time or another. Why his mother had seen fit to discharge her was beyond his torturous reasoning.

How much better it would have been had he been able to deal with her once and for all on their return. Even now he could have had her safely in his clutches. Bedded or wedded, it was all the same to him. Forty thousand pounds would be within easy reach. He could only hope now that she would keep her mouth tightly sealed about the events of the masquerade. It would not redound to his credit were she to reveal the shortcomings of her sojourn at Surrey Manor!

His ruminations were brought to a timely conclusion by the arrival of the morning's mail. The silver platter was laden with watermarked envelopes, very few, he noticed, bearing the coveted franks of the elite. Those that did were pointedly directed to the Honorable Miss Beaumaris, a circumstance that made a foul day fouler still. A cursory glance at the remainder revealed bills, bills, more bills. How he was to fight off the duns was well beyond his knowledge. Wedding the unwilling second cousin was now a compulsory measure if he wished to show his face about town. At least few could quibble at the size of her portion. How maddening it was that all his well-laid plans were confounded. He would have to contrive again, that was all there was to it.

Vague instinct made Sir Robert look up and notice the uniformed lackey hovering in the vicinity. His eyes narrowed as he caught the singularly anticipatory expression that conveyed life to his habitually wooden features. Remarking this, Harrington frowned. Perhaps there was a missive he'd missed. He screwed up his eyes thoughtfully, wincing from the shock of unexpected pain as he did so. The footman, one of his own creatures, would be unlikely to lose his composure at the sight of yet another statement—they were too commonplace by far.

"Cat got your tongue?" He sounded waspish as he rounded on the servant. "Stop hovering, man, and tell me what you find so particularly curious!"

The footman muttered something inaudible under his breath and Harrington dismissed him in disgust. Alone, he pushed some of the shattered glass to one side, then peeled off his tan riding gloves. Placing the salver gingerly on a small but elegant occasional table, his hand alighted finally and with decision on an envelope franked impressively in blue and red. It was at once remarkable for bearing the seal of state.

Eagerness etched his features as his fingers clumsily ripped at the single wafer. Here, he hoped, was the answer to his nightly prayers. Confirmation at last of the demise of the sixth Earl Surrey. Lord Frances Beaumaris could surely be no more. He smothered an anticipatory grin. He could not help but feel the missive to be in the very nick of time. His mind wandered feverishly as his fingers made short shrift of the letter's folds.

He'd hold a banquet and invite all his creditors. Serve them humble pie, too! He sniggered. Then they'd regret their insinuating ways and niggardly harassment! Debtor's jail indeed! Those days were gone as surely as he was the Lord Robert Harrington, seventh Earl Surrey. What a pleasant ring the title had, to be sure!

The paper rustled as he unfolded it. He smoothed it down hastily with a practiced flick of the wrist. The words jumped out at Harrington unpleasantly. For a moment he thought he must have misread, but the hope was dashed instantly. Disappointment turned Harrington's sallow features haggard, then calculating, as he took stock of the contents.

In all Robert's long and decidedly eventful life, he'd never suffered such a devastating setback to one of his lifelong obsessions. It was funny how three formal sentences, iterated on His Majesty's stationery, could have such a profound effect. For an instant the room spun round. When it stopped, the germ of a notion had begun to formulate.

The second footman, standing in an agony of suspense outside the heavy wood door, found himself recalled to the room. If he suffered disappointment at his failure to catch a glimpse of the missive, he was certainly not granted sufficient opportunity to bewail the fact. Before he knew what he was about, he'd been ordered to the Running Footman, a dubious little watering house on the outskirts of the Surrey estates, there to exchange pleasantries with a fellow answering to the rather unlikely name of "Cutthroat Jake."

The said person was in his late forties and looked altogether like a pugilist gone to seed. Heavy framed, the stubble that arose from his chin was of the hard, black variety, harshening his already asymmetrical features. When all was said, his appearance went a long way to reminding the unfortunate servant of a bull terrier on a very short leash. This impression remained unaltered, even after the consumption of two long draughts of the innkeeper's finest.

The black stout served its purpose by means of introduction, but also went a long way to causing the beleaguered lackey to fair pass out. Lolling on the inn's beechwood benches, he came close to casting up his accounts, an event that did not elevate him in the eyes of the seasoned likes of Jake. The interest of the said highwayman-cum-jack-of-all-dubious-trades seemed to increase in direct proportion to the amount of silver the footman now saw fit to lay across his palm. He was awake to the fact that he had within easy grasp a pigeon ripe for the plucking.

By the time he'd pocketed his sixth shiny piece and ascertained there was more to be expected on completion of a small, but unspecified "consideration," he was prepared to bestir himself from his slothful state and balefully head for the door. It was all the lackey could do to prevent himself from succumbing once more to the somewhat demeaning effects of the stout.

Sir Robert found that he'd judged his man aright: Jake was most gratifyingly receptive to the scheme he'd devised in the ill-fated moment he believed all lost. It seemed singularly unfair to the second footman, however, that after all his trouble he should be dismissed so summarily. The door had been firmly shut in his face, only minutes after presenting his charge. It was an insult he found unbearably hard to swallow. Cursing his luck, he bent down low, straining to hear snippets of the conversation taking place from within.

It was not to be expected that this transgression should go unnoticed. Indeed, the first footman, who caught him bending with his ear pushed tight against the keyhole, had much to say on this score. Since his misdemeanor was compounded by intoxication, he was fortunate, indeed, to escape the requisite dismissal.

On consideration, the penalty had been vetoed by the redoubtable butler. With more than a hint of regret he'd decided against turning the man off without a character. If truth be known, his mercy had more than a little to do with his own curiosity. Although he would die rather than admit it, he was extremely anxious to hear of the proceedings taking place under his very nose.

The second footman, spared the indignity of a dismissal, was constrained to satisfy his peers with lengthy descriptions of the rogue Jake and his manner of business. The servants' quarters fair hummed with speculation. What Lord Harrington wanted with such riffraff was anyone's guess, but it was many—including Stanford—who offered up a silent prayer for Miss Beaumaris's safe return.

"Cutthroat Jake" would have to live up to his unsavory name if he were to pay his way. Sir Robert found himself fervently hoping that the appellation was rightfully gained and not an idle boast. It was a strange thing, he'd noticed: people were perfectly willing to rob and maim and loot. When it came to a question of murder, however, the average Englishman balked at the thought.

He scoffed in contempt. Not a flicker of doubt shadowed his mind as he went through the possibilities logically and without incident. He marveled at how easy it all was. Hardly even a challenge. Why he'd not had this plan formulated as contingency before he could not say. How fortunate Cassandra had mentioned the little sloop Surrey kept anchored off the coast of Brussels. The very thing, he was quite certain! Jake would sail posthaste to France, then travel by mount cross-country to Antwerp, where the sloop would be anchored. He, of course, would commute at a more leisurely pace to the coast and await Jake's arrival with the jubilant news of the unfortunate earl's safe disposal.

After the whole matter was satisfactorily settled, he'd deal with Cassandra. How much better in the unchallenged position of peer of the realm. The thought excited him. He wished, suddenly, to be alone. A lifelong dream was but an ocean-length away. The moment was too exhilarating to share with a lowlife like the rapscallion before him.

With a conspiratorial flick of the thumb that nevertheless conveyed an element of deep contempt, the dubious Jake was ushered from his presence.

Time enough in the morning to discuss contingencies and refine further upon the details. The evening was one to savor and savor it he would. Silently, he lifted his glass in half salute to a man lying in a hospital camp some way off from La Hay Sainte.

An acid laugh saw him toss his head back and drain the drink whole.

A discreet cough broke in on Lord St. John's innermost thoughts. It is to be inferred that these deliberations were definitely on the pleasant side, since a tiny gleam of humor was to be detected lingering at the edge of his wide, wholly masculine mouth.

His lady love had just flung down the gauntlet and he was

not the man to resist. What self-respecting fellow would turn his back on such a challenge, after all? Especially one that came wrapped as delightfully as this one did. How his heart's delight had sparkled as she named the stake. A throw of the dice, a hand of cards, a game of chess. Winner to take all. Well, well, and well! She must have been very sure of herself, the wench, to hazard so high.

He could only guess at the feelings that had willed her on to provoke him in this manner. Like chess, indeed like most earnest challenges, attack was the best form of defense. It troubled him that she still had cause to be defensive. He understood her, however, and made allowances. Besides, he admired her. He was hard put to think of another who would so willfully throw her fate to the gods. What a dear, spirited, brave girl to make light of life's troubles in the singularly novel way she had done.

He knew—perhaps more than most—what it was like to be fettered by society and its expectations. She'd defied the social code, and nothing short of a miracle could restore her to her rightful position. Well, for better or worse he intended to be that miracle. It seemed the most natural thing in the world to shield her, to devote himself to her preservation and safety.

That she refused the ultimate protection of his name only endeared her to him more. Whether she knew it or not, she would be his. She belonged to him in more than just the physical sense, although that was certainly a part of it.

The thought of releasing the clips of her hair and running his fingers through smooth, silken, unencumbered locks was fast becoming an obsession with him. The dull ache within his body was yearning for a matching passion. Never before had he been so sensitive to a warm, laughing presence. They belonged together and not to be bonded in the most ultimate of all ways seemed an incalculable sin.

He had known her for a few snatched hours long ago and now this. Another mere sprinkling of time, but the hours were an eternity unto themselves. This was no passing fancy—he was all too well-acquainted with those—this was the real thing, Shakespeare's stuff of dreams that he had been so cynical about. Before the fortnight was out, she would be his wife. The special license he'd been carrying on his person all day bore testimony to this most incontrovertible of facts.

Miss Cassandra may rest easy in the belief that she'd won herself a reprieve. Miles knew better. For starters, he was an old hand at playing cards. How fortunate that Rupert had not been present to warn her off. The young gadabout was forever complaining—often quite volubly—that he had too uncanny a grasp of the order of play.

Spectators seemed awestruck that at the end of a game His Grace the duke would next to always be holding the royal flush. Few had insight into just how much skill was involved in achieving that situation. Not sorcery, just a degree of calculation and logic. It was a thoughtful Miles who fingered the deep sapphire and silver handkerchief Cassandra had dropped from reticule to floor soon after she'd laid the terms of her bet.

When she'd finally flounced from the room with the trace of an impudent grin and self-confident swagger, he'd decided there and then to keep it as a small memento. An heirloom with which to amuse his children and grandchildren. In the meanwhile, he intended to keep it close to him. Perhaps he was fanciful, but beneath his shirt, tucked away in the recesses of his muscular body, it would be close to his skin, close to his touch, close to his very heart.

Vallon would grow slowly apoplectic at the sight of his bulging cambric undershirt. Nothing, to him, would justify a wrinkle in Islington fabric—not even passion. With fortitude Miles ignored this consideration. With due respect to his fastidious valet, some things were best endured.

Pickering coughed a little louder, hoping this time to divert the attention of his master to more pressing matters. The matter, for instance, of a rather sorry-looking fellow kicking his heels in the second receiving chamber. Also, and decidedly more auspicious, the circumstance of a wafer having been hand delivered by the lord high chancellor himself.

He'd not stopped, but had admonished the under footman to see it delivered into the duke's hands with due urgency. The lackey, knowing his duty, had passed it on to Pickering who was now relinquishing it—with deference—into the appropriate hands. St. John smiled his thanks.

"What would I do without you, Pickering? You were right, of course, to deposit young James in the blue salon. Always so discerning! Sometimes I wonder how you do it."

Pickering glowed inwardly at the praise. Outwardly, his features remained as immobile as ever, a fitting testimony to a butler of impeccably high standards. He held out the heavily sealed missive and made as if to withdraw.

"One moment, if you please!" Miles stretched for his glass and languidly depressed the seal. The envelope opened with ease, the paper crisp in his gloved fingers. Scanning the short enclosure, he nodded positively before breaking out into one of his rare but brilliant smiles.

As if instantly energized, the duke began rapping out some succinct but urgent orders. If the butler was surprised, he had the good breeding and civility not to reveal it. He merely bowed and promised faithfully that His Grace's orders would be carried out to the letter. He also promised to apprise Mr. Everett of all the details the duke had seen fit to outline. St. John smiled perfunctorily as the butler made to withdraw.

"No wait, Pickering. I may need more."

The duke's brows furrowed as he thought furiously. The foreign office had made short work of his request for information regarding the status and whereabouts of Captain Frances Sedgwick Sinclair Beaumaris, Sixth Earl Surrey and regimental leader of the Fourth Hussars. If his suspicions were confirmed, he'd have no time to lose.

"Send word to the stables that I want the chestnuts set to. Also, I'll need Vallon to ensure . . ." His instructions were interrupted by the sounds of hoofed feet on the cobbles. "Who the devil can that be?"

Pickering cleared his throat. "That, I rather think Your Grace, is a hack."

His Grace looked incredulous. "A hack? Now who would call a hack, I wonder? Don't, I pray you, gammon me into believing master Rupert's pockets are as to let as all that! However desperate he may be, I don't see him resorting to that type of conveyance, do you?"

The butler permitted himself a small smile at this allusion to young Lord Rupert's penchant for high steppers. Though his team was not nearly so fine as that of His Grace, they were nevertheless extremely good goers, very well matched, and the envy of all his friends. The viscount was fast developing expensive taste in horseflesh. Not a likely candidate to be jaunting around in a hired pair! Flat-sided, too, if he guessed it right.

He turned to his master. "No, Your Grace. Not the viscount! Miss Beaumaris, I believe. Something about a governess in Bath?"

Light dawned. Miles's passing interest evaporated into definite concern.

"Send him away at once, Pickering. At *once!* Kindly convey to the household that Miss Beaumaris is to be a lengthy and valued guest in this establishment." He hesitated a moment, then added, "Unless by express orders of myself or master Rupert, she is not now nor later to be abetted in any foolish attempt to remove herself. Do I make myself clear?"

Heavy lines furrowed Miles's brow as he made this declaration. In circumstances other than the one in which he now found himself, he'd have no option but to assist Cassandra in her endeavors to achieve a modicum of respectability.

As it was, he had no choice. The communication he had only now received made it all the more imperative that he protect his loved one from possible danger. He hoped fervently that his imagination was merely hyperactive. There was no indication, after all, that Harrington's inclinations would run to murder or extortion. Left to chance, though, he'd rather not take the risk.

Pickering bowed. He'd known his master since he was in short coats and trusted his unfailing judgment. If the situation seemed strange to him, it was not his place to comment. No doubt St. John knew what he was doing. He would stake his life that the man would not trifle with a lady's reputation unless he had just cause.

Even so, the butler could not help but hope the matter would soon resolve itself. He would have his work cut out depressing the curiosity of the chambermaids and kitchen staff, who were already agog at the circumstances of a lady of quality putting up at a gentleman's establishment.

NINE

Cassandra had time to reflect. She realized, to her exasperation, that she was now honor-bound to remain under the duke's protection. A wager was a serious business, not to be lightly dismissed. She'd contracted to play and so she must. It seemed madness to her that she'd got inveigled into such a situation. If St. John had been a gentleman he'd not have countenanced it!

Honesty compelled her to admit that in all possible ways he had, in truth, been a gentleman. It was her own judgment that had been at fault. How could she have suggested such a thing? And such stakes, too! He must think her wanton to fool with her honor in this way. Marriage was no golden guinea to toss around wherever the dice may fall.

She breathed a sigh of relief. Thank heavens her sanity had not so left her that she'd suggested a horse race across the commons or some other such thing! Judging from the looks of the duke's splendidly frisky cattle, she'd not wager a farthing at the chances of her besting His Grace in that particular pursuit. If ever there was a way to settle this ridiculous issue of matrimony, it was this. At the risk of immodesty, she knew her chess game to be superior. She was relatively satisfied, too, that she'd comport herself well in the card stakes. Frances had always had the edge on her in this, but only just. She was proud of her masculine sense of logic. The dice would be luck, but she'd have to stand the odds.

Looking out from the French bay glass, she caught sight of the conveyance that had been sent at her request. The hack was patiently trotting up and down the pathway, in momentary anticipation of her arrival. Cassandra realized, with a sigh, that she ought to go down and tell the poor driver to cease his exertions. The one horse looked suspiciously lame, and it was with no great sorrow that she resolved to send him off with a shilling for his trouble. She may yet have need of his services, but for the moment, at least, she'd be remaining a guest of the duke and his refreshing family.

Holding her skirts as she hurriedly took the steps two at a time, she came close to colliding with a very harassed looking Grace. This lady, it must be noted, was carefully balancing a dish of water in the crook of her right arm. In her left was an aromatic bowl of leftover jointed chicken cutlets that tantalizingly filtered the air. Apologizing with a smile, Cassandra had just time to wonder what the minx was up to before reaching her allotted goal outside the front door.

Once there, she was astonished to find that the man had already been paid and was in the laborious process of turning his horses around. Her eyes flashed in anger. It was one thing for her to decide to remain, quite another to be held hostage against her will. How dare His Grace make that choice for her! She determined to tackle him at once, just as soon as she'd unpacked the valise.

These contained the few gowns and oddments she'd brought herself to select from the overflowing wardrobe His Grace had seen fit to acquire for her. If she were to remain under the extraordinary and often irksome protection of the duke, the least she could do was make every push not to inconvenience the staff. Alice had very kindly packed for her. She would do the unpacking.

Making her way back to the glorious sun-filtered room on the landing, she could not help but hear the frequent and ill-concealed whispers of excitement hailing from one of the lesser-used morning salons. Debating whether to enter or not—she'd scarcely like to be called a snoop—the decision was wrested from her hands by the advent of a great, bouncy, velvety-pawed puppy who proceeded to lick her to death with all the buoyancy of month-old youth.

Cassandra chuckled, her anger momentarily abated by this new development. Changing course, she turned from the stairs and pushed the mahogany-paneled door a little wider as she stepped inside. It would hardly have taken a genius to deduce that the cutlets and water had been intended for nonhuman consumption.

The suspicion was confirmed by the wet ring around the puppy's nose and mouth. Cassandra did not like to reflect what had become of the bones in this cozily furnished chamber. The Lady Georgina emerged from behind the curtains, urging her twin to do the same. "It's all right, Gracie, you can come out. It's only Miss Beaumaris!"

Cassandra didn't know whether to be pleased or sorry at this summation of her character. "We thought it might be Pomerey, you see. She'd be bound to give us a regular scold." Georgie beamed seraphically at Cassandra, patting the animal as she did so. Puppy, loyal if anything, instantly transferred his attentions back to his young mistress.

Grace patted down her dress as she emerged from behind the chaise longue. "I think Max wants to go out," she murmured with charming discernment.

Cassandra gave a groan as all eyes fixed on the bouncing bundle of canine life.

"Stuff!" Georgie returned mockingly. "He doesn't. Can't you tell, Grace? Look at his face. You know how he crunches it up when he needs to go out! He's hardly got a wrinkle right now!" She turned engagingly to Cassandra. "Can you see a wrinkle, Miss Beaumaris?"

Cassandra very circumspectly adjudged that wrinkle or no, the dog was to be given the benefit of the doubt. Just in time she opened the doors leading out to the shaded garden. Grace veritably shouted in glee. "See, I told you so!"

The Lady Georgina at least had the decency to look abashed. "Well, I was not to know, was I? He didn't look as though he needed to be put out. Perhaps it was the water?" With a doubtful glance she consulted Cassandra.

"Most likely! Dare I ask what you are doing with—Max, I think you said?"

"We're looking after him! Aren't we, Gracie?" Georgie sounded triumphant, her pixielike features twinkling with mischief.

"Uncle Miles says he has to remain in the stables. Have you ever? Dear little Max doesn't want to be out in the smelly old stables! Here Max, come back in. It is true, isn't it? You don't want to live in that nasty big barn?" In answer, the dog proceeded to lick his protector, tail wagging at a dangerous velocity. "You won't tell, will you?" Gracie suddenly looked anxious, her dark eyes pleading.

"Don't be such a widgeon, Grace!" The Lady Georgina looked scornful. "Of course she won't! You can tell she's not a prattle-pated gabster like some I can name!"

Cassandra assured them gravely that she was not one of those most noxious of creatures. She was rewarded with beams of pleasure.

"We're trying to get him into spanking good trim. Chivers—he's the under groom, you know—well, he reckons if we take good care of him and brush his coat just as he shows us, we'll be allowed to keep him. Not for hunting, you know. For com-com-companionship." Gracie was visibly pleased at the term she'd used. Cassandra couldn't help but feel a rush of warmth for the two young scamps.

"Well, I certainly won't give you away. Just make sure you take good care of him, though. I shall expect a full report from Chivers."

The children clapped their hands with glee, Cassandra's ruling approved without question. They seemed to accept her appearance in the household with none of the reservations of their elders. Cassandra could only be glad.

"But," the indomitable Miss Beaumaris continued, "in return I shall expect you to take your lessons, pay good attention to your governess, and practice very hard with your pastels."

There was a wave of protest, which Cassandra quickly squashed. "A bargain is a bargain, you know. If you like, you can take out your watercolors and paint Max. No sneaking off without consent, mind!"

The twins bashfully acquiesced, each hoping Cassandra would never guess that at that very moment they were in fact truant. If she half suspected as much, she had the good sense to hold her peace.

Making her way toward her chamber, she chanced upon the very man who had begun to fill her thoughts. A flash of lightning ran through her frame as she found herself face-to-face with his stark white shirt ruffles.

His scent was so masculine, so uniquely Miles that she had to shake herself to prevent succumbing to its heady magic. Summoning up all her dignity, she coldly asked if she might have a private word with him.

Miles cocked his brow and grinned. As he indicated the way to one of the morning chambers that led off from the conservatory, he reflected somewhat wryly that the gentleman in the blue salon would just have to kick his heels a while longer.

Closing the doors behind him, he made his love an elegant bow before adjusting the line of his snowy cravat. He removed his morning gloves, watching her all the while from out the corners of his twinkling eyes.

"This is an unexpected pleasure, madame. Ready to concede defeat before the game commences?"

"No!" Cassandra blushed to the roots of her hair, then chided herself on her lack of self-control.

"I came, Your Grace . . ."

"Your Grace?"

"Yes, *Your Grace!*" Cassandra glared at him balefully.

Miles chuckled. "Well, that's a bit of a dowser. I thought I was to be Miles to you, fair enchantress."

Cassandra stamped her foot in exasperation, her dignified pose vanishing rapidly in the face of this obdurate man. "Will you listen to me, please?"

Unexpectedly, the duke cast aside his mocking air. Cupping Cassandra's face firmly in his grip, he looked deep into her eyes, and the words that spilled out were words of love and enduring warmth. "Always, my Cassandra. Always. What is it you have to say?"

Shaken, she averted her eyes and paused for breath. Thinking wildly she could not for the life of her remember her complaint. The man had cast a spell on her. She was certain she'd been bewitched. Never before had she acted like such a veritable widgeon. Her grandfather would have scolded her for even thinking in such cant.

His Grace waited, arms crossed, watching the fleeting thoughts as they danced across her expressive face. She was a delight to behold, a constant source of joy and amusement. He experienced a sudden and quite overwhelming desire to enclose her in his arms and keep her there. He shook himself. Later. There'd be time enough later, when she was his affianced. When the matters that had primarily occupied his morning's attention had been duly concluded, he would return to claim his bride. Until then, he must be the soul of propriety. A lady's reputation was at stake, and he was not the man to sully it no matter how irresistible the impulse.

The definite and distinctly unwelcome sound of a dog's bark broke the moment. Cassandra was obliged to cough discreetly to mask the sound.

"What was that?" Miles asked.

With a sigh Cassandra knew it was incumbent on her to prevaricate. She could only hope against all hope that her sudden coughing spasm would not be exposed by the advent on the landing of Max himself. "Oh, nothing."

Somewhat disobligingly, the duke was not distracted from

his first impression. "It sounded suspiciously like an animal!"

"No! Oh, no! It couldn't be! Not here in the house! In . . . in . . . the stables maybe!" Cassandra protested.

The duke looked at her, then looked again. As if satisfied, he hid the slow smile that was beginning to tremble at the corners of his mouth. He bowed. "If you say so, my dear!" He opened the door and fixed her with a brilliant smile as he waited for her to pass him.

His presence lingered with her long after he had taken the rest of the stairs.

TEN

The duke's conversation with the mysterious seaman of the blue salon proved fruitful. Nodding firmly when the transaction was finished, he concluded the arrangement with a tenner in the hand of young James and a last minute instruction to his groom.

He thoughtfully rang the bell before heralding out his visitor, with strict adjurations to his groom to ensure the curricle was light and well sprung.

New bolts had been fitted not two months before, but it was important that the wheels be carefully inspected. The roads were damp from the storm and the coastal pass was treacherous.

It would have been better, perhaps, to take the barouche, but His Grace was anxious to make haste. Some small instinct told him that there was no time to be wasted.

The duke looked over a few points of the missive he was holding. His eyes squinted narrowly as he thought on the treachery he suspected. Like as not it was all a hum. God will it be so! All the same, it was best to be prepared.

The hunch was confirmed when Rupert appeared, elated, in response to the bell. Without preliminaries he rushed into speech. "Blow me down if you weren't right all along, Miles!"

The duke lifted his eyes from the narrative and raised his brows questioningly.

"I just took a peek in at Surrey Manor, and the whole

establishment is agog with the news. Seems young Harrington got a sudden whim to travel cross-country." Rupert could hardly contain his excitement and indignation. "By the sound of things, he's traveling with a rather unlikely character. Not quite up to the snuff from all that I gather!" His face grew glum. "I set Belinda to talking to one of the second housemaids, but either she is singularly dim-witted or else very close. Nothing could be gained from her but that the bedsheets are all to be aired."

Rupert looked his disgust. "Women, I tell you! They don't look to see what's under their very noses. There was evidently some story gabbled out by the second footman, but the butler seems to have made short shrift of the gossip. Good man, that, but poker-faced as they come. Told me Cassandra was indisposed. What a rapper!"

St. John smiled. "What would you have, Rupert? Thank God the man is discreet. If Miss Beaumaris's secret can be kept safe just a little longer, we might be able to turn events around."

"I'm sure you can pull it off, Miles. Anyway, by all accounts a message of some sort was delivered on Friday, but none can quite say what it contained. I dare swear if I were to nose about, the butler might . . ."

"No!" Miles was firm. "I want you to say nothing of this, Rupert. Do you hear? Miss Beaumaris must not become embroiled in a scandal of our making. If I can scotch the gossip, then so I will. I may even be wrong in my suspicions. But I doubt it." His voice was dry. "The important thing is to get to Mont Saint-Jean and find young Beaumaris. From what I gather, he was transported there in an open cart by one of the villagers of La Hay Sainte. A long way to travel, I warrant."

His voice changed. "He was found under the body of a dead hussar. What an ordeal to live through, poor boy. I just hope that he is recovered a little. Communication is still damnable from across the channel, despite Napoleon's safe custody."

"But the Lord High Chancellor . . ."

"Yes, I know, Rupert." Miles's voice sounded weary. "Even his sources are not always accurate, or at least they are quite often delayed. All we can do is pray for Frances's safe return and hope that, in the meanwhile, we'll be the first to get to him."

Rupert shivered at the implication of his guardian's words. "May I not accompany you, sir?"

"No!" Miles smiled at the disappointment etched on his young ward's face. If the lad lacked anything, it was certainly not zest for adventure.

"I have a special, possibly more important task for you."

The young man's eyes gleamed in hopeful anticipation.

"I want you to watch over Cassandra—Miss Beaumaris, I mean." The disappointment on Rupert's face was palpable. Had Miles been anything less than deadly serious on this score, he would have been amused, ever one for a good joke. Now he tried soothing, dulcet tones with his high-spirited relative.

"Try not look so woeful, young man. I am charging you with a very great responsibility and you look as though you've just been whipped. Cheer up, I must beg of you! Has it not occurred to you that Miss Beaumaris may be in a measure of danger?"

"Danger?" Rupert brightened considerably.

The duke nodded. "I want you to see to it that she is well protected. I'd not put it past that cur to set one of his confederates to snooping. Sooner or later, they'd be bound to spy out this estate."

Rupert looked interested, then frowned a little and shook his head. "I doubt he'd have the impudence. Why, Pickering would send him the rightabout for sure. He wouldn't get past the first bell-pull. Besides, how is he to know where Miss Beaumaris is residing? I hardly think he'd suspect you, Miles, a man of the first stare! I daresay he'll send posthaste for Harrowgate or some such place. He'll think her at some watering hole or other, you can count on it."

Miles looked at him fondly. "Can I, cawker? Sir Robert

Harrington is hardly a fool, you know! He knows I'm one of the few of last night's party likely to take the northbound road. He is bound to suspect I may have stopped or noticed her predicament."

"Yes, but . . ."

"Listen, Rupert. You know as well as I how disastrous it would be if he found her now. Just think a moment. Her ruin would be in his hands without a doubt! The blackguard will stop at nothing to secure her fortune, believe me!"

His tone changed, his jaw set intractably. "I have good reason not to wish for this eventuality."

Something in Miles's voice made Rupert yield at once. He could not but feel proud to be in his guardian's confidence and charged with such a trust. All thoughts of accompanying Miles disappeared.

"And Rupert?"

"Yes, sir?"

"Wish me happy."

Rupert did not miss the duke's meaning. Like the twins and the butler and the maidservant, he had taken an instant liking to the auburn-haired beauty who'd confronted him at the breakfast table that morning with such good-humored aplomb.

There'd somehow been such a sympathetic twinkle in her eye as she'd caught sight of him grappling with the fall of his fob. He'd had the devil of a time trying to get it to swing in just the same, unobtrusive manner as his guardian. To this moment he was not sure whether it had been his imagination, but he could have sworn he felt a light palm brush his hand as a helpful tap alighted on the shiny gold ornament. Imagination or no, he was quite as much at ease with her as ever he was with his young sisters.

"Wish you happy? You may be sure I will, Miles! Very happy! And be sure I'll look after her as if she were the greatest treasure on earth!"

"She is." Miles uttered this softly, looking past his young

nephew as if to something very beautiful and quite, quite unexpected.

His eyes twinkled. "Tell her I love . . . but no! Tell her I'll be back shortly to test her skill against mine. Have ready a pack of cards, my brass dice, and the chess set left to me by the Baron of Stratford-Hithe. Polish it up, will you, Rupert? I reckon on a very interesting series of games."

He caught sight of the look of bafflement on his ward's face and chuckled. "Better sport, I wager, than hunting! And a better prize, too." This last, murmured softly, escaped the attention of the young viscount.

"Games? Why games? I thought you never played?" Rupert looked puzzled. As light dawned on him, bewilderment changed to shock. "You're not thinking to fleece her in cards, are you? Miles, that's monstrous!"

A gleam appeared in his mentor's eye. "The lady claims she can win, Rupert. Who am I to say nay? It does promise to be a worthwhile match, however. Perhaps I'll invite you to keep the score!"

Rupert, deciding there and then that his guardian was becoming a bit touched in the upper works, screwed up his face and politely declined.

"Be off with you, sir! If you want to catch the tides, you'd best start now. Changing at Dartford, are you?"

When Miles nodded his assent, the young buck appeared satisfied. If he knew anything at all it was how to judge blood cattle.

"Good. I don't much hold with the livery-stables at Worthing, I must tell you! Now at Dartford I'll warrant you'll pick up a trustworthy pair. Not like your grays, of course"—he hastened to qualify himself—"but some sound trotters nonetheless. Just make sure they're fresh when you change."

He looked thoughtful. "I reckon with a well-paced pair you could cover the fourteen miles from the Roxburgh Tollgate in Dartford to the Red Lion in Rochester in under an hour. If the weather holds out, that is."

He stopped as he saw the light of mirth shining in Miles's eyes. Since the said person had taught the viscount all he knew on the subject of horseflesh, it was hardly surprising that he saw an element of humor in the lecture he was receiving.

It was one of Rupert's particularly appealing qualities that he could laugh at himself when the situation arose. Realizing his mistake, he joined in Miles's amusement wholeheartedly, adjuring him only to take heed of what he'd said and make sure he chose a team with a clean pair of heels on the Kentish change.

For his trouble he received a light-hearted cuff, but ducked dexterously to avoid the impact. Pleasantries thus observed, His Grace took his leave, setting his pair a spanking pace as they galloped before the gleaming curricle, heads proudly aloft.

The groom was afforded a fine view of country England as His Grace took the whip, driving the thoroughbreds with a light but well-practiced hand. It must be said that Miss Beaumaris, chancing to look up from the depths of her portmanteau, gave a deep sigh. Relief that His Grace had granted her a reprieve battled with immense anguish at his departure.

No word of explanation, save a boyish "hey-ho" and an impudent wink that sent her senses reeling. No indication of plans or of whether he intended his trip to be short or long. He'd intimated that he'd be leaving and that he held her to her wager, but nothing more. Damn the man, he'd sounded so urgent, so caring she had not had the gumption to confront him as she had determined to do. Surely he could not expect her sojourn at Wyndham Terrace to be indefinite? She could only reflect on the scandal!

As the curricle vanished from view, Cassandra had to admit she was puzzled. She determined, however, to make the most of her brief but tranquil stay. Old Grandfather Surrey had ever been a one to quote the dictum of making the best of every predicament, no matter how noisome.

As he had time and time again asserted, if a man had not the spunk and rambunction to make a go of every situation, he was hardly a man at all. Cassandra smiled at the memory. A gruff old man, but she had loved him. If only she knew for a certainty what had become of Frances. She quickly put the thought from her.

For the moment, at least, she would live in the present. The house and the estate, filled with noise, with bustle, with laughter was her peace. Even in happier times she had never truly understood the meaning of tranquility. Here, she found it. Here, amid the housemaids and the twins and the chirping dovetails. Here, paradoxically, where peace of mind had most been challenged, dormant sensation most awakened. She determined to savor that peace, short-lived though she knew it would be. Sooner or later the realities of her life would impinge once more. Until then, she would endeavor simply to be happy.

ELEVEN

Quite according to plan, the Surrey family sloop glided out of the port of Antwerp. That it did not travel a straight route but stopped first at a small but unknown cove in the heart of France raised few eyebrows. Equally, that her crew was a motley lot did not surprise any of the harbor officials who may have interested themselves in the business. Times were rough and seamen were not what they used to be.

There were few respectable people who wished to sail the seas right now. No doubt the sloop was to be used to ferry shipments of velvet and lace or the odd keg of matured rum. Even with the restrictions lifted, it was still nigh on impossible to get hold of the real thing in England. The channel crossing was too risky, the last of the rattled French legions still too desperate to make the attempt.

The sloop was sufficient to fetch a rare price in cargo for whoever dared brave the crossing. The tide at this time of year was enough to make any unseasoned mariner quite green with illness. To Jake, however, bobbing up and down the oceans like a veritable cork was no great hardship. Blessing his good fortune, he had time enough to take stock. How fortunate that he was to have free run of the sloop and its dubious shipment.

This of course included ill-gotten burgundy, Parisian perfume, and rolls and rolls of fine point d'Angleterre. Just where he acquired these luxuries was to be his business, no

questions asked. When he had accomplished the trifling task
for which he was employed, he was to sail home, docking
the sloop at one of the small English enclaves in the south.
Now there was the rub! It did not suit the fine Jake to have
his profitable trade overset by details of this nature.

What is more, it suited him even less to satisfy himself
with the meager consideration Sir Robert had seen fit to
offer. True enough, at the time it had seemed a windfall. That
was then, however. When a man has not a groat with which
to pay his ale, he has little choice. When he has command
of a sloop, a few dozen yards of Brussels bobbin lace, and
numerous barrels of the finest French hock, it is a different
matter entirely. Truth to tell, Jasper Meredith—for that was
his true name—at last had the world at his feet.

The sea breeze and the saltwater slapping up against the
sides did much to exalt Jake's confidence in the vagaries of
fortune. For once, he felt lady luck had favored him, and he
was anxious to seize the moment. His eyes gleamed at the
possibilities before him. It seemed life had landed him a
plum ripe for the picking, and he was bound by his code to
make the best of it.

He stroked his chin, considering. It must be said that the
man was not averse to going to the highest bidder. Unlike some
he knew, he was seldom troubled by inconvenient moral scru-
ples. That he was already contracted to do a piece of work for
Harrington would not weigh with him if he thought the alternative more lucrative. Unfortunately, on reviewing the odds,
he regretted to have to admit that Harrington's proposition was
the most promising. It was hardly likely that his victim would
be in sufficient funds to buy his freedom.

The chance of Lord Frances Beaumaris being in a position
to outbid his employer was scarcely even worth the contemplation. What was worth a moment's thought, however, was
that tantalizing little word beginning with "b." Blackmail. And
why not? As a little side activity to the current venture it could
prove most profitable. The thought conjured up an involuntary

smile of cunning on the seaman's face. He would have to chew it over carefully, but there was no obstacle he could immediately divine to extortion at its highest rate.

If Lord Harrington wished to be invested with an earldom, he would have to pay for it. Not large sums, mind you, just small installments over a great many years. A great many years! Jake's eyes gleamed as the plan gained some shape in his head. Wicked, perhaps, but not so wicked as the foul deed Harrington had conceived.

As he took another swig of proof French hock, he ruminated on the likely course of events from that moment forward. The thought stimulated a warm glow of contentment. Life, he anticipated, was going to take a very interesting turn. Very interesting indeed.

It must be said that in the mountains of Mont Saint-Jean, life was a whole lot less interesting for Jake's intended victim. Frances Sedgwick Sinclair Beaumaris, Baron Hancock and the rightful Earl Surrey, if truth be told, had quite lost his customary jauntiness. Small wonder, since he was immured on a narrow stretcher in an unknown locale leagues and leagues away from the comforts of his ancestral home.

True it was that the battle was over, but for Frances, stranded and alone, the prospect of England seemed far away indeed. Dizzy with fever, he rolled over and permitted himself a small groan. The events of the past month—or was it years? or perhaps a week?—were too hazy to try to focus on. The smell of death and the round rosy cheeks of a small country urchin were jumbled together in the most peculiar and distressingly puzzling manner.

Indeed, the juxtaposition of bayonets with horses and carts, artillery fire with the neighing of cavalry horses were almost too much for his aching head to make sense of. He smelled gunpowder in his nostrils, and this was confused with the minty smell of liniment, zinc potions, and lint.

It is strange, though, how perverse the human mind is. It likes to sort patterns into images and images into logic. As long as Frances Beaumaris was alive, he knew his mind would give him no rest until he made the effort to make sense of the swirling shapes and smells around him.

Memories had to be formed and molded into whole pictures, just as the stuff of dreams and nightmares had to be edited to formulate some meaning, some ultimate sense. Lying on his pallet in the icy mountains of Mont Saint-Jean, the sixth earl of Surrey wrestled with the problem of making light out of his darkness.

His efforts were greatly facilitated by the presence of a gentle hand, ever so often cooling his brow, checking his dressings. The nurses of St. Christopher of Albans were renowned for their quiet efficiency and their healing touch. The officer in the bright, debonair uniform of the Fourth Hussars had had a very narrow shave with death. It had taken all the healing skills of Suzannah De Bonhuit to nurse him back to the world of the living.

Two months it had been before they collectively pieced together bits of his story and so were at last able to trace his name and family. When they had, it had simply been a matter of waiting for the right weather before undertaking the descent into the nearby town of Vert Coucou and contacting the appropriate English authorities.

All day, Suzannah and Sister Monica tended the sick, giving hope to the lost, time to the needy. Between rounds they established links between the conquered and the vanquished, housing French, English, and Spanish soldiers alike. It was with sublime indifference to political concerns that they discharged patients into the welcoming hands of family and country, whichever was the first to respond.

They expected his lordship to be contacted any day. Their prime concern was to see that he was fit for the journey. His fever had broken and his wounds were healing well—it was simply that he was not yet ready to tackle questions or risk confusion.

Sister Suzannah sat with him as often as could be spared, sewing samplers, mending ripped sheets. From time to time her voice would break into song, and the notes would form part of the patterns in the young captain's head, introducing an element of gladness to all the pain and burdensome confusion.

After his groan, the good lady had moved closer, whispering words of encouragement and peace. When darkness faded into the small shelter, the lilting pluck of a delicate harpsichord did much to ease the gloom of the crowded, makeshift hospital. It was during just such a time, when the soothing strains of Handel wafted through the cutting cold, that Frances had opened his eyes and beheld an angel.

An angel in white merino with faded chip-straw hat and a welter of dangling ribbons that looked ridiculously modish given the unorthodox setting. His head ached as he focused on very dark hazel eyes and well-worn slippers peeping out from under skirts. He had smiled, then, and the worst for him was over.

Sister Monica was the first to look up from her ministering and find a lean, swarthy-looking gentleman staring at her intently from out a mocking gaze. His toothy smile made her shudder and wrap the flimsy shawl she had set around her shoulders just a little tighter across her body.

"May we help?"

"I'm sure ye can." Jake inhaled deeply of his distinctive brand of tobacco. His eyes raked the sister up and down, undressing her as they did. Perhaps, when the task was over, he'd pay another little visit to the quiet, isolated community. First things first, however.

"Lord Frances Sedgwick Sinclair Beaumaris. I hear you be havin' a patient answerin' to that name?"

Sister Monica's eyes were searching. Somehow, she did

not equate Frances with the appearance of this man. There was something wrong with his cocky manner and makeshift cart. She was hesitant to turn him away, so short was she of beds, but his general demeanor did not please her in the least.

"May I ask who is inquiring?"

Jake tittered. "What's it to ye, sweetheart?"

Sister Monica blushed crimson, thankful that Suzannah had entered the small, bare entrance parlor. Her clear, crisp tones brooked no argument. Though her bouncy curls were charming, they were now severely encased under a no-nonsense chip-straw bonnet. Jake, under the circumstances, did not demur. Perhaps best not to make waves. The last thing he needed was to be bathed in a haze of suspicion.

He bowed low, and although his manners were unobjectionable from then on, there was something faintly disturbing behind his eyes. The young ladies both felt the menace, but at the same time chastised themselves for being judgmental.

Their fears were slightly alleviated when they heard that Mr. Jasper Meredith was merely acting as emissary for the captain's sister. Clearly, he was not quality, but that could be understood in the light of the times. Miss Cassandra Beaumaris—his lordship in his more lucid moments had spoken often of her—must have hired this seafarer to convey the earl across the channel. It was plausible, but there was still a bitter ache in Suzannah's heart as she prepared the still-weak captain for his departure.

The way he looked at her, lightly brushing her brow with his fingers, was infinitely gentle. She'd said farewell to many a handsome officer but never before had she felt so bereft. The truth was, she had come slowly to love this youthful young earl with his indomitable spirit, fine sense of humor, and blithe disregard of pain and confusion. She of all people knew of the depression of spirits like to beset men cast down in their prime. Not one word had she heard of complaint, not one murmur when he found he was in danger of losing his leg. That the wound had healed so cleanly was due in some part to her skill and in great measure to his common sense. He had submitted unwaveringly to their often painful ministrations and had desisted from rising too early as was his inclination.

Suzannah gave a tremulous smile and wished fiercely that their paths would cross once more. The crumpled note she had carelessly crushed in the pocket of her capacious apron suddenly promised much. For the first time, she thanked her good fortune that her work here was soon complete. Sister Patience of Navarre was shortly to relieve her, and with the fighting at an end she realized she need feel little guilt.

Repressing an urge to tell Frances of her circumstances, she held her tongue. It would be unconscionable to trap him into saying something he might later regret. Restored to his family, it was all too possible he would forget the gentle moments they had shared together or the fierce words he had uttered, half asleep, half delirious. She would never forget. But then, how could she? She shrugged her shoulders with Gaelic good sense and smiled up into his troubled face.

"Au revoir, Monsigneur. Be good! And do not, I tell you, get your dressings wet!" Her voice was scolding but her eyes betrayed her. Frances had the sudden urge to tell the waiting minion to be damned. He did not. Thoughts of his sister put paid to his momentary overwhelming selfish and utterly compelling urge to tarry.

"Au revoir, ma cherie! Be sure I will return!" His eyes turned dark, then his irrepressible humor surfaced once more. "And it will be with a very fetching bonnet, I can promise you that!" Suzannah dimpled and curtsied. Jake shifted his feet impatiently.

After thanking the staff of the tiny hospital and bowing particularly over Sister Monica's dainty hand, he turned once more to Suzannah. His eyes were speaking.

She gave him a no-nonsense pat and boldly told him to "Be off!" The smile in her eyes matched his own as he was carefully set in the wagon, a far cry from the Surrey coach that was his by right of birth.

TWELVE

Viscount Lyndale was making much of the task the duke had assigned him. Indeed, it was no hardship, for he found Miss Beaumaris to be quite the most approachable young lady of his acquaintance. He felt himself losing the shy reserve he usually experienced with ladies of quality. The fact is, the viscount was experiencing that unfortunate time in life when making conversation with the gentler sex left him feeling gawky, stiff-lipped, and irremediably gauche.

Cassandra engendered no such feeling in him. On the contrary, her company seemed to stimulate and fortify, imbuing him with the unassailable impression that she was altogether a "great good gun."

His Grace would have chuckled to see him strutting about the estate with such a look of youthful self-importance that needs make all but the kindliest of people laugh to see. Cassandra, being one such person, merely allowed herself the veriest glimmer of a grin before hiding her merriment meekly behind her hands.

It would not become her, she knew, to press Rupert about his uncle's plans. Nevertheless, she felt such a burning curiosity that she could not help but pave the way for him to introduce the subject, if he so wished. His secretive look startled, then amused her. Obviously, he was in his uncle's confidence and relishing that situation with all the enthusiasm of youth.

Miss Beaumaris remained undaunted. An hour of his company made her realize she could wrest his secret in a trice if she so wished. Though she scolded herself for giving way to her baser instincts, in the end could not help herself. The twins were giving chase to Max on the lawns of the great, sprawling mansion, and in a moment of unlooked for freedom she removed her wide poke bonnet and allowed the sun to shine on her lustrous hair.

She looked such a picture that Rupert was quite dazed. For the first time he saw her as his uncle must. Kneeling down by the small stream, her eyes as wide as saucers, almost violet in the light, she would have been hard for any man to resist. Rupert was simply no match for her. Before he knew what he was about, the secret of Beaumaris's whereabouts was wrested from him. To his credit, he did not mention Harrington's role in the affair.

"Rupert!"

Cassandra's eyes were alight with joy and hope. With a burst of energy she jumped up and ran right across the garden, shedding her slippers as she went. Rupert was hard-pressed to follow, while the twins squealed with delight, and Max romped with frenzied joy at this unexpected bliss. Poor Rupert! He could only stare in baffled bewilderment at the quiet young miss he had transformed with a few ill-considered words. Worse was to come. Before he knew what he was about, he was receiving a quite emphatic hug and was being pulled with great gusto by not one but six eager hands, right into the fray.

The servants chancing to look out from quite a few of the many great windows of Wyndham Terrace might be forgiven for thinking themselves in a dream. It had been a long time since such merriness had been witnessed on the noble estate. Certainly not since the tragedy of five years previous, when the duke had succeeded not only to his title, but also to the upbringing of his sister's vibrant progeny. A regular handful they were, that was for sure. For all their energy, the tragedy had a mellowing effect on the duke, moving him to a more adult approach to life than perhaps his years had warranted.

There had somehow been no space or inclination for boisterous romps such as these, more was the pity. The housekeeper broke rigid precedent by allowing her upper maidservants a glimpse of the festivities, an action that earned her their approbation for a long time after.

In the garden, meanwhile, Cassandra was plying the hapless Rupert with question after question, shouting above the din of the dog and the restless chorus of her charges. The Honorable Miss Beaumaris was nothing if not persistent. Rupert had an uncomfortable suspicion that his guardian would be none too pleased at his disclosures. Nevertheless, the look of wondrous hope on Miss Beaumaris's face made all worthwhile. Rupert decided at once to make a clean breast of it to Miles and not to dwell too deeply on his reaction.

How St. John had got wind of her brother's whereabouts was a mystery to Cassandra, save what Rupert had hinted as regard to the Lord High Chancellor. So like a man to succeed where a woman had failed! Had she not herself been haunting the foreign office these days past? How should it be that the duke was privy to such information when she, as next of kin, was not?

He must have been funning her all along! Not getting a special license, but rather investigating Frances's whereabouts. No doubt he had spent the better part of the morning gleaning all the information he could. How perverse that she should feel a small twinge of regret. After all, she'd never countenanced marrying the man. At least now he would not press her. With Frances reinstated, she need have nothing more to do with her loathsome relatives. The earl would know how to scotch any scandal attaching to herself, of that she was certain.

Rupert demonstrated a deploring lack of knowledge as to his guardian's immediate plans. How long he would be, whether or not he'd stop at one of the many inns dotted along the countryside, whether he planned to stay in Brussels with Frances or return with him swiftly were all as trifles to the young man, who invested an extreme degree of faith in his mentor and would be brought to think no further of the matter. Resigning herself to the fact, Cassandra settled down, preparatory to a long and impossible wait.

How strange that fate should intervene by way of the servants. Had it not been for the fact that the duke's second maidservant was something in the way of affianced to the Surrey's first footman, the matter might have gone no further. As it was, word has strange bedfellows. Strict though the edict had been on Cassandra's presence in the bachelor establishment, it could hardly be expected that the two lovers would not exchange a moment of delicious gossip.

A word in the right ear and the redoubtable butler Stanford was apprised of the new scenario. It came as something of a relief to him to know that his erstwhile mistress was safe and unharmed, although her residence at Wyndham Terrace came as unpalatable tidings.

It would not, he knew, become his station to make judgments on the actions of his betters. Indeed, he may privately have shaken his head at the way the world was going, secure in the knowledge that the third earl would have brooked no such shenanigans. Publicly, however, it was incumbent on him to defend Cassandra's honor, while at the same time deploring her necessity. He'd never been taken with the new earl and was now even less so. The possibility that the Honorable Frances Beaumaris might yet be alive filled his earnest being with something approaching delight.

What he heard, therefore, set him to thinking. Stanford, as all who knew him would concur, was a ponderous man. It was not often that he found himself in a situation where he was called upon to utilize his intellect, his calling being such that the fewer questions he felt impelled to ask the better. Now, however, he felt himself saddled with a somewhat ticklish problem.

Laying the particulars before him, he came up with a number of incontrovertible facts. The second footman had lately hand-delivered a missive to Harrington that must have held some degree of importance. This was gathered from the fact that it bore the state seal and had caused Harrington to have dealings with certain unsavory elements at the Running Footman, a haunt not too well patronized by the nobility.

Here, the services of one Cutthroat Jake had been commissioned, the said Jake being a right bad apple if ever there was one. Further adding to the mystery, the first footman had been ordered to set the Surrey sloop aright. Jake had left the house. It had taken a night and a morning before the butler had come to his conclusion that two and two spelled something rather more than three. The uncomfortable task now rested with him to apprise his mistress of the facts. What those facts were he was not quite certain, but he was sure enough to be aware that she might wish to be informed.

Accordingly, after a degree of deliberation, he hired a hack to take him to No. 4 Grosvenor Square—known to polite society as Wyndham Terrace. None could have been more astonished than Cassandra when his arrival was discreetly brought to her attention by Pickering.

He, incidentally, had found himself at a rare loss. In all his years of dealing with the gentry, he had never yet found himself in the position of announcing a fellow butler. Not wishing to insult his compatriot by relegating him to the kitchens, nor of offending Miss Beaumaris by treating him as a guest, he had decided at last on that useful little blue salon to which the duke had so lightly referred.

Stanford's revelations left Cassandra in little doubt as to the extent of the danger confronting her brother. It was too much of a coincidence to suppose that Harrington would negotiate a channel crossing at the selfsame moment as St. John without there being some urgent cause. The description of the cutthroat sent shivers down her spine, rendering her quite incapable of speech for some few moments.

When she had to some degree regained her composure, she collected herself enough to thank Stanford and slip him a small token of her appreciation. He appeared gratified and accepted with a customary display of pomposity that would ordinarily have sent Cassandra into paroxysms of laughter.

As it was, the moment was not one for laughing and she could not help but grimly recall St. John's last words to her. He had thought her in need of protection. She now understood that he'd not merely been engaged in an attempt at looking heroic. Harrington was at his malignant worst and there was nothing she could do to prevent it, save warn St. John. At this realization, she was spurred to action.

Throwing a cape over her shoulders, she rang for the viscount and apprised him of her intention to follow in the wake of the duke. Rupert's face was a picture of dismay. In the face of his protestations, Cassandra shrugged her shoulders impatiently and begged Chivers to set the horses to.

Countermanding all his lordship's attempts at rationality, she swung up onto the duke's chestnut and gave the animal a light spur before even Rupert could arrange for a more suitable mount. She was halfway down the path before the beleaguered viscount caught her up and reminded her of the imminent shower, the footpads, and the penury that awaited her if she set foot without benefit of chaise, manservant, or brass farthing.

Something of his frantic gabbling must have penetrated, because it was a very relieved young man who watched the hell-bent Miss Beaumaris perform an admirable turn, coaxing the stallion every inch of the way.

His alarm was not long to be assuaged. The glint in Cassandra's eye was such that no man could put asunder. Despite Rupert's protestations that the duke was already apprised of Harrington's intent, she would not be turned from her course. Pacing up and down the gallery, the faces of St. Johns past and present staring down at her from out their weathered canvasses, she formulated a plan that was as shocking as it was bold. Rupert winced on hearing it, but his remonstrations were lost on his willful charge.

In clear, bell-like tones she set out to decry all his former objections. Money. That was no problem. She'd draw on her bankers that very day. If they thought it odd in her, well so be it. They'd think it odd. Footpads, maidservants, chaise. No trouble at all. She'd dress as a gentleman and arm herself with one of Miles's well-balanced dueling pistols. The sight of such an object would make any knave blanch. Besides, she'd set such a cracking pace no footpad would be able to catch her.

Chaise. A paltry problem. Rupert had a curricle, and if she guessed it right, spanking good horses. She looked at him sideways, hoping she had hit the mark. She half-suspected that her reference to his high steppers would do the trick. She could not, of course, be certain, but she did detect a slight lessening in the young man's protestations.

When she stopped to draw breath, Rupert interposed. "I say, Miss Beaumaris! I have the most marvelous plan! No need for you to get all bothered. I'll go myself!" This magnanimous conception would be bound to satisfy both his uncle, Cassandra, and his own yearning for adventure. Now that he thought on it, the opportunity to give his team a good run simply could not be missed.

"Oh, Rupert that would be wonderful of you. So wonderful!" Viscount Lyndale heaved a sigh of relief, his eyes gleaming at the prospects before him. "Only . . ."

His heart sank. "Only?"

"Only it won't do, you know! How are you going to recognize the Surrey sloop when you're over on the other side? You hardly even know our crest. You surely don't expect to make inquiries of every vessel docked? Even if Harrington does not set sail under your very eyes, your questions will certainly get back to him and arouse suspicion. I want no chance taken with my brother's life, you understand."

Rupert groaned. "Miss Beaumaris."

"Cassandra. If we're going to be confederates, call me Cassandra."

"Cassandra, then. You have to see, I can't let you go. My uncle was very specific. I was to stay here and make sure you kept out of harm. He'll scalp me if I go along with this crazy scheme."

"And I'll never forgive you if you don't! Can you live with the death of my brother on your conscience? I cannot! I assure you I know I cannot! Do not make me, Rupert, I beg you. If you say no I'll find a way to get there on my own. Who knows what horrible fate will befall me then? Footpads, drowning . . ."

"Stop! What do you want me to do? Think of your reputation!"

"Reputation?" Cassandra smiled a trifle dolefully. "I seriously doubt I have anything left by now. Even so, my brother is worth more to me than any ballroom whisperings and social approbation. If you're concerned, though, let my departure be a secret. Let me dress as a man and no one need know that I've accompanied you alone across the seas. No one need know anything. Not even the duke."

"Especially not the duke! If he knows what I've let you in for, he'll kill me. Promise me that, Cassandra. This will be a secret between the two of us."

"I promise." Her eyes were shining, vivid and violet, a sore temptation to any man. Her enthusiasm was infectious, and it was not long before Rupert had entered fully into the spirit of the plan, issuing orders and hunting avidly through old chests in a quest to find garments of a suitable size.

Strong willed though Cassandra was, he had somehow managed to prevail on her not to draw from her banker. Miles had made it very clear that her whereabouts was to be kept secret, and it was hardly to be expected that Mr. Pratt of His Majesty's Bank Royal would not display some degree of curiosity.

It did the viscount justice that he did not draw on the

duke's personal fortune for the journey. Instead, he regretfully conveyed his emerald cuff links and lapis lazuli-embedded snuffbox to Upper Wimple Street, where he sold them for a fraction of their market value. It was well for Cassandra's peace of mind that she knew nothing of this little transaction.

If Pickering was surprised at the young Viscount Lyndale's sudden intentions of conveying mistress Beaumaris to Bath, he knew enough to keep his peace. It was unthinkable that the young scamp would embark on such a venture without His Grace's blessing. No doubt they knew what they were about. Perhaps they were right, too. The duke wanted scandal averted. Removing the unwitting but constant source of gossip from his household might be sufficient to accomplish just that.

Entering into the spirit of the expedition, the lady in question donned bottle green breeches, an unexceptional Marseille waistcoat, and slightly underpolished topboots as if to the manner born. It is not to be denied, however, that she suffered a few anguished moments in front of the glass before summoning up sufficient strength of will to undertake the first few snips of her luxurious locks.

It was fortunate, indeed, that the viscount arrived on the scene at this very unprepossessing moment. With all the powers of persuasion he could muster, he succeeded in convincing her that a hat was sufficient to cover her tresses. Seizing the scissors from her hands, he offered thanks to immortal God that he had caught her in time. What Miles would have said in response to a shorn fiancée was enough to make him shudder.

The matter thus satisfactorily resolved, Cassandra was left only to shrug herself into morning coat and cravat before surveying herself once more in front of the glass. The effect was admirable. Hastily scrawling a note to the twins, the duo's next endeavor was to ensure her safe incarceration in the carriage. It would not be to their advantage to be forced to explain their actions to the numerous lackeys and household staff that the duke saw fit to employ.

Cassandra had just time enough to gasp at the splendor of the traveling chaise that confronted her, gold-mounted harnesses shimmering like diamonds in the afternoon sunlight. The inside squabs looked curiously inviting as she was bundled inside with due lack of ceremony and uncompromisingly little fuss.

The crest of Duke Wyndham, Earl Roscow, and Baron of the Isles glinted with fine pomp as the door flashed shut. She was later given to understand that although Rupert's conveyance bore all the marks of being "a prime one," even he, in his more sober moments, would not consider it fitting for a hastily conceived cross-country flight.

The groom beamed at his instruction. "Set them to, Brentley! As swift as the wind, mind! We'll change at the first posting station and get a fresh pair. No need to save their stamina."

With a bow and slight flourish of the whip, the groom took his young master at his word. The carriage gave a sudden jolt and started on its way, the clip-clop of horses sounding resoundingly in Cassandra's ears as town was left far, far behind.

So it was that the Honorable Miss Cassandra Beaumaris, previously of Surrey House, found herself clad in buckskins and topboots, alongside a young gentleman of good breeding, great impetuosity, and little sense, on the great market road to the coast.

THIRTEEN

"Where is the sloop, Jake?"

Frances was doing his best not to fall back into a swoon. The tramp down the mountain was wearying indeed for anyone in a full state of good health. For Frances, it was torture. The only light at the end of the tunnel was that it would soon be over. The whole nightmare would soon be over.

He could not wait to be with friends again, to slowly heal from the trauma of seeing all his companions at arms downed under Ney's cavalry. The picture of the young infantry officer who died atop him would forever haunt his dreams. There was little consolation that Napoleon was captured. So many lives! So many lives! It had seemed like a game going in. Now it just seemed a travesty.

Jake leered, but held his tongue. No point enlightening his young victim just yet. Plenty of time for that later. Right now, they had a mountain to get down and a stream to ford. Better to have a willing participant than a surly one.

Frances shrugged. He found it very odd that Cassandra should have chosen so cantankerous a man. Strange, too, that she had organized it at all. Surely grandfather Surrey . . . ? No use trying to ponder. No doubt all would be revealed in good time. Such a pity he was feeling as weak as a kitten. It was churlish, perhaps, but he could not help but hope for a good crossing.

Time seemed to stand still, an endless ebb and flow of

light and dark. The air was dry and cold, biting into the thin buckskins and well-rinsed coat of his battle uniform. All the braid was frayed, and the bright scarlet of the Fourth Hussars had dimmed. Frances did not allow his hope to fade in the same way. His will to survive was great.

If he could only make it to the safety of his sloop he'd be home and dry. He could picture Cassandra at the helm, perhaps even his old friends Sir Reginald or Freddie Althorp. If he could just sustain himself enough to bear with the steady clip-clopping of the mares, he'd get there. Gritting his teeth, the young lord permitted exhaustion to overcome pain.

Not for long. It was growing dark, and the nags were inclined to stumble. It was a great effort not to wince at every jolt. Frances closed his eyes and imagination took over. The calm, soothing voice of Suzannah as she mopped his brow, singing all the while. His breathing became easier, his pallor less distinct. Jake glanced at him sharply and shook his head. Wouldn't do for the blighter to recover altogether!

He began a monologue, his agile brain looking for every crack in Frances's defense. Wear him down, that was the ticket! The weaker the man, the easier his task. Frances opened his eyes and groaned. The barely audible mumbling made it impossible to slip back into the hazy half world between dream and reality. It seemed he was to be firmly ensconced in the real world, and he was not sure whether to be glad or sorry.

The candles burning aboard the sloop did much to revive his spirits. The Surrey heraldic crest blazed bright in the new gaslight of the wharf, engendering a warm feeling of triumph in his breast. So far he'd come, so far! He closed his eyes and blinked back sudden, relieved tears. So many good friends had died in this battle. It was a miracle—truly a miracle—that he had been spared.

Climbing aboard brought back a shock of pain and weariness. The earl of Surrey bit back several peculiarly unsavory curses in his efforts. Jake grinned at the stifled oaths and lent a grimy hand. Frances thanked him, a fact he was later to regret quite bitterly.

And then, it was done. Dusk was casting pink streaks across the clouds and his lordship finally was aboard his sloop. But what a shock! Not the waiting servants, the banquet, the sight of a beloved face. Not even, at least, a familiar one. Instead, he found himself being roughly handled and dragged to the stern. Jake's sneer had turned suddenly malignant. His slothful veneer had disappeared without a trace.

Without ceremony he reached under the sacks and hauled out a long, yellowed piece of gutting used for the mast. Before Frances could make sense of the turn of events, he was trussed to the rigging and gagged in the bargain. There was no reasoning with Jake. Even if he could, he realized it was useless. The man had begun a fervent whispering, his eyes glazed at the thought of the bounty. Night had fallen, the gaslights dimmed of their own volition, and it was pointless leaving the calm of port.

Jake checked the mainsail and decided that another night could be of little harm one way or the other. Besides, there was still the little lady bird of the night before. If he could but be certain of his captive's compliance, there was no reason why he should not pay the Villa d'Esprit another nocturnal visit.

Again, he checked the bonds that to Frances were as heavy as chains. Talking all the time, he feverishly calculated the sum owed by Harrington and the likely interest off that sum. To Frances, it was just a blur of words. Nothing made sense. He was startled when his tormentor addressed him.

"I don't suppose you can do the dandy? Your pockets to let like the rest of 'em or what?"

The speech was incomprehensible to the sixth earl of Surrey.

Jake loosened the gag. "I said your pockets to let or what?"

Receiving no comprehensible response, Jake shrugged his

shoulders and made as if to tighten the bonds. A sudden spirit of self-preservation overcame Frances. "Money. Do you mean money?"

"Well, of course I do, you blighter! Ain't that what I been saying all along?"

"This is a kidnapping, then?"

Jake sniggered. "Well, there be some as would call it that. I like to call it an unfortunate accident, that's wot. Better ask your mate Harrington what this is all about, then. I don't half like the word murder. So nasty sounding, don't you think? But for an earldom and some of the ready like folks says you got stashed away, murder don't seem so bloody terrible, now does it? Come to think on it, you won't have much of a chance to ask, buddy boy. Better ask me—like as not I'll let you in on it if you behave. Still, it won't do you much good, you know."

The last part of his sentence was lost on Frances, who was still trying to glean sense out of the first.

"Harrington. What's Harrington got to do with this?"

Jake positively guffawed, in an expansive mood now that the serious business of getting his hands on Beaumaris had been accomplished.

"I don't usually give away no secrets, mate, but seeing how you're going to be fish food afore long, I reckon it don't matter too much. Come to think on it, maybe I won't tell you. Matter of professional pride, you understand."

Frances felt compelled to inquire further, then gave it up in disgust. It was only too obvious that Jake meant simply to torment him. Why give him the satisfaction? On the other hand, the more he knew of what he was up against, the greater chance he stood. Weighing up his pride with his natural curiosity and life force, self-preservation won out.

"Tell me more, Jake. You were hired by Harrington. Why? Where is the earl of Surrey?"

Jake guffawed with enjoyment. "I be staring at him right in the face, you cawker! What a joke to be sure!"

Bewilderment then realization crossed Frances's pain-racked face. "Surrey? You mean Grandfather Surrey is dead?"

Jake winked. "As dead as a doornail he be! As dead as you're going to be in a few hours! No use frettin' now, what will be will be. Died of the pox, very like."

The vulgarity angered Frances intensely. He moved toward Jake, unconsciously handling his flaccid gag as he did so. Instantly his enemy was on the alert, menacing once more.

"Now don't you take it into your head to start hollering, mate. Just remember. I can do it nice and swift or I can do it nice and slow." The eyes that glinted in the starlight were deadly.

Frances felt the sweat pour from his palms and forehead. In his weakened state, he wouldn't have a chance against this assassin. As far as he could see, he'd reached the end of the road. What a bizarre place to end it, after all he'd witnessed on the battlefield! The horror was slowly sinking in, leaving him breathless.

Jake tightened the gag. His concentration was momentarily diverted by the sounds of footsteps along the gangway. Pistol at the ready, he left Frances at the stern and made his way to the helm, his tread heavy and dangerous. Low voices followed. Frances strained to hear snippets of the conversation but failed dismally.

Occasionally, the words "bale" and "barrel" wafted through the silent night air, but nothing he could make any definite sense of. Jake seemed to be arguing, then listening. By the time the footsteps receded and he was back to the aft, his face was transformed in a veritable wreath of smiles. The fiver, it seemed, had paid off.

"Slight change of plan, mate!"

Frances sat up as far as his restraints would allow.

"Nothing to get too excited about, mind! Noon tomorrow I've a small meeting in the way of business, you understand. Taking delivery of a few kegs of choice proof cognac. A couple of bales of triumph lace, too, if those blithering fools are to be believed. Times are aripe for merchanting around here, I reckon. I couldn't well turn down such a likely cargo just because of you, now, could I? You may just as easily be drowned Tuesday as Monday, can't you then?"

As Frances could hardly be expected to agree, it must be assumed that this monologue was largely rhetorical. As it was, it offered the beleaguered Beaumaris a small reprieve. For that gloomy night, at least, he could rest easy. Jake checked the bonds that were slicing now into Frances's wrists. Satisfied that they were still secure, he nodded abruptly, gave a farcical doff of his cap, and skipped over the moorings to the dry land ashore.

For the earl, it was the start of a solitary night.

FOURTEEN

The dawn was cold and damp, mist curling and unfurling around the masts like lone sprites unsure of their way. On deck, Frances was battling to keep his wits about him, half-way between swoon and slumber. His wrists were etched in blood, for the gutting was tight and cut into him with every move. The captain had long since given up plans of escape. For one he was too weak, for another the situation was simply impossible.

The sloop was dipping and swaying, bobbing like a cork on unchartered seas. Sickness had passed then passed again. There was no energy left, hardly even the last vestiges of a will to survive. Given the choice, Frances might well have chosen death than the perpetual motion of the rocking boat. There'd been no sign of his tormentor throughout the long and icy night.

From time to time a gull called then subsided, its voice an eerie echo of freedom and loneliness. The gag tasted foul. Frances opened an eye, willing himself awake. This was worse than the battlefield, where dying had a meaning, some small glory, and a purpose that was forever England. This experience held no consolation whatsoever.

The quiet was shattered all of a sudden by the thud of boots and the piercing whistle of a man well satisfied by the night's events. Frances was too sick by far to make out the shabby breeches and slightly soiled buckram that he'd come to recognize as uniquely Jake's. The man towered over him, his overhearty voice exquisite pain to one as deprived of company as Frances had been.

"Morning, me hearty! Sleep well?"

Jake removed the gag, a trifle roughly but with all the manner of a man bestowing great largesse.

"Good! You do not scream. I like to see a man what is sensible!"

Frances tried to murmur some reply, but his throat was so parched that response was hardly possible.

"I have business today, my man. No need to tell you that silence be what I'm after." Jake looked Frances over critically.

"You will hold out, won't yer now? Can't be having yer drop down plumb dead in front of me mates, now can I? Fact is, I'd rather yer be snuffing it later when the sloop's outa dock. Think yer'll make it till then?"

Frances remained silent. Following the gist of the lingo, there was not much he could—or would want to—contribute to the particular conversation at hand. It was a pity for him that Jake was in an expansive mood as he checked the rigging and rinsed the deck.

His former malignancy seemed to have vanished, leaving in its place an equally unappetizing quasi-comradeship that left the earl quite sick with disgust. The way the blackguard referred to his impending death as a fait accompli—just part of the day's chores—was enough to make even the strongest man balk. Frances, in the best of times weak, was utterly sickened.

Disgust turned to horror when the assassin unbound his wrists and placed a dank, dark length of burlap sacking over his head and trussed him up like a chicken. Almost apologetic, the cutthroat explained that the sacking was best for "when his mates came round." He seemed to have an inordinate fear that on seeing Frances they would want a cut in the blackmail bounty. Jake was too sharp a man to run that risk.

The sloop was moored gently at dock, awaiting its ill-gotten treasures. The pennant of the Surrey dynasty, the brave raven and peacock, fluttered helplessly in the breeze, itself a prisoner to the fluctuations of wind and fate. When all seemed lost—when it appeared that the last surviving earl of Surrey be doomed to listen to the cant, highly volatile words of his captor for the rest of his remaining life—Jake jumped off the boat.

The peace was miraculous, but not for long. Beggars from around the small peninsula had trickled to the yacht at first in twos, then in droves. They were hopeful in their quest for sustenance, chattering and calling as if with one voice. Enraged, Jake had taken a broom and jumped onto the shore, scattering the vagrants as he did so.

One poor unfortunate who did not quite make it to safety had been thrashed in such a resounding fashion that the thuds echoed across the bay. At last, Jake was done. Casting the beggar from his clutches, he'd stood up, waving the broomstick menacingly before him. "The next one of you lot 'oo 'as a fancy for a trouncing, come mess with me and my boat. If yer don't want me to dust the jackets of the lot of yer, ye'd better scarper now."

The boys looked at him in awed wonder. Beatings came upon them as often as a rainy day and some of them none too pleasant, but this man certainly knew how to administer a rare trouncing. The luckless youth had stood aside, still rubbing his rear from the smart. His grubby little hands were struggling to wipe back the tears each fresh blow had caused.

"Scat. I mean it!" Jake stepped toward them meaningfully. They did not wait to be told twice. Before the seaman could blink, they'd vanished into thin air, their squeals the only tangible reminder that they'd ever had the temerity to approach a regular dab like Jake.

The loading of the boat commenced at noon, when most of the afternoon watch were away at tea. The sounds of the brigand were muffled to Frances, who lay meshed in the burlap, bound head to foot. Jake kept to the fore and it seemed his men had orders to do the same. From time to time the odd keg was rolled to the aft, but in the main the booty was strapped to the front decks and covered in ground sheeting and cod. The smell was paralyzing. Fine for a regular sailor like Jake. Impossible for Frances, who categorically loathed the stench of rotting fish. In the main, a good ploy. It kept the overeager watch and customs officials well at bay.

On shore, Viscount Lyndale and his confederate were at something of a loss. They had crossed the channel without incident, taking advantage of the strong tides to make record progress. Now, however, they could only groan as they surveyed the busy port. Somewhere, they were convinced, birthed the Surrey sloop. Quite where this would happen to be was beyond their somewhat limited powers of imagination.

They were tired and sticky. The travel had scarcely been one of luxurious comfort, despite the well-sprung carriage and the swiftness of the crossing. They had been fortunate, indeed, that the winds had turned in their favor and that the vessel just putting to had been convinced to wait.

Rupert had to admire his conspirator's pluck. She was a game one, that was sure. No hint of complaint, despite looking a trifle peaky and sporting suspiciously bright eyes. He would book her a room and set off to catch his uncle.

No doubt Miles would know what to do. The fellow was bound to be putting up at the best establishment in town. No good dragging Miss Beaumaris along, though. For one, the duke had an uncomfortable omniscience that would in all likelihood penetrate her disguise. For two, he might well have taken himself a bird of paradise to while the time away.

He half expected Miles to have the young earl safely tucked away. Privately, Rupert doubted Cassandra's reasoning. He could never quite believe in danger that lurked in every corner. He would, however, humor her. After all, it was her adventure. Time enough, if he failed to catch up with the duke, to do some investigating of his own.

It did not help that he'd quite forgotten the direction of the hospital Miles had mentioned. Rather a bother, but with the optimism that sat so easily upon his nature, he made light of the problem and very wisely chose not to voice it to the lad in bottle green breeches sitting so impatiently at his side.

"Where are you going, Rupert?" Cassandra's voice was filled with dismay as they rounded the corner on the harbor and kept on walking, away from the sea and out toward the bustling town. If she felt conspicuous, she need not have worried. No one was paying the smallest heed to a young gentleman clad in wrinkled attire and breeches that bore all the marks of a darn above the right knee.

The other gentleman that had arrived that morning, well now, that was another thing! A regular out and outer he was and that was for sure. Arrived in fine style, he did, complete to a shade in black velvet and ruffled lace, a gold fob dangling idly from out the side of one of his fine-fitting pockets.

Not green about the gills, either. Young Ned, the baker's son, had tried to prig him for the watch but to no avail. His fingers had been caught in a vice, and the eyes that met his were as stern as stern could be. He reckoned as how he'd escaped lightly from that one, but he was as sure as anything he'd not try it again. A couple of his friends had nodded in gloomy agreement. The lord was a prime one for the plucking but too gamey by far! They all solemnly averred he must be a "dook" or even a king.

The gentleman in question was seated in the first parlor of the Duc du Barry, delicately wiping his lips after a light luncheon of quail's egg, Chardonnay truffles, and cream of peach suzette. The fire was gently ebbing at the fender and his glass was closer to empty than full, the light catching at the crystal as he idly scrutinized the stem.

His day had been arduous but on reflection, not ill spent. It was fortunate for him that the weather was in his favor, reducing altogether his need for haste. He was perfectly certain that for a good few hours at least, no ship would be game enough to leave the safety of the bay. At all events, if one particular vessel made that mistake, it would probably find itself regretting it.

The harbormaster had proved most helpful on this point. If truth be told, the man had succumbed to His Grace's authoritative air with as much alacrity as the young pickpockets had done a little earlier in the day. It was a blow that Beaumaris had been discharged from St. Christopher of Albans. The nurses had been shocked to learn that their patient had been discharged into dubious care. Finding a sympathetic ear in the duke, they made bold to voice the doubts that had assailed them all morning. Piece by piece, His Grace was able to formulate a pretty accurate idea of the extent of Harrington's machinations. The presence of the Surrey sloop in port confirmed his convictions, and from there it was but a short step to the magistrate and port officials.

Waiting for a warrant was a wearying business, but the duke was a meticulous sort of fellow. Not one to do things by halves and that was the truth! He would stake his life Frances was on board and unharmed. It would hardly make sense to do away with a body on shore when one could have the expanse of the ocean to commit the deed.

How much greater the chances of detection in port than out of it. If, as the duke hoped, Harrington was aboard the vessel, he would wager his fortune that the man would not have the pluck to commit the deed in cold blood. If he left it to professionals, they would undoubtedly await the most auspicious moment. Criminals took very good care to cover their tracks. They would not recklessly put themselves in jeopardy for want of thorough planning.

The duke closed his eyes and instantly the vision of Cassandra flashed through his mind as it had done a thousand times before. He knew every tremor of her lips, every downy wisp that escaped her tight coils of shining hair. He had noticed that her nose tilted ever so slightly when she was amused. Her eyes sparkled her moods. Lavender for peace, violet for passion. Miles cupped his hands in his face and leaned forward over the table, elbows hard on the cream damask tablecloth.

He loved her. The words echoed in his head like spirals of dizzying light. He, who had at two and thirty scorned to find a woman who matched his moods and dreams in every way. A woman who was maddeningly adorable, confusingly honest, muddleheaded but witty, considerate, innocent, seductive, funny, and solemn. A woman who was hasty and zestful, yet who had known suffering and patience. A fine, healthy, charming lady who burst with impetuosity and exuded pride. What a plethora of contradictions, but how delightfully they all mingled in such a unique concoction of pure delight. Cassandra was that special something. That treasure that can take a man a lifetime of searching to find. Were it not for the Harringtons, he may not have noticed her at all.

The very thought afforded him pain. Perhaps he owed them something after all. The thought was amusing. Opening his eyes with a slight chuckle, he was startled to find a pale, wide-eyed face staring at him from behind the mottled green window of the Duc du Barry.

He raised his glass in salute at the woolen-capped urchin. He, the duke noticed, was being jerked firmly away by a young man in a navy hooded cape. Intriguing. The duke directed his eyeglass to the window. Strange what boredom could do. Ordinarily he would not have had the slightest interest in the pair's affairs. This particular moment, however, he had nothing whatsoever with which to occupy himself.

As far as he could discern, the private parlor that he'd

bespoken held no items of amusement or entertainment. If he stirred himself the landlord would no doubt procure for him a newspaper of some sort, but he was in no mood to put his flawless French to the test. He was biding his time, and if that included witnessing a slight altercation between two young and obviously English gentlemen, who was to say otherwise?

The lad who'd first attracted his attention appeared to be tugging urgently at the taller youth's sleeve. Rain was just beginning to spatter from the sky, and the duke could have sworn he heard an oath muttered from the latter's mouth. The younger, clad simply in waistcoat and breeches, was gesticulating wildly and earnestly pointing in the direction of the window.

The flag of Le Duc fluttered pompously in the breeze. The duke lolled back in his seat and smiled. If he guessed it right, the sprigs were as green as could be. Doing "the grand tour" or some such thing. No doubt he hadn't eaten for a while. By the looks of the younger, he could do with some fattening up. Perhaps that was why he'd stared so urgently through the window.

The duo seemed locked now in hot debate. The nobleman stoked the fire somewhat absentmindedly, then came to a sudden decision. Picking up his silver-topped cane, he threw his greatcoat around his shoulders and stepped back into the polished foyer. The innkeeper scurried toward him, a servile expression etched on his features. Bowing low, he inquired whether there was ought at all that His Grace required. The duke shook his head languidly and smiled that brilliant smile that made him so adored among servants and peers. The housekeeper, just passing, vowed she'd never seen the like. The serving girls were already close to a swoon whenever he passed their way.

The cold hit him like a knife as he opened the double oak door. Nimbly he took the stairs while shaking the greatcoat on. Where was the pair? Damnation, after leaving the warmth of the embers, he'd jolly well seek them out and demand their company! Bureaucracy being what it was, the warrant would be at least a half hour yet in coming. That was, if the dock officials bestirred themselves. The duke had a nasty suspicion that the letter of the law would in all likelihood not take much precedent over afternoon luncheon. More like two hours before anything of importance could be achieved.

He rounded the corner. The pair was heading in the direction of the King's Arms, a small posting station not too far out of the town. Miles called to them. Was it his imagination, or did they quicken their step? Now genuinely intrigued, he broke into a run and caught up with them.

"Rupert!"

"Your Grace!" The young scamp always called him that when he felt he might be in trouble.

"What in God's name are you doing here?" Miles's voice was grim, taking in the travel-soiled clothes and staring at the lad next to him with a piercing gaze that left the youth awkwardly hopping on first one foot, then the next.

"Miles, listen! I . . . uh, we . . . uh . . ."

"Yes?"

"This is Mr. Marshall."

"Indeed."

Miles gave the lad in bottle green breeches a sweeping stare before making him a bow. In somewhat more civil tones, he suggested they repair back to the Dorcester, where there would be time enough for explanation.

In silence the trio returned, the younger casting imploring looks in the latter's direction. If the duke noticed this at all, he seemed sublimely indifferent.

The footman at Le Duc Du Barry raised his eyes somewhat at the rather unprepossessing appearance of the pair. Had they not been in the company of so prestigious a nobleman as the eighth duke of Wyndham, baron of the Isles, and an earl to boot, it is doubtful whether they would have acquired entrance. As it was, the innkeeper looked askance when the duke called for a hot luncheon and a new bottle of burgundy, long laid down.

The duke raised his quizzing glass. "What are you waiting for, my good man?" The tone was languid, but a hint of steel was to be detected behind the penetrating eyes. The innkeeper responded at once. There was no fathoming the ways of the gentry, but he knew where his bread was buttered. With a servile bow he began shouting orders to the kitchens and hurried off with a slight shake of his head and a smiling backward glance at the willful duke.

FIFTEEN

Rupert looked decidedly sheepish as he entered the parlor on the heels of his good friend Mr. Marshall. The duke closed the door behind him with a sharp click, then turned to face his ward.

"I assume you have an explanation of some kind?" He turned to Cassandra. "Forgive me, Mr. Marshall, I do not generally air family matters in company, but I must confess to a certain curiosity. You will forgive me if I proceed to satisfy that interest?"

Cassandra nodded dumbly. She had stopped dead in amazement when she'd first caught sight of Miles through the rippled glass of the hotel. Here, it seemed, was the answer to her prayers. It puzzled her that Rupert had not demonstrated the same degree of enthusiasm. It had taken a great deal of urgent whisperings, not to mention a firm grip on her arm, to prevent her from flying headlong into the private parlor and pouring forth all her hopes and fears.

In the few moments Rupert had, he'd reminded her in no uncertain terms about their agreement. Miles was never to suspect that she had accompanied him on the perilous voyage across the sea. He'd broken the trust the duke had invested in him and should His Grace ever find out, he shuddered to reflect on the consequences.

If Miss Beaumaris found his reasoning somewhat melodramatic, she had to agree that for the sake of her own reputation and peace of mind it would be better that St. John remain in ignorance. A niggling adjoinder to this was the fact that she herself had agreed to remain incognito. For Rupert's sake, she was honor-bound to stick to that pledge.

The viscount convinced her that her disguise was not to be trusted under the shrewd scrutiny of his uncle. For safety's sake he'd leave her at the King's Arms before backtracking to the Duc du Barry. There he would find the duke and apprise him of Stanford's tale. There was no need at all for Miles to know that the viscount had been accompanied.

The logic made sense to Cassandra, who had sensibly ceased struggling and in return extracted a promise that Rupert would waste no time in speaking to his guardian. The plan had seemed admirable until they'd been confronted by the man himself. Now the pair were forced to brazen it out and hope to God the duke had enough else to think of than to pay too close attention to a slight young man of indeterminate age and rank.

"Miles! I came to warn you!"

The duke removed his greatcoat and seated himself, indicating the two men to do the same. A slight smile gleamed in his dark eyes as he gazed at the disheveled pair, but he remained silent.

Rupert, seizing his chance, rushed headlong into the tale. Before he knew it, the story of his flight—with a few minor modifications—had tumbled from his lips. When he'd done, the duke remained speechless. It fascinated Cassandra that in the light of what had just been disclosed, he remained so unutterably still.

Rupert began to feel uncomfortable, especially as his guardian had become intricately absorbed in removing an invisible particle of dust from his gleaming white shirt ruffles. As the miscreant well knew from past misdemeanors, this was not a good sign. The duke rarely raised his voice when angered. Instead, he became deathly quiet, and the nerve of his left cheek twitched in a manner that was barely detectable to the uninitiated. The nerve was twitching now.

Miles stood up. "Thank you for your concern, Rupert. And yours, Mr. Marshall." He bowed in Cassandra's direction.

Rupert heaved a sigh of relief. Perhaps he'd been wrong about that nerve.

The duke's gloved hands moved behind his back. "There is one thing, however!"

Rupert's heart sank. "Yes?"

"It's the small question of Miss Beaumaris. Forgive me if I'm obtuse, but I thought I'd commended her to your care? Your exclusive care?" The duke rapped out the words.

Viscount Lyndale looked extremely uncomfortable. So, for that matter, did the young Mr. Marshall, who was now seeing fit to kick at the heels of his topboots in a manner most unbecoming to a gentleman of breeding.

"You did, Miles!" Rupert's face brightened. "And I can assure you she's safe! Never better, in fact! Sends you her good wishes. Really." The viscount coughed.

In other circumstances Cassandra would have burst into a peal of laughter over the mull he was making of his story. As it was, she lowered her lashes and felt awfully small. If the duke were to discover the truth, all that inner anger would be directed at her. The thought made her squirm. She tilted her head proudly. What cared she what the duke thought? And why wasn't he doing anything? There was simply no time to waste!

"Your Grace."

The duke turned to her in surprise. "Yes, Mr. Marshall?"

Rupert stared daggers at her. Cassandra decided to ignore it. "Can you not set out at once for the hospital? By all accounts there is a lot at stake!"

The duke raked Cassandra up and down. Slowly, deliberately, he flicked open his snuffbox and took a somewhat large pinch. For an instant, the aroma drifted across the room.

"Would you care to enlighten me on just what the viscount has been saying?"

Cassandra colored up. The duke could really offer a set down if he so chose. "Well, it's just . . ."

Rupert interposed. "Leave us . . . Andrew." The name just popped randomly into his head. "Wait for us in the foyer. We shan't be a moment!"

Cassandra was doubtful. She'd never been alone in the foyer of an inn before. Then again, she'd never before donned breeches and hat. She was about to drop a curtsy when she remembered herself. With a casual swagger, she made for the door.

"One moment, if you please." The duke stopped her midstep.

"You will repair to my private chamber. It is much warmer there, and I'd prefer not to arouse curiosity." Cassandra drew in her breath. Things were not moving the way she'd planned. Rupert gave an audible gasp.

"Sir . . ." The duke scowled. One look at his face and Cassandra quavered. A bell tinkled. Before she knew what she was about, a footman had entered and been instructed to lead the way. Without another murmur, she left the room.

The duke's chamber was sumptuous in the extreme. The room smelled of leather and oak and had long, heavy drapes that blocked out the sunlight. A fire was crackling at the hearth and the bed looked temptingly inviting, its covers turned back so that the sheets remained well aired. A snowy cravat was carelessly flung on the pillow and beside it, a sapphire kerchief that looked vaguely familiar. The rain had ceased it's sputtering, and Cassandra pulled back the curtains to let in some of the fading morning light.

If she closed her eyes and stood on the great mahogany desk, she could just make out the dock and its moorings. Helplessly, she counted the vessels in port. Too numerous by far! How the duke ever intended to locate Harrington's sloop was a mystery. She felt a stab of impatience overwhelm

her. If anything were to happen to Frances, she'd never forgive herself. Not now. Now that she knew he was alive. Sigh-
ing, she let the drapes drop back.

As she did so, she started in shock. The green and black
of the raven and eagle! She drew back the velvet and squinted
out for a closer look. No, she was not mistaken. Her eyesight,
as always, had served her true. The Surrey family sloop was
sandwiched between the earl of Hampstead's yacht and the
crimson pennant of the Deloras dynasty. Cassandra may not
immediately have recalled these crests. Her own, however,
was most certainly familiar.

There was no time to be wasted. Taking the stairs two at
a time, she had just an instant to straighten her hat before
being ushered once more into the private parlor. What an
annoyance! The duke and Rupert had quite vanished. The
quiet scent of His Grace's snuff was the only indication that
he'd ever graced the room with his presence.

Cassandra thought quickly. No use wondering where they
might have been headed. The sloop was ashore for the present but could well set sail at any time. If her brother was
onboard, it would be the worse for him. She came to a decision. Climbing the stairs once more, she entered the duke's
chamber, withdrew a wafer from the drawers of the great
desk, and scribbled a note.

She slipped out as unobtrusively as she had come in. When
she was well past the stables she broke into a run. Faster and
faster until, out of breath, she reached her destination. Instinct warned her to hang back. She'd been right. Two
swarthy men appeared on deck. She felt goose bumps down
her arms. If Frances had tangled with them, there was little
hope. To her surprise, they appeared about to disembark. A
third, more wily looking fellow, appeared behind them. They
exchanged words that bore structural resemblance to English
yet remained unintelligible to Cassandra.

What relief when all three nimbly jumped to shore. They
spared not a glance for a weak-looking sprig in bottle green

breeches. The man they called Jake appeared to be absorbed in an account of the antics of a local bawdy house. Cassandra could not be certain. The three appeared to be sauntering off in the direction of an ale house, and the resourceful Miss Beaumaris seized her moment.

Blessing the Lord for her pantaloons, she hoisted herself on deck with the aid of a rope that hung dangling from the side. Her heart beat so audibly that she could hear little else. A traitorous voice kept murmuring that there might yet be more danger lurking on board. Perhaps even Harrington. She quelled the voice and shuddered.

She had just had time to tiptoe to the aft when the boat tilted once more, indicative of someone embarking. The heavy thud of a seaman's boot confirmed those fears. Diving under some old sacking, she held her breath. Jake. The man Jake was back!

He was indeed. Cassandra gasped as she peeped out from under the pungent sacks. He was talking and by the sound of things, not to himself. Someone was beneath the burlap.

"All's well, me hearty!" The great man gave a chuckle. "Ye'll pardon me if I don't untie yer, won't yer now?"

Silence. "All right, have it yer way then. I'm not a bloke what insists on talkin', yer ken. Just a few more hours, I reckon. The wind be to the west. When it lets up a mort, we'll be off."

Frances groaned. His body was too worn to exert itself in any way. In a few hours he'd be lying on an ocean bed. Perhaps it was a fate more appealing than the one in which he currently found himself.

Jake loosened the bonds slightly and allowed a rush of fresh air to flow into the sack. Patting his victim in an absurd parody of comradeship, he announced that he "be getting a morsel to eat." Frances retched. In disgust the seaman stepped aside and moved to the front. The earl rolled back in despair.

Cassandra crawled under the sacking and reached the victim on the other side. "Frances! Frances is that you?"

Beaumaris closed his eyes. He must be in heaven. He could have sworn he'd heard his sister's voice. Why did it sound so urgent? Why was it hushed and insistent? Angels should be restful, at peace. Cassandra prodded the burlap.

"Frances!"

Frances started. This was no angel! For that matter, this was no heaven! "Cassandra?"

"Yes, it is I. Cassandra." Huge tears welled up, then fell unbidden onto the hard wood deck. "Just hold on and I'll untie you, Frances. You hang in there, you'll be all right, I swear!"

Gritting her teeth, she set her mind to unknotting the ropes that twined the sacking. It was tough, and she was forced to use her teeth. Resolutely ignoring the foul taste of the moorings, she doggedly worked until the last twine loosened. Frances, granted new hope and life, found strength to help her.

His wrists ceased to feel pain as he wriggled doggedly to loosen the last remaining bond. He had so many questions they tumbled from his mouth two at a time until Cassandra hushed him, her voice a low whisper. Her heart raced uncontrollably. At last, when it seemed as though it would never happen, the last knot came unstuck. The fresh, cool air enveloped Frances's senses as the sack was unceremoniously pulled over his head.

The change revived him. He breathed deeply, his bloodshot eyes becoming much more focused as he took in Cassandra, dirty, disheveled, and boylike. He opened his arms, and she hugged him, tears streaming now unchecked. Then the fear again. Fear and a hint of panic. How were they to get off the wretched boat? Frances was clearly too weak to be diving out to sea, or, more difficult still, creeping past the likes of Jake. It was a dilemma. Of that there was no doubt.

More and more Cassandra found herself wishing she had not rushed off so precipitously. If only she had waited, the duke would have organized something. He was so dependable, so sure in everything he did. If only she had listened to Rupert, trusted in His Grace's ability. Perhaps he'd find the note. If so, what then? No, she must not pin her hopes on so passive a plan. Strategy! That was what she ought to have! No good. It didn't matter how much she chided herself, the fear remained.

Frances's arms encircled her. Despite his weakness he was strong, a real anchor. She looked up at him and love shone bright in her eyes. He was family. The only family she had now. His fingers tightened. His lips were so dry and parched. If only she'd thought to bring a flask! But then, she'd had no idea of the terrible condition she was to find him in.

Regrets were useless. The thing that was critical was the here and now. Painfully, Frances made the effort to speak. His voice was little more than a whisper, but he was fighting for more than just his own life. He was responsible for his sister's well-being, and the knowledge brought with it a surge of unexpected energy.

He eyed the distance to the bridge critically. There was always the chance that Jake would disappear once more, leaving them free to creep across the deck and climb ashore. The only alternative would be to dive overboard, but he could not altogether rely on his strength to keep him afloat. Too risky for Cassandra, too. The North Sea was icy. There was no telling that they'd be able to slip past the sloop and make it back to the dock. Jake sported a nasty-looking blunderbuss. If he shot it would be to kill.

The winds were fast subsiding. By Frances's estimation it would not be long before the seaman deemed it safe to leave the shelter of the bay. It was imperative that their escape be complete by the time this happened. On consideration, the pair decided that a half hour wait on the off chance that Jake would leave the sloop was warranted. After that, it would have to be a deep, cold dive into the rolling gray ocean.

Cassandra tried to steel herself to the thought. The boat lunged. A flicker of emotion crossed Frances's face before he was goaded to action like a highly sprung pistol. Pushing Cassandra under the sacking, he threw himself over her body and covered himself as best he could with the remaining burlap. Her disheveled form was visibly trembling beneath him, her breathing uneven and ragged. Instinctively, Frances reached out to stop her mouth, fearful of every sound. The stress of the ordeal overcame him and he was suddenly very afraid. Afraid for her, for himself, for the whole impossible predicament.

His instincts had been correct. The familiar thud of Jake's boots on the planks resounded in their ears. The sloop veered to port slightly. Cassandra stirred beneath her brother's frame. In response, he grasped her hand in a silent vise. Now was not the time to make the smallest movement, the slightest flutter. Every tiny stirring could spell out death and discovery.

Instinctively, Frances felt Jake's eye upon him. His flesh shivered as he sensed the penetrating gaze. He dared not breathe. He willed Cassandra to remain still. From the corner of his eye he could see one of the ropes that had bound him, lying in a telltale pile on the floor. He prayed that Jake would not do the same.

"Well now, me hearty." Jake's voice sounded, to Cassandra's petrified ear, much like a cackle. She kept telling herself that this could not be true. She could not truly be lying in a bundle under her lost brother's body, afraid for her very life. That sort of thing simply did not happen!

The voice obtruded into her thoughts, an unwelcome menace. Her finely tuned ears could just discern the splash of an empty bottle tossed to sea. "Reckon we can heave ho right quickly, me mate. Wind seems to have let up a bit."

The cutthroat pulled yet another bottle out from his coat pocket. The glass flashed brown in the daylight. He took a swig. Frances could hear the gulp as it slithered down his throat.

"Not bad stout them Frenchies brew. I'll say one thing for them, they know how to make yer proper drunk." Jake teetered slightly. He wiped his lips on his sleeves, then laughed a little foolishly.

"Must sail. Won't do to be anchored here all day, ye ken.

Got precious cargo aboard." He looked at the tangled form of his prisoner. "Not you." He broke into a mirthless snigger. "The contraband! On second thoughts ye might have some snoopy relatives for all I know. Can't have them pokin' about, now, can we?"

Another hideous guffaw. Frances remained silent. Disappointed, the cutthroat saw fit to kick at the sacking. "Cat got your tongue or somefing?" Receiving no response, he bent down closer. The smell of hock was overpowering. His voice dropped to a whisper. "Not long now, I reckon. Ye'll be shark bait before I can say Blarney stone. Now what have ye to say to that? Huh?" Once more the mocking chortle. Cassandra was sickened.

The assassin turned to go. Frances could almost feel himself breathing again. The boots stepped. Then stumbled. Frances's heart sank. The rope! The stupid fool had tripped over the rope! Panic seized his gut. Unless a miracle happened, they both were doomed.

No miracle was handy. Jake was too much of a professional to let a little drink cloud his judgment. It took not two seconds before he'd drawn a knife and approached the sacks with caution. Two more and the Beaumarises were miserably exposed. Frances stood up, defiant. Cassandra did the same. She shot her brother a warning glance, and in an instant he understood. The cutthroat would never know it was a woman he'd murdered onboard the sloop.

SIXTEEN

Jake approached the sacks with cunning. If his victim had extricated himself from the ropes, then he was more game than he'd imagined. He drew his long, deadly knife and advanced with caution. Frances and Cassandra could only look miserably at one another and pray for a miracle. Although they could not actually see a weapon, they were pretty certain that struggle would be useless.

It was worth a try, though. Anything was better than being at the mercy of a villain like Jake. Cassandra could feel Frances tense, his muscles flexed and ready to spring. As Jake whipped off the sacking, Frances dived for Jake's ankles. Cassandra jumped up and searched wildly for something with which to stun their captor. Frances yelled at her to escape. She ignored him, running for the heavy metal grid that covered the cod nets. If she could use it she would.

Frances forced Jake back, utilizing every vestige of his remaining strength. For an instant he was on top, trying desperately to wrest the knife from Jake's grasp. Cassandra started screaming, her cries echoing in the wind. The grid was obstinate, refusing to be dislodged.

She gave it up and ran to the struggling pair. Jake was gaining the advantage and his knife was coming perilously close to slashing Frances's cheeks. Without thinking, the Honorable Miss Beaumaris struck out her foot and delivered an almighty blow. Thank heavens for the topboots! The force of the kick sent the knife flying from Jake's grip. He was momentarily diverted, but not for long. Before she knew what she was about, she'd been drawn into the fray, screaming and kicking with all her being.

Jake was incensed as he shook off Frances and dealt Cassandra a backhand that sent her sprawling across the deck. As she made to recover, he turned on the young earl and struck him with a final, unequivocal blow that left him dazed. For Jake the danger was over. He towered over his captives as the snide amiability slowly returned to his features. Frances and Cassandra involuntarily shivered, their eyes never once straying from their captor's face. The game was up and they knew it.

The cutthroat's voice was menacing, his wits about him. There was no trace of the drunkenness that had absorbed him a few moments before.

"We have a visitor, I see."

Cassandra stood up, her heart pounding wildly. His tone had not been pleasant. Shaking off fear, she made a bow. Frances could only marvel at her flourish.

"Yes. Andrew Marshall. A friend." Her voice was crisp and clear, a far cry from the wobbly blancmange she felt inside. Chin up, she cast her enemy an appraising glance.

The boatman seemed amused. "And how, Mr. Marshall, do ye come to be tarryin' on me sloop?"

"Your sloop?" Cassandra feigned ignorance. "Oh, Lord Beaumaris's sloop, you mean?"

Frances gasped at her temerity. Once started, Cassandra was not to be halted. He knew this of old. Where the baiting would lead them, though, he could not guess. There'd be nothing stopping her now that she'd got a grip on her initial fear.

The cutthroat laughed. The sound was dry and nasal. "Sense of 'umor, I see. It be a pity I 'ave to nabble yer so soon. Yer might 'ave done for a spot o' company. No relation of this 'ere earl, I take it?"

"Earl?"

Jake scanned her face carefully. Mr. Marshall passed the test. He seemed ignorant enough of Beaumaris's identity. The villain's tone relaxed and became conversational. "Yes, he be a earl orll right, but not for long, I reckon."

The teeth flashed white. " 'Ands be'ind yer back. Both of yer." He stooped to grab the rope. Frances saw his chance. He lunged toward the criminal, but to no avail. Jake was not one to be caught twice. In less than a twinkling the cutthroat's boot had made excruciating contact with his face. Frances fell back, blood oozing from his left eye.

"I've 'ad just about enough of yer." Jake's face darkened ominously. He turned to Cassandra, finger extended. "Don't yer try any fancy tricks now me mate. I've got me knife. One scream from yer and yer friend is dead. Dead, dead, dead. Got that?"

Cassandra nodded miserably.

"Now get down onto that floor next to 'im. Ready?"

Cassandra edged herself down, her eyes glued to the weapon.

"Good. 'Ands be'ind yer back and make sharp!"

Cassandra did as she was told. There was no hope now. None at all.

She felt the man pull roughly on her skin and concentrated on not crying out. If she was going to die then she'd do it with dignity. She was a Beaumaris when she was born and she'd behave as such when she perished. Frances was looking anguished. Cassandra smiled at him and it seemed as though a great weight departed from his shoulders. Even in a situation like this she exuded an inner glow that brought comfort. It did not take long for Jake to gag the pair, secure their hands, and place Frances in full bonds once more.

The episode had unnerved Jake slightly, and now more than ever he was aware that the sloop ought to depart in haste. He stepped over the sacks and made his way to the fore. The duke was waiting.

The tussle out the back had not prepared Jake for an eventuality of this nature. Normally guarded, he'd let his watch slip in his concentration over the prisoners. The sleek footsteps of the duke of Wyndham had gone unnoticed above the screams of Mr. Marshall. The click of a pistol primed had not been heard above strong sea winds. Too late! The duke was advancing on him, and he had nothing but a knife. He moved forward. A shot rang out.

The bullet met the mast just inches from the cutthroat's head. Jake ducked. An icy laugh met his ears. The biting words of the implacable man before him sounded like a death knell. "Have the goodness to drop your weapon." A moment's hesitation. Another shot. This time, the bullet grazed the silken hairs of his ear before nesting deeply, irretrievably, in the wood pylon. Jake dropped the knife, his eyes never leaving Miles's face.

"Thank you." Miles inclined his head, arms still outstretched. His eyes did not waver, and Jake experienced the sobering, overwhelming sensation that he'd at last met his match.

"What can I be doin' for yer?"

Miles raked him up and down. "That is hardly to the point, my man. I rather think it is more a case of what I can do for you!"

Jake stared, uncomprehending.

"Look behind me."

Jake looked.

"Look again. You will note that behind the tree there is a gentleman." Jake nodded. "That gentleman's name is Lyndale. Viscount Lyndale. Understand?"

Jake nodded quietly, hardly noticing the sprightly young man who bestowed upon him an impudent wave. His attention was focused wholly on the duke.

"Behind the viscount there waits a brigade of excise men." Miles waited for the words to sink in. Jake blanched. The duke nodded. "I thought so. I rather think they might be interested to see what lies beneath the cod. They may cast a blind eye to the smuggling, but there's a price on the head of the man who made away with the burgundy. I suppose you know that?"

Jake nodded dumbly.

"Good. Then I think we understand each other. You have on this sloop two passengers. A Mr. Marshall and the sixth earl of Surrey. Am I correct?"

Jake had ceased to be amazed at the omniscience of this unknown nemesis. He nodded.

"You will unhand them and you will divulge who paid you to bring about Beaumaris's death." Jake's eyes held mutiny. Miles kept the pistol cocked and reached into the folds of his greatcoat. Drawing out a sheet of paper, he indicated that Jake review its contents. There was no need. Jake knew the looks of a warrant when he saw one.

"Enlighten me as to your employer and the viscount need never call upon his friends the excise men."

Mile noted with satisfaction the glimmer in Jake's eye. He was interested. "Personally, I am not particularly concerned about the whereabouts of a few odd barrels of contraband. No doubt you will get your comeuppance in time. Had harm come to either the earl or Mr. Marshall—" The duke stopped and swallowed hard. No, he would not dwell on that thought. His voice cleared. "Had anything happened to either of them, I'd have had you hanged, drawn, and quartered. As it is, you're lucky."

Jake did his damnedest not to reflect on the bruising that must now be surfacing on Beaumaris's face. If this madman with a pistol were to see it, who knew where things would end? He tried to steer the conversation.

"If I tell yer what flash cull it was 'oo 'ired me, you'll let me go? Not set them dratted customs culls on me?"

Miles relaxed infinitesimally. "If you play your cards right, are careful not to cross my path in any way, and are prepared to sign testimony to your words. Moreover, if you repair back to London from whence you came, shut your mouth, and never breathe a word of this despicable little episode to anyone. Got that?"

Jake nodded. He got it.

SEVENTEEN

The Duc du Barry was full. The footman shook his head sorrowfully and pronounced it positively full. His Grace had fixed him with a stare as cold as ice and as haughty as the devil, and a room was miraculously procured. A disheveled and pathetically weak Frances had been helped up the stairs by Rupert and the duke himself.

Cassandra fluttered about helplessly. The relief after her trauma had been so great she'd experienced an insane desire to throw herself in the duke's arms and confess to all. The stupid masquerade, the foolishness of their flight. If only she'd trusted him! She wanted to sob and be comforted, to put her hands in his and forget the ordeal past. She wanted Miles. Above all else, she wanted him. She loved him. The strong jaw, the comforting strength, the transient eyes, sometimes warm, sometimes steel, sometimes an expression she could not understand at all.

It was funny. She still did not know how the duke had found the sloop. How he'd boarded it at the fateful moment when she'd believed all lost. It didn't matter, somehow. The duke was strong. Always resourceful, he was the type of person who could be relied upon in time of need. Almost like magic. Cassandra's lips curved dreamily. That was it, magic!

How she longed for the enrapturing comfort of his strong, muscular body. The warmth of his form against hers, caressing and gentle. The impulse to cling to him as he'd helped her off the boat and out of harm's way had been immense. Cassandra prided herself on her strength of will. It was that strength that was going to see her through the long and weary night ahead.

The viscount and his mentor were ensuring Frances's comfort. A doctor was on the way. There was nothing more for the strange young man in bottle green breeches to do but wait. Miles, considerate to the last, had noticed how peaky she'd appeared and ordered her to bed, to rest. Cassandra had demurred, but what could she do? She was hardly in a position to beg to nurse her brother. Of all things that would be out of character for a friend of the viscount!

When Miles had pushed her firmly in the direction of his chamber, there'd been no convenient excuse ready at her fingertips. Rupert had thrown her an anxious glance but had merely shrugged helplessly in the face of an unstoppable force. Frances, too, had seemed resigned. He'd frowned ever so slightly but relaxed at the sound of the duke's cool, calm, efficient strictures. What the man did not know could not harm him. If he believed Cassandra to be a young male companion of his ward's, her virtue could not possibly be under threat.

How circumspect of Cassandra to maintain the masquerade. It was essential to her honor that the charade be played out to its end. Not even a Beaumaris could commit a social solecism of this magnitude and not expect to pay the price. Cassandra was too young to be ostracized from Almack's, to be forever cast to the fringe of the monde. No gossip must envelop her name. None, ever! As for the duke, he appeared a good enough fellow. They had a lot to be grateful for.

Later, Beaumaris would have cause to wonder. His Grace had expended a great deal of time and energy in coming to his assistance. It was possible, after all, that his lively young sister had gotten it wrong. It hardly seemed plausible that a pink of the ton like Wyndham would go to such lengths out of altruism. More likely by far he'd seen through her disguise and was motivated by more than just kindness. No doubt he'd be offering for her hand before he knew it. On that amusing thought, the sixth earl of Surrey closed his eyes, lost to oblivion at least for the while.

His sister was close to the same fate. Tiptoeing out of the sickroom, she crossed the landing to Miles's bedchamber. Her feet were aching, she felt exhausted, the chair next to the desk was uncompromisingly hard, and before she knew how it had happened, she was lying, fully clothed, across the length of the four-poster bed. Her recumbent form was covered somewhat haphazardly by a light quilted coverlet of the same hue as the velvety drapes.

Day became night and the candle burned down low as Miles gazed at the sleeping figure. His face was filled with tenderness as the shadows danced and flickered across her face. From time to time, her little white hands would clench and unclench and His Grace discovered in himself the most passionate desire to hold them, to stroke each finger, to kiss the tips and to never stop. Her gorgeous mane of hair was tumbling down from the ridiculous woollen cap she'd chosen to affect. Thank goodness, at least, she'd had the sense not to crop it.

He considered putting an end to the charade, then laughed. If this was the way she wanted it, he'd play her at her own game! It would be interesting to see what would come of it. Life was suddenly full of promise. Her gentle snores had deepened, indicating a sleep of great depth. Seizing his opportunity, he tenderly tucked the soft tendrils back in their woolly prison. Shrugging, he gingerly found himself a space in the great bed and rolled Cassandra over so that she was properly tucked. Her legs were very close to his, her breathing deep and calm.

The duke closed his eyes. This was harder than he had expected. Her small frame exuded such warmth, such promise. If only he could cradle her gently in his arms, he was convinced he'd sleep. No! On his honor as a gentleman he could make no move. No matter that before the week was out she'd be his wife, like it or not. Less, if he could arrange it. Unfair to take advantage. He was bound in conscience to let her be. He sighed.

She shifted. Drat the girl, what was he expected to do? Her body moved closer to him, her scent pure torture. Despite the muddy clothes and the faint smell of cod, her own unique perfume wafted maddeningly into his nostrils. He wanted to shake her awake. She wasn't playing fair.

No, by prolonging the charade he was not playing fair. She was tired, that was all. Her arm dangled across the bed. What could he do but climb under it? He'd wake her if he tried to put it back. Her head snuggled forward, a hair's breath away from his chest. This was madness! The duke groaned. Hadn't the wench caused him enough trouble for one day? Her lips blushed with promise.

Firmly the duke closed his eyes. His body was taut as he tried desperately to think of a distraction. Sheep did not help. He'd counted seventy before Cassandra's little nose had touched his chest. That did it! There was no way he could endure another hour of such sweet and unrelenting torture. With a sigh he extricated himself from her delightful tangle and wrapped a gown firmly around his rigid form. Tiptoeing down the hall, he made his way resolutely to the sickroom where Frances was fast asleep and Rupert in much the same state.

The duke resolved not to be too hard on the young scamp. Honesty compelled him to admit that Cassandra was a handful. Far too strong-willed to be left in the charge of someone as good-natured as Rupert. It was all partly his fault for leaving her in the first place. He should have guessed she'd lead his ward on a regular song and dance. The girl had pluck and courage. Not, however, a particle of sense when it came to affairs of the heart.

Poor Rupert had looked so dejected at his ticking off. The duke had maintained his cold grandeur the whole course of the evening. He was angry, really angry. If something had happened to his life's treasure he would have been forever anguished. He'd lived with tragedy. That would have been as nothing in comparison with Cassandra's death. Thinking on it, his body tensed. All was well now. He must dwell on that and let the past be forgotten. Rupert and the twins were his joy. He'd be lenient with Lyndale.

As if sensing this new mood, Rupert opened an eye. The duke grinned the engaging smile that had made him the idol of his family. Rupert sat up, bathed in happiness. He could not stand to be estranged from his guardian. Darling Miles! It was so good to have him back and in spirits!

"How is Mr. Marshall?" Rupert asked.

Miles cocked his head quizzically. Well, he could hardly expect the scamp to betray Cassandra's secret, now, could he? "Fine. He'll be just fine. Resting soundly as a log, I can tell you that! Couldn't sleep for the snores!"

Rupert could not resist a boyish whoop. "Snoring, now, is he? Well, I never! You'd best catch some sleep, Miles. Long day ahead tomorrow. Good thing you hired Messrs. Brandon, Brandon and Longey! After our last crossing I could do with some traveling comforts!"

"Hard, was it?" The duke looked sympathetic.

"Hard? The devil! You have no idea . . ." He broke off, unwilling to divulge more. No need for the duke to scrutinize the details too carefully. He was too astute by half! He gave an elaborate yawn.

The duke cocked his eyebrows, then relented. "Good night, old fellow. Sleep well."

"You too, Miles. Hope old Andrew doesn't keep you up all night!"

Miles neglected to say he was certain that he would. Instead, he closed the door lightly and padded back to his chamber.

A candle was burning. Alert, the eighth duke opened the door cautiously. Any prowler caught by him would have a lot of answering to do. No prowler. Only a hungry Mr. Marshall reading notes by candlelight.

"Good evening."

"Good evening." Suddenly shy, Cassandra felt the whole world had burst into masses of shining stars. Strange how Miles had such an effect on her. It seemed like years, not days, that they'd known each other.

"Care for a glace fruit?" she asked.

Not bad, since she'd been munching from the bowl intended for him all along. Miles grinned. "Why not? Are there any cherries left?"

Cassandra looked dubiously at the bowl. "I rather think I ate the last one. Sorry!"

"Never mind, a nut will do." Miles picked up a nutcracker and looked at his love curiously. "Can't sleep?"

"No! I can't think why not, rather stupid really." Cassandra came dangerously near to a blush. How could she tell the man that waking up in his bed had the most curious effect upon her, leaving sleep quite out of the question?

Miles teased her. "Well, you seemed to be doing just fine an hour or so ago. I left you snoring most amiably."

Cassandra gasped. "Me? Snoring? Never! Why, I never snore! Besides, you've not been in the room this evening! I took particular note to wait up for you."

The duke cracked his nut. "Did you? Why?"

Cassandra blushed a definite crimson. The conversation was getting difficult. "Oh, I don't know. Wanted to thank you, I suppose."

"Yes. Most extraordinary circumstances, were they not? I can't help but wonder at your precipitancy. What you did there was really above and beyond the call of friendship, you know."

Cassandra bit into a peach. The duke had a right to be astonished. There was little she could say in explanation. She hated being tangled in a web of lies. It seemed the more she came into contact with him, the deeper she became enmeshed.

"When exactly did you meet my Rupert?" The devil was

in the duke and he knew it. He was beginning to enjoy himself.

Cassandra was vague, muttering some unintelligible nonsense. Miles could just make out "Oxford" and "horse" in the gabble. He nodded, as if accepting the offering. Cassandra looked relieved.

"Take off your hat, Mr. Marshall. I'm sure the fire will suffice. It's warm enough in here."

Cassandra's heart lurched. Out of the frying pan into the fire! There was no doubt that sweet though this time with the duke was, it was nevertheless going to be fraught with pitfalls. "No!"

The duke feigned surprise. "Why ever not?"

"I . . . uh . . . personal reasons!" Even to Cassandra the excuse sounded lame.

The duke took pity on her. "Personal reasons. Yes, I think I understand. You wear the hat out of sentiment. I too have a lady love. At home. In England."

Cassandra's heart sank. This was not what she wanted to hear. Why should she be surprised that the duke had an attachment? It was only natural, after all. She had no claim on him. None whatsoever. If anything, the duke's words confirmed her desire to keep her identity a secret. If he discovered her in this compromising situation he would certainly be compelled by honor to wed her. She did not want that. Not at all.

"I also have a keepsake. I like to keep it with me. A trifle really, but nonetheless comforting." He hesitated, a small smile of impish mischief sparkling behind his eyes. "Would you care to see it?"

Cassandra's heart was heavy. The day had been filled with so many wild emotions. Those that fluttered in her heart now were the heaviest.

"No!"

"No?"

"No!" Cassandra shook her head vigorously. The masquerade was bad enough. She refused to invade the duke's privacy in such an underhanded way.

"Why not? I'm proud to show you. After your behavior today I deem you a friend. It is good, at times, to unburden oneself to a friend."

The duke turned his back to Cassandra. Pulling back the coverlet, he let his hand wander until his fingers grasped the object in question. "Here. Look at this."

The sapphire lace kerchief. In a wave Cassandra knew why it had looked familiar. It was part of the wardrobe the duke had procured for her. She'd lost it the first day she'd confronted Wyndham. And here it was, in a foreign land, across seas, in the duke's very own bed!

What could it mean? She was in no state to grapple with its significance. The duke had spoken of love. Was it possible? Possible that he'd offered marriage out of affection, not duty? Adoration not chivalry? The thought was too precious to just dismiss. She'd ponder it on the trip back. Tonight she'd just savor for what it was. Time alone with her heart's delight.

"Do you play cards?" Miles pulled the belt of his rope tighter and looked Cassandra directly in the eye. If only she knew how much he wanted to take her in his arms and kiss away the madness. Still, life with her could never be said to be boring!

"Cards?" Cassandra was lost.

"Yes! Piquet, poker, rummy, that type of thing. Go in for a little flutter now and then?"

It was on the tip of Cassandra's tongue to deny she ever gambled. She stopped midthought, the vision of the challenge she'd thrown to the duke fresh in her memory. It might be interesting to get a glimpse of his style. Not cheating, really. Just a little firsthand observation.

"Yes. Yes, I do from time to time."

Miles looked at her quizzically. From out the great desk came a new deck, clean and glowing in the half light.

"You cut?"

Cassandra nodded. There was no way she was going to get any more sleep that night. Not with Miles so very close. This evening was precious. The last they'd ever spend together. It surprised her how much the thought pained her. She dealt the cards quickly. The duke was impressed by her expert handling. Obviously no novice, this one. A lady of many talents!

Cut after cut. Deal after deal. They were well matched, Cassandra fiercely concentrating, the duke languid. The first few rounds went to an exhilarated Miss Beaumaris. The duke hardly seemed perturbed.

The next few went to himself. After that, there was no stopping him. It seemed that the more Cassandra concentrated, the more he won from her. It was annoying and delightful at the same time. The man offered a real challenge to her intelligence. Not even her wily brother could hold his own as well as this man did. If truth were told, Cassandra was actually having fun, the large pile of nutshells gradually diminishing before her eyes as the duke systematically won them all back. Thank heavens the stakes were so manageable! Cassandra could not help but breathe a satisfied sigh.

By the time they finally did fall asleep, he over his wine, she over her last remaining nutshells, the sun was just beginning to dawn over the horizon.

EIGHTEEN

Consistent with their reputation, Messrs. Longey, Longey and Brandon had done the duke proud. The *Prince Regent* was a vessel to be reckoned with. Stable and strong, it bore little resemblance to the dingy that had ferried Cassandra and Rupert across the morning before. His Grace's yacht could well have been regarded by some as a national treasure.

What was more encouraging was that its crew comprised a good deal of the trusted servants of His Grace's household. Though Pickering and Pomerey were absent, Vallon was to be spied brandishing a full set of ducal coat hangers and any number of well-starched neckties. Familiar, too, were a couple of poker-faced footmen who, with much aplomb, graced the portals of the castle on sea.

The duke was led to remark that it was a pity the grooms had not come along, too. He could have done with a morning's ride. Cassandra detected the humor lurking behind the chance remark, and her eyes gleamed. What fun the duke was when one got to know him! Not at all the man she'd imagined. Had she really called him a gilded lily? The thought made her want to cringe. How could she have?

The duke exuded more forcefulness and energy than ever she had seen in a man. Though he gambled, he gambled with purpose. And he won. Always he won. Cassandra thought of her impetuous challenge and sighed. Her wager had been too precipitate by far! Perhaps, now that circumstances had altered, he'd release her from the contest. She hoped so. Or did she? Her heart was crying treason. It was best she busied herself with something else.

Rupert was at her side. "You all right?"

Cassandra nodded.

"Look, I'm awfully sorry about this whole mess," he said.

Rupert looked so contrite Cassandra had to laugh. "Don't be. It was me who got you into it, not the other way round!"

The young man eyed her ruefully but did not have it in him to gainsay her. "I think you're an awfully good sport you know." His smile deepened, shyness returning.

"Well, I thank you." Cassandra made a grand bow. "I confess I'll be very pleased to see land again. Also, a long, clean lacy dress would not go all that amiss. I can hardly stand to wear these breeches any longer. As for this hat, well, it's so scratchy I can hardly bear it, and my hair keeps threatening to come tumbling out! I have the most unmanageable mass, you know."

Viscount Lyndale grinned. "Yes, I'd gathered! Not long now, Mr. Marshall. I've rather missed Miss Beaumaris you know."

"Have you?" Cassandra cocked her brow. "I daresay she's missed you too!" Her tone altered. "I expect she'll be utterly delighted to see Frances."

"Yes. Don't forget, it's imperative you act surprised. Miles has the most uncannily suspicious mind, you know. He'll skin me alive if ever he gets whiff of this exploit." Rupert looked whimsical.

Cassandra grimaced. "Well, we've made it this far. Let us hope our luck continues. Harrington is in for a shock! I can hardly wait to see his face when Frances walks in. Violet will have an apoplexy, I'm sure."

"By all accounts she deserves to. Hush, here's Miles."

Cassandra whirled around in time to see His Grace fixing her with a rather penetrating stare. Remembering herself, she made a hurried bow. His Grace inclined his head.

"It looks as though we're set for a smooth passage. The men are just casting off. You're not prone to seasickness are you Mr. Marshall?"

"Nnooo . . ." Cassandra did not sound convincing.

Miles smiled sympathetically. "I see you need something to take your mind off the passage! I have a good cheroot in my cabin. I'd be honored if you'd join me there."

Rupert, somewhat uncharacteristically, broke in on his guardian. "I don't think so, Miles. You see . . ."

"I don't believe I was addressing you, Rupert! Mr. Marshall?"

"Well, I uh . . ." Cassandra was at a loss for an excuse. The duke was gazing at her with a fascinating twinkle, and she found she was no match to his will. The man was impossible! One look from him and she lost all her composure. It was unheard of.

"Thank you. Yes. Thank you." She was burbling like an idiot.

Rupert shot her an anguished glance. The yacht lurched. "I'll join you!"

The duke relented and bowed. "By all means, Rupert!"

In no time at all the trio was headed for the sanctum of His Grace's cabin. The sixth earl of Surrey was already there, perched somewhat precariously on the tip of a rose brocade chaise longue. His old spirits were rapidly returning, and he greeted the party with a broad smile and an eloquent handshake for each. Cassandra's eyes met his as she made her requisite bow. The twinkle in his bright eyes matched her own. What a relief it was that she had the support of Rupert and Frances. Between them, they should be able to dupe the duke long enough for the landing.

Miles moved over to his bureau and drew out a long, slim case. His arm extended as he passed around the cheroots, remarking conversationally that he would be very pleased to hear their opinion. Frances shot Cassandra an anxious glance. He need not have worried, she was gamely selecting her cigar. The hint of a smile lingered in the duke's eyes before he moved on to the next of his guests.

"Fond of tobacco, Lord Beaumaris?"

"Frances. Please call me Frances." His lordship was regarding the duke with something approaching hero-worship. That same expression was mirrored in Rupert's eyes. Cassandra felt a slight impatience. She nonchalantly dangled the cheroot from her mouth. It was all her traitorous sibling could do to stop laughing.

Miles was at her side. "Allow me, Mr. Marshall." With a deft sweep of the wrist he hit the cheroot. Cassandra inhaled with a swagger. She'd watched it done dozens of times.

The smoke curled inside her, escaping through her throat and down her nostrils. For an instant she felt she'd choke; then she needed to breathe. With a splutter she opened her mouth and coughed, desperate to inhale clean air.

In a trice Miles was at her side, his hand firmly tapping her back until the fit had passed. Eyes streaming, Cassandra was still bewilderedly holding the cheroot.

"Not to your taste, I fancy." The duke gently removed the offending cigar. "The aroma is uncommon. A blend unique to the East, I gather. What think you of it?"

The remark, addressed to Frances, was conversational. The earl shook his head. "After Mr. Marshall's reaction I dare not! Thanks all the same!"

The duke shrugged. "Rupert?"

"Yes, please!" The young man lit up with a casual air. He did not fool his guardian for a moment.

"Like it?"

Rupert coughed discreetly. "A little on the strong side, I reckon!" He turned to Cassandra. "My uncle is forever purchasing exotic substances. You're not the first to fall victim to his peculiar tastes!"

Cassandra nodded. "That's all right, then. As long as I have not offended you, sir?"

Miles's eyes softened. "Not at all, my dear Mr. Marshall!

Not all of my friends are partial to my tastes, you know. Come, let us amuse ourselves. First person to throw two sixes wins." The duke drew a pair of heavy, golden dice out from his waistcoat. "I always keep a pair handy. It whiles away the time, you know. My nurse taught me that trick. By the time I'd finally thrown a pair of sixes we were always well on our way to Bath. I used to hate those journeys. My father, Lord rest his soul, never believed in well-sprung carriages."

Rupert was interested. "You never told me that."

The duke looked quizzical. "Ah, I daresay there are a great many things I've not told you, Rupert."

The viscount grinned. "I daresay!"

His Grace looked pointedly at Cassandra. "Sit down, Andrew. Lord Beaumaris—Frances I mean—you roll first."

Frances inclined his head. He shook vigorously. A five and a six. "Damnation!" His oath brought a jolliness to the proceedings. Rupert threw two ones, Cassandra a four and a three. The duke flicked the dice with astonishing speed. Another five and six. The round started again. The cabin was silent, all eyes on the dice. Round after round, it seemed perverse that none among them seemed to strike the sixes. The *Prince Regent* was well on her way to England before the long awaited moment arrived.

Cassandra had just affected another of her peculiar flicks. The throw had landed a six and a four, but the die had trembled, then trembled again until landing with decision on the six. A twelve! The company clapped in unison. Mr. Andrew Marshall grinned broadly.

"What's the prize, Miles? We never agreed on terms!" Frances had entered with zest into the spirit of things.

A strange light crossed the duke's handsome features. "That is for Mr. Marshall to decide, is it not?"

Cassandra almost blushed. Instead, she disclaimed and deftly turned the conversation. The winds held up. Every wave was a wave nearer England.

* * *

On shore, Harrington paced up and down. Jake was a day late by his summation. Andover was a dreary place to be that time of the year, and the innkeeper was vulgarly keen to see the glint of gold. Impatience spurred the usurping earl to action. All morning he was to be seen on the wharves, eyeglass extended, waiting. It would take only the flash of the raven's black or the peacock's green to send him scurrying officiously alongside the most unlikely of vessels. He was disappointed every time.

The arrival of the *Prince Regent* held no interest for him whatsoever. The vessel was too large by far and was carrying a crest of crimson and gold. A good deal of the port officials seemed to be shaken out of their inertia, but this fact was merely a mild irritant to the edgy earl incumbent. When the whole episode was satisfactorily over, he'd dock Jake's pay for the delay. The tension, he was convinced, was slowly killing him.

The minion in question, Jake, had well and truly spilled the beans. Harrington would have cringed to know the extent of his outpourings. Even now, as he strutted up and down the moorings, his days of freedom were numbered. Miles knew where he was waiting, what he was waiting for, and with exactly how much of the ready. It was only a matter of time.

The waiting continued. A small sloop was gliding in to port. Harrington was momentarily arrested. His eyeglass went up then fell again. A dinghy, no more. Silently he stamped his foot in impotence. A sibilant voice uttered his name. He whirled around thinking it was Jake, and that he must have missed him somehow.

It was not Jake. The eighth duke of Wyndham, earl of Roscow and baron of the Isles stood before him, a veritable nemesis. Dressed in black, he was impeccable as ever, his signet ring flashing ruby in the sunlight. Harrington suppressed an inward rush of anger. This man was the most meddlesome, unwanted specimen he'd ever come across. So cocksure! He wanted to plant him a flush hit there and then. It wouldn't do, he knew. The duke was a master. He still had the faint tenderness and cheek bruising to prove it.

"What do you want?"

The duke smiled, his teeth gleaming a perfect white. "Who are you waiting for, Harrington?"

"None of your damn business!"

"Ah, but that is where you are so very misguided! I believe it is very much my business!"

Harrington glared at him.

"Perhaps we will wait for this mysterious arrival together. You do not mind, of course?" The duke's tone was silky, but the usurper was not fooled. He knew the game was up, and in a flash he had his sword drawn.

It was fortunate, indeed, that His Grace had anticipated such a course. Their steels clashed at one and the same moment. Sir Robert was good, his point just winging the duke more than once. He did not, however, reckon on St. John's dexterity and force of thrust. Just as the sweat was beginning to pour from Sir Robert's forehead, he felt a sharp pain in the shoulder blades and knew himself to be pinked.

His Grace stayed his sword in grim satisfaction.

Harrington cursed. "Now look you . . ."

The duke held up his hand imperiously, watching the erstwhile nobleman closely as he did so.

"You look, Harrington! I have enough evidence to have a rope around your neck. No, hold your peace! Your man Jake has been very cooperative with the runners. I say very cooperative." His meaning was not lost on Sir Robert, who was glaring at him balefully, his eyes narrow with anger.

"Not that it is your concern, but I intend to wed Miss Beaumaris and have no wish for her name to be linked with a scandal entirely of your own making. Do I make myself clear?"

Harrington could only nod, the oozing sight of his own blood making him feel distinctly queasy.

The duke continued. "I therefore intend to show you a degree of clemency you do not deserve, although if you show your face in England ever again, I may well change my mind. Do I make myself clear?"

Sir Robert nodded dumbly.

"There's a packet leaving Andover tomorrow. Where it's going I know not and do not much care. Just see that you're onboard, or I'll have my not inconsiderable friends at Bow Street making inquiries." St. John looked his utter contempt. Then he turned on his heels and walked away.

NINETEEN

"The duke of Wyndham, ma'am!" Cassandra looked up from the fresh daffodils. Her heart gave a sudden, unaccountable lurch as she bunched the flowers in their vase with a complete lack of ceremony. How strange that her heart should flutter so when she'd rehearsed this scene a dozen times or more in her mind.

A good night's rest, a fresh velvet riding habit, and a brisk morning's trot had done much to revive her habitual good looks. Frances was still sleeping, and she'd ordered the servants to keep it that way. After the ordeal he'd been through, an afternoon slumber could do no harm.

It was fortunate, indeed, that the duke had accepted without question the news of Cassandra's return to Surrey Manor. This had made Mr. Marshall's task so much the easier. By dint of shinning up the drainpipe, the resourceful young man had gained unlawful—but perhaps discreet—access to Surrey Manor through the west wing.

It had taken a great deal of scrubbing, the ceremonious burning of breeches, and a well-earned nap before the transformation had been complete. Cassandra had spent all of the previous night alternating between giggles, tears, and tender exchanges with her prodigal brother.

Strange to think he now occupied the role their grandfather had always done. Well, that was as it should be. Violet and her brat would be looking for new premises soon.

Frances could not easily forgive or forget the wrong done Cassandra. He had been incredulous to hear her story and vowed with a twinkle that he would make well certain of a more appropriate heir in the near future. Cassandra looked at him questioningly, for Frances had never before shown matrimonial—never mind paternal—tendencies.

Her brother had only smiled secretively and told her to be patient. She let it pass, but had a strong suspicion she'd missed something somewhere along the line.

The sixth earl of Surrey drank deeply of a cold, clear apple cider and looked annoyingly smug. If Suzannah would have him, he would be wed long before Cassandra need worry about the earldom. For the moment, the last of the Harringtons remained confined to their chambers, uninvited and unwanted reminders of a very ugly chapter in the Beaumaris past.

The duke was waiting! Cassandra straightened herself up. The pretty cambric looked extremely fetching with long bands of pastel ribbon cascading from her hair. Cassandra touched her dress self-consciously and moistened her lips. Now that the time had come, she felt surprisingly shy. She walked across the passage and headed toward the drawing room, where she knew her fate was waiting. Her hands trembled slightly, but otherwise she was the picture of composure as she stood at the threshold of the salon.

If ever there was a moment the duke would remember it was this one. Cassandra looked so beautiful, so freshly feminine that he could but gape. Transfixed, he moved toward her and the words came of themselves, for he was lost for expression.

She saw the gaze and blushed. Why, oh why, did this man always have such an effect on her? Her pulse was racing, her hands suddenly, unexpectedly, clammy. The duke was magnificent, as ever, in emerald morning dress and shirt so crisply tight it molded to his very form.

His dark, cropped locks were a stark contrast to the gleaming white of his shirt points. His presence was so masculine that Cassandra shivered, his nearness a physical pain. If only she had the right to throw herself in his arms and beg never to be released, what heaven, what bliss that would be! She pulled herself together and executed a model curtsy.

The duke bowed over her hand as he brought the delicate, pink flesh into contact with his lips. The touch was brief but the sensation lingered on intolerably.

Cassandra withdrew her fingers. "Your Grace."

The duke stopped her, his hand to her lips. "Why so formal? I thought we'd agreed on Miles."

Her face lit up, the ice broken by her irrepressible sense of humor. "Oh, we're not going to start that again. Miles, then. There, I said it. Miles!" She spat it out at him, cheekily.

The duke grinned, the impudent smile taking years off his face. "Good girl! Now come along, we've got an engagement."

"An engagement?" Cassandra looked bewildered.

"Of course we have, silly girl. We have a wager to attend to."

"But . . ."

"No buts about it! A hand of cards, a throw of dice, a game of chess. Winner decides your fate. Don't say you've forgotten?"

Cassandra's heart beat so fast she was breathless. "No, of course not, but things have changed. Circumstances . . ."

"Ah, I see. A debt of honor and you're backing out. Am I understanding you correctly?" The duke looked very fierce, a sudden scowl blackening his features.

"No!" Cassandra was indignant at the suggestion. "I would never do that, but don't you see . . ."

"Stop arguing, woman! Gather up your muff, call one of the housemaids to chaperone you, and step into the chaise. You may leave a message for Surrey if you like. Well, come on!"

Cassandra was left no choice. After scribbling a hasty and

somewhat unintelligible letter to her brother, she sought out Natty, bade her accompany her to Wyndham Terrace, and sedately followed His Grace down the stairs and out through the main gate.

As the horses neared the cobble of Wyndham Terrace, the duke leaned toward her and whispered that he hoped Natty was still as reprehensible a chaperone as she had been on the day he had first set eyes on her. Cassandra blushed but assured him the little maid had mended her ways. He gave a comical scowl, and she felt an inordinate surge of happiness.

The great portals of the mansion that had once seemed so threatening were now familiar, thrown open, and bathed in afternoon sunlight. The twins were to be detected peeping through one of the windows, boisterously waving a handkerchief and vainly seeking to suppress the telltale barks of a frolicking dog. The home had such a welcoming familiarity that Cassandra was compelled to press back unbidden tears. What a dope she was being! She just hoped the duke had not noticed.

She hope in vain! It was scarcely likely the duke would miss even the slightest nuance that pertained to his lady love. Cassandra should only have known how close he came at that moment to pulling her into his arms and kissing away the shining sparkle that appeared so rebelliously at the corners of her violet eyes. If it weren't for the presence of the Surrey maid looking very demure in mobcap, he might have done just that. As it was, Cassandra remained in complete ignorance of his intentions.

The duke's library was just as she remembered it on that first memorable night. The smell of rosewood and mahogany mingled to create that distinctive, masculine aroma. The book collection, bound in leather, remained just as impressive. The up and coming Keats vied with Livvy for a place on the duke's shelves. A cursory glance revealed also the works of Galileo, Homer, and Milton. Peeking out from some of the lower shelves were the latest works of Lord

Byron and—yes, Cassandra had seen right—several serial copies of Miss Austen's literary works. Cassandra resolved to borrow them if she could. His Grace's interests were diverse, to be sure!

The collection was completed by a very interesting looking thesis on the mechanisms and history of hot-air ballooning. Seeing her surprise, the duke laughed. "Are you interested in aviation, my love?"

She chose to ignore the endearing term and answer the question. "I am, indeed. Ever since Dr. Jeffries's astonishing channel crossing I have quite longed to see such a contraption."

"Well, so you shall. Not Dover to Calais, I'm afraid, but Lord Lyndale is passionate on the subject and has made several ascensions already. You can imagine the crowds he drew from my estate. Quite festive, I do assure you!"

"I should imagine so!"

"The housekeeper offered to make up the silk, but the task was so daunting that even I was commandeered to make up the sewing team!" He shook his head ruefully, and Cassandra gurgled sympathetically.

"I would like to have seen that," she said.

"I wager you would have, you widgeon. The stitching took so long that we nearly tired of the plan."

"But?"

"But what do you think? Grace and Georgina would not hear of such cow-heartedness, so the balloon was completed after all. But come, we are not here to discuss such diversions. We have much more urgent matters at stake, have we not?" His tone became silky, and Cassandra eyed him warily as he gestured for her to take a seat. He rang for the under butler before pouring himself a glass of burgundy and offering Cassandra a drink of ratafia. She demurred, requesting instead, some iced lemonade. The duke laughed.

"Keeping your head clear?"

"Yes!" Cassandra sparkled defiantly.

"So be it, then. May The best man—or woman—win."

The under butler appeared, and Miles asked him to procure the brass and silver chess set that had been bequeathed to him by the baron of Stratford-Hithe. Cassandra was awed by its beauty. She'd played on many a board, but none had been wrought with as delicate a care as this one. Her fingers ran over the pieces with pleasure. Heavy, well defined, and smooth. The game would be a pleasure, circumstances apart.

The duke placed the queens behind his back. Cassandra chose. Silver. Her start. She focused her thoughts and determined to concentrate fiercely. This was her strongest game, and she willed herself to win. She opened with a queen's gambit. The duke responded swiftly, his fingers scarcely hesitating over the pawn. Cassandra attacked. St. John responded in kind, forcing her to defence. Unlike Frances, he was slow to take pieces, preferring instead systematic control of the board.

Cassandra waited as he thought through the next couple of moves. His face was endearingly animated with strength and skill. She took the time to notice that his raven-black hair just brushed his epaulet. She was glad that he did not affect the powdered wig of some of his contemporaries. She noticed, too, his full mouth, slightly pink, and she remembered his kiss. . . .

His grace initiated an exchange, and a veritable bloodbath occurred, her knight being traded for a bishop, his pawn for a pawn, her knight for a rook. Piecewise they were equal, Miss Beaumaris claiming some slight advantage. Position wise, Cassandra was stressed. Her moves became defensive. The man was stretching her to her limits. Only her grandfather Surrey could claim to have done the same. In matters of chess, Cassandra was generally regarded as invincible. Too sharp by far!

Move by move, the duke gained advantage. Cassandra ceased her daydreaming and concentrated as never before, unwilling to lose ground to the man who so unwittingly held her heart. Her remaining knight pinned the duke's king and castle in a fork. She virtuously tried not to be exultant, but she could not help feeling a slight twinge of triumph. The duke moved out of check and she swiftly removed his rook from the board. Miles's queen shot forward.

Exultingly, Cassandra moved the knight back to its square of origin. Bishop forward, the silver king was threatened. Cassandra made to move it. She stopped. Brass queen was in the way. She looked again in disbelief. Grandfather Surrey had always admonished her not to be too confident, and he had been right. If she was not careful, she would be checkmate in the next move, rook or no. She surveyed the board. There was only one move that would prevent sure catastrophe. If she moved her pawn en passant she would protect her piece and put pressure on the gold queen. Her fingers dangled as if to play.

At that moment, her eyes fluttered up to that of the duke's and she felt herself lost. Her fingers withdrew. With an imp of mischief, she played the king.

The duke's eyes gleamed in appreciation. She was too good a player to make so simple an error. He moved toward her, his voice husky with passion. "You do know what this signifies, Miss Beaumaris, don't you?"

Cassandra stood up nervously, her heart pounding in her ears. There was a strange excitement about her that she could not describe if she tried.

"What does it signify, Your Grace?"

The duke encircled her in his arms. His touch was exquisite torture, her face tantalizingly close to his chest. He smelled crisp and utterly, indefinably male. "It means I have your honor in my hands. Your fate is mine to decide."

His face bent toward hers, his voice throbbing with ill-suppressed love. Cassandra stared steadfastly at the plush rose carpet. If she looked up now, his mouth would touch hers and there'd be no way back. The moment was broken.

"Let me go! You've not yet won!"

The duke looked at her quizzically. Cassandra flushed crimson. His voice was soft. "Have I not?"

"No! You still have to play a hand of cards and throw the very elegant dice I see you sport! You've not forgotten, I assume?"

The duke turned to face the shelves, his hands behind his back. "No, I've not forgotten, Cassandra. A hand of cards, a roll of dice, a game of chess. Best man wins. Those were the terms, were they not?"

"Well, then?"

The duke turned toward her. "You look enchanting today, my love. Pastel suits you."

Cassandra looked bewildered. She smoothed the rosettes on her dress.

"Thank you."

"Not like bottle green."

Cassandra's eyes flew open. She was instantly alert. What can the man have meant?

Miles elaborated. "I must say, my love, a dress is infinitely preferable to knee beeches. Remind me to tell Vallon to get rid of my childhood vestments. They've got darns in them."

Cassandra gasped, his meaning now quite clear. "You knew?"

"Do you take me for a fool?"

There seemed no suitable response to this. "I . . . It is just . . ."

"No need to explain. Do you have any idea, my love, of the agony you've put me through? Can you imagine how I felt when I discovered you'd left the safety of my chamber and waltzed off by yourself to the docks? One would have to be very blind or very drunk not to recognize the beauty you are beneath those breeches!"

Cassandra blushed, tears stinging her eyelids. How she must appear to the duke! A veritable wanton. He would be within his rights, now, to take her honor. There was nothing she could say in her own defense.

He tucked his hand under her chin. "Darling Cassandra, don't, I pray you, look so woeful. Do you not know that I must have loved you from the very first moment I set eyes on you? Yes, all blackberry-stained on the Greensides land. I could have killed Harrington when I came on him in the arbor with you. Perhaps I should have done, after all the trouble he's caused. And your hands! Your poor, dear, darling hands! When I saw how that rascal Jake had tied you, I could have throttled the man!"

Miles's voice became serious, and he relaxed his grip. "It would not have been long before he discovered the truth, and what then? I cannot bear to reflect! The risks you have taken, my angel! My dear, brave, wonderful girl!"

Cassandra was overcome. Instead of shame, he was covering her in glory. He was murmuring to her words of love, not of disgust. She dared look at him. His eyes were tender. He opened his arms. She came to him. Somehow, their lips touched. At first gently, then urgently. Her body just melted against his.

Such joy, such pure happiness. Cassandra gave herself up to it, unaware that Rupert had looked in, grinned, and quietly closed the door behind him. It was a long time before the pair became disentangled enough to speak. When they did, Cassandra found she was seated on the duke's lap, her hair tumbling relentlessly from its ribbons.

"Leave it!" That was an order. Cassandra stopped fumbling, ceasing her vain attempts to tie it back. The earl touched a strand. Cassandra quivered at his touch. His voice was deep and husky, his tongue just caressing her ear. "You don't know how I've longed for this, my love. How I've yearned to touch the softness of this mane of gorgeous hair and unpin it from all its clips and ties. As for that hat, that damn, dratted, godforsaken woolen hat! Burn it! I never want to see it again!" The command was imperiously given, but tinged with the strongest hint of laughter.

Cassandra disengaged herself from the duke's tongue and took leave to chuckle impudently. "You cannot know how much I loathed that hat! It was all scratchy and smelled far too distinctively of rotten fish."

The duke looked at her, then burst out laughing. "I know. Consider it a punishment, you naughty widgeon! You are many things, but not a good liar, I'm afraid to say. Which reminds me. . . ."

"Yes?"

"Next time Max barks it would not be wise to start coughing. Not a good cover, my dear."

"You knew?"

"Of course I knew. Those scamps get away with murder. They have been caring for him well, though, so one of these days I might rescind my edict. I'm not such an ogre. The thing is, my dear, you must learn to trust me."

"But you didn't say where you were going or why. You just mysteriously walked out of here without a word."

"I knew that if I didn't get your brother back right as nine pence, I wouldn't have a hope of marrying you. You would have gone off to that odious Plum woman, and I would never have laid eyes on you again."

"She is not odious!"

The duke afforded her a steely glare. "Do not interrupt, I beg. Odious! You would have given me a million and one arguments why you couldn't wed me. You would have insisted you were entrapping me, that I only offered out of honor, that . . ."

"But it was true!"

"Listen to me, Cassandra. It was not true! If I can't marry you I'd rather starve in a garret! Since I have no wish to spend the rest of my remaining days hungry, marry me for goodness' sake!"

Cassandra prevaricated. "I still don't see why you rushed off to save Frances like that."

Miles looked exasperated. "All right, I'll tell you." His face grew serious. "I wanted you to know that I was not offering out of misguided charity. I had a notion that if your reputation, your home, and your brother were restored, you'd begin to believe me. I made inquiries of the foreign office and discovered Frances's whereabouts. I also had a pretty strong suspicion that Harrington would not stomach his return in good faith. I had no idea the lengths to which he would go, but I determined to fetch Frances back anyway. I had a feeling that the *Prince Regent* would offer him a more comfortable passage than he might have got otherwise. The rest is history."

"So simple."

"So simple. And now, my dear Miss Beaumaris, will you please marry me?"

"What about the cards and the dice?"

Miles looked at her for a moment, then a mischievous twinkle appeared in his eye. Cassandra was to learn to be weary of that particular twinkle. Before she knew what he was about he'd lifted her off her feet, flung her over his shoulder, and marched her up to his desk. There he unceremoniously deposited her and administered a light but nonetheless definite spanking with the back of the mahogany hairbrush he'd been saving as her wedding gift. He would delight in brushing those tresses!

Amid indignant screams of laughter and protest, he set her down on her feet once more and smoothed down the back of her ruffled dress. This done, he exasperatedly inquired, "What were those games I played with Mr. Marshall? Do you think I played them for nothing?"

"You mean you played them for the wager?"

"Of course I did! Why else would I while away the time at dice? Do you think I have nothing better to do?"

"Well, I don't know . . ."

The words were never finished, Miles's mouth once more blissfully upon her own. A great many moments later, he looked up at her and smiled.

"Perhaps if I ask you like this!" He dropped to his knees, his hands dipping into his waistcoat and emerging with a blue velvet box. "Open it, Cassandra."

Wonderingly, Cassandra did. Embedded deeply in the white satin was a ring. An elegant contrivance of heavy gold filigree work adorned only by a single, solitaire diamond that flashed blue with purity. The stone sparkled light, its facets refracting the brilliance in a radiant cascade.

Cassandra stared.

"It was my mother's. The last duchess of Wyndham. It is fitting now that it be passed on to the next generation. To the new duchess."

Cassandra could not speak.

"Here. Let me do this." The ring was slipped on her finger in a trice. It felt cool and unfamiliar, yet it flashed fire. A reflection of her feelings. The duke was still on his knees, his eyes infinitely tender.

"Now will you marry me, Cassandra? I have won the wager and you have won my heart. For your honor I choose marriage. Will you have me?"

There was no longer any doubt. "Yes!" Cassandra wanted to shout yes and keep on shouting. The ecstasy was too great. Miles stood up and swung her in the air.

"Let us tell the others. The twins will be in seventh heaven, I know! You are quite a hit with them, Miss Beaumaris!" She smiled. "And I daresay Rupert may have an inkling . . ."

"Yes. And Frances! I suppose you'd better ask his consent!" Cassandra gurgled at the thought.

"I already have!"

"What? When?"

"This morning when you were out riding. He was not asleep all day as you seem to have imagined. What is more, my dear, I can only say he was not in the least surprised! Said he'd guessed it the first night we rescued him."

Cassandra looked indignant. "Well! What a cheek! He never said anything to me!"

The duke took her in his arms. All else was forgotten. The future duchess of Wyndham gave herself up to the most improper of advances. Moments later, the library door clicked open. The giggles of the twins and the mock sighs of their lordships Viscount Lyndale and Earl Surrey went unheeded. The gathering was forced to come to the very definite conclusion that the couple was beyond hope. Moonstruck beyond repair. The door quickly clicked shut.

TWENTY

TWENTY

"What is it, Everett?" The duke took pity on his long-suffering secretary and sat up with a sigh. This is not to say that his hold on his affianced lessened any more perceptibly, or that the necktie he'd been at pains to tie that morning in the most impeccable rendition of "The Cascade" looked any more likely to be retrieved from the floor.

If anything, he had to be admonished by his young mistress, who was not so lost to her sense of propriety that she did not seek, with belated modesty, her pins that lay scattered in the velvet folds of the great chaise longue. Seeing her confusion, Mr. Everett coughed once more and found himself apologizing for the intrusion that even a veritable nodcock of the first water would know to be unwelcome.

He was sincerely relieved when the duke favored him with the roguish grin that had not blessed his face for many a long year. His dark, unconsciously saturnine look had yielded to the hidden depths within himself. He appeared most unrepentant as his lady love scolded him for his conduct and gently eased her waist out from his tightening grip. Regaining her customary composure, she welcomed the duke's secretary with a likeable smile and a gracious offer of her hand.

"How do you do, Mr. Everett? I believe I have you to thank for the trouble taken over my missing brother, Frances! No! Do not disclaim! The duke has informed me where the credit lies, and I find myself quite irredeemably in your debt!" Her eyes sparkled merrily as they came to rest on the portly gentleman hovering indecisively in the doorway.

"Come on in! We were just admiring the fine morning, were we not?" She cast careless appeal to her suitor. He rose admirably to the occasion, discoursing for quite half a minute on the fortuitous state of the weather. Since this gentleman had never before waxed lyrical on the subject, Mr. Everett found himself agreeing that the afternoon promised a rare sunny day with some degree of bemusement.

The duke sympathized with his plight, reflecting with wry humor that his well-ordered household would never be the same again. If the Honorable Miss Beaumaris could bring around his crusty old bachelor secretary, she could do the same again with his servants and his wards.

To his astonishment, he found himself looking very much forward to the time he'd be living under the cat's paw. Well, that was a turn up for the books to be sure! His lady love caught the glint of amusement in his dark eyes and responded in kind. Fluttering open her pale feathered fan, she very properly engaged Mr. Everett's attention while throwing His Grace a delicate but decidedly saucy wink.

His most gracious lordship, accustomed as he was to the sycophantic civility of his underlings, found the experience most novel. Indeed, if truth were accurately to be told, the earl of Roscow, baron of the Isles and duke to boot was quite undone. He doubled up in mirth, leaving Mr. Everett uncustomarily bereft for words. The poor man felt strongly that he should leave, but really, the matter was most pressing!

Cassandra resumed her scolding as she presented St. John with a sheer, starched handkerchief of the finest lemon lawn. He did not miss the significance of this act and cocked his brow appreciatively. Wiping his eyes with the said item, he quite deliberately placed it in the pocket of his tightly fitting morning coat before diverting his attention to his long-suffering employee.

"Speak up, James! Am I being dunned by my tailors?"

"Your Grace!" James was shocked at the suggestion, however humorous the tone.

"My nieces in the mire again? I hear the Lady Georgina has an eye to my new roan." The duke's eyes gleamed.

"No, Your Grace!" James denied, then qualified his words with a cautious enjoinder, "Well, at all events not mischief of that kind!"

A gurgle of happy laughter escaped Cassandra. The duke rounded on her suspiciously. "You know what the young rapscallions are up to now, I'll bet my best nag!"

Miss Beaumaris looked prim. "What, another wager so soon, Your Grace?"

The eighth duke of Wyndham chuckled but was not deterred. "I reckon it's a safe bet, my lass!"

"Possibly!" Cassandra's tone altered. "But I'll not be carrying tarradiddles, Your Grace!"

His Grace groaned. Clearly the little varmints had a new champion in the house. Vallon would be as mad as fire! He had to admit, however, that his fastidious valet would find no fault with his bride. Indeed, quite the reverse if he judged his fine French taste aright. Miss Beaumaris looked enchanting in her cool, lemon-trimmed jonquil cut enticingly low at the front. His eyes moved to the pale flesh that promised such sweet delight, then turned once more on the waiting Mr. Everett.

"Come on, James. I know it must be important. You'd not knowingly disturb me for a trifle." His voice held a slight hint of impatience that was not missed by Miss Beaumaris. She, it must be said, was engaged in examining the handsome effect of a set of fine muscles, ill concealed behind a tight-fitting shirt of the sheerest silk. When her thoughts strayed to the immaculate fit of his snowy morning pantaloons, she blushed scarlet and looked up straight into the knowing eyes of her lord.

His Grace delivered of himself a wide, impudent grin before returning to the more serious affair that his able secretary felt himself at such pains to impart. "It is the small matter of the Lady Suzannah, Your Grace."

"The lady who?"

Mr. Everett shuffled his well-polished boots and coughed deprecatingly. He cast a miserable glance at Miss Beaumaris before suggesting in a sotto voce somewhere between a whisper and a rasp that perhaps His Grace would like to accompany him to the sanctuary of his office.

Miles declined with alacrity. He had too much catching up to do with his lady love by far! A quick review of his latest paramours inclined him to believe with a fair degree of certainty that the name Suzannah did not feature among the somewhat lengthy list. Besides, he had sent his latest cher d'amour a fabulously generous gift upon the occasion of his second encounter with the enchanting Miss De Laney.

"Spit it out, James!"

Mr. Everett polished his spectacles, then replaced them with care upon the bridge of his nose. "Your Grace will recall that your great aunt Elthea—the dowager marchioness of Langford . . ." He stopped as the duke struck his hands dramatically to his face.

"Curses and double curses! Aunt Elthea!" Mr. Everett bowed, relieved that the implication had finally struck his employer.

"Quite so, Your Grace."

Cassandra looked intrigued. She had taken up a stitching hoop and was idly selecting a thread of flamingo pink, which she deftly wound around her little finger. As her hands hovered over the silks, she could see consternation written clear over the duke's chiseled features. She held her peace, but listened with growing bewilderment to the conversation that ensued. She was no more enlightened, however, by the time Mr. Everett had received his instructions and bowed himself from the room.

"Well, Miles?"

His Grace grimaced as he plucked the stitching frame expertly from her grasp. Ignoring her protest, he slipped his arms around her waist and began resuming where he had formerly left off.

Miss Beaumaris wriggled free. "Miles!"

"What?"

"Tell me what that was all about!"

"That was me being recalled to my arduous duties, ma'am!" He made a face.

"Oh?"

The duke placed a feather-light kiss on her nose, but it missed, landing instead on her rather endearing cheek.

"Miles!" Cassandra brought him up short. "Be serious!"

His Grace's eyes twinkled mischievously. "Are you always this persistent, my love?"

Cassandra relented for a moment and replied with her customary humor. "Always!"

His Grace chuckled at this sally, which annoyed her curiosity excessively. She stamped her foot. The duke's eyes glinted as they fell on her neatly turned ankle. "Do you know, my dear, that is the prettiest sight confronting me in a long time?"

Gasping at his effrontery, Cassandra somehow found herself entangled in his strong grip. Since he smelled so positively, deliciously masculine, and since his shirt strained so invitingly across his broad chest, she gave up the ghost and snuggled deeply into his waiting arms.

It was only much later on in the day that the mistress Cassandra was apprised of St. John's intention of escorting his aunt to her country seat at Shropshire. Sensing there was something more to this venture than immediately met the eye, she probed a bit further. She was more than a little disconcerted to discover that somewhere in England there was a young lady other than herself who cherished ambitions of becoming the newest duchess of Wyndham.

When she tentatively voiced this, His Grace quirked his eyebrow ironically. He informed her with due emphasis that she had better reconcile herself to the idea, for there were several young ladies who could fit that description. Lest she thought him vain, he added with cynical sarcasm that most of them he had not yet even met, nor was ever likely to. She giggled appreciatively, but understood the note of resigned exasperation in his tone. "The title holds the most nonsensical attraction," he informed her with a deceptive shake of the head. Instinctively, she understood.

When he teased her about her own ambitions, she was indignant. She told Miles with a fair degree of asperity that she was not wishful of the title at all. His Grace was perceptive enough to believe and love her for this, but he did not pass up the opportunity to roast her a little. He very unchivalrously demanded to know exactly what it was that she did desire of matrimony with him. When she colored up delightfully, he declared that they would need the special license sooner than she thought if she wished to remain at all respectable.

Cassandra sobered. Her active imagination led her to believe that the announcement would be a most mortifying blow to the absent Lady Suzannah. While she realized that an offer had not actually been made, her sense of honor could not allow her to accept a proposal that would come at the expense of severe disappointment to one less fortunate than herself. Perhaps her recent experiences had made her more sensitive to the plight of others. Whatever the case, she repressed the deep feeling of chagrin that seemed to whelm up from her depths and shook her head at the man who had now become so dear to her.

"It won't fadge, my dear!"

His Grace took up his position by the bay window and looked down at her with mild surprise. "What won't?"

"A harrum scarrum marriage that you might well come to regret! Your aunt, Elthea, will not like it, and I daresay a whole brace of relatives won't either!"

The duke looked into her wide, intoxicating eyes and thought them delightful. Privately, he wished all his relatives in bedlam, but he chose not to say so. Instead, he caught up her well-sprigged bonnet and began making sense of the tangles. He cast his mind back to that other time he was engaged in this activity and grinned.

"Frills and furbelows! I see you need a man's help!" He playfully wagged his finger at her and his ruby signet gleamed. She longed to take his hand, but resisted the temptation with an effort. He was being annoyingly, endearingly, frustratingly obtuse! Talking of head wear when she felt the world likely to cave in! There he went again . . . his fingers were so nimble and firm. . . .

"However do your bonnets get in this unseemly state of disarray? I could swear there are any number of knots in these ribbons!"

"Miles! You are not paying attention!"

He looked her up and down, from the tips of her toes to the crown of her head, and she felt a delicious shudder suffuse her body. He grinned wickedly. "I am, my dear, I assure you I am!"

"You are what?"

"Paying attention, you goose! What else?" His eyes were velvety as they rested on hers. "You were saying? Ah, yes, I recall. Some addle-pated nonsense about my family deploring our match. Why ever should they? Your antecedents are impeccable. Not even the most toplofty, exacting of my exasperating family could ever find fault!" The duke was emphatic.

Cassandra bit her lip. "That is a matter of dispute, Your Grace. Your great aunt clearly had other designs for you. Besides, a hasty, nimble-shamble union is not what is owing to the consequence of His Grace of Wyndham! Not to mention your numerous other titles that date back to goodness knows when!" She drew breath, and the duke availed himself of the opportunity to stem her flow.

"A nimble-shamble, harrum-scarrum marriage, as you term it, would be just the thing for me! Only think how detestable it will be if we have to wait for the petrifyingly pompous ceremony the ton will no doubt insist on according my position!" He dropped his hand and watched her, his eyes never leaving hers for a moment. "The endless invitations, the countless carriages arriving from who knows where for who knows how long, the bickering over what honors should be bestowed where, who takes precedence over whom in the seating arrangements, which choir will preside, which archbishop shall be in attendance . . . the mind boggles!"

Cassandra sympathized but remained firm. "I am sorry, Your Grace, but I cannot!" She did not want people whispering that the great St. John had been snared into an unpalatable alliance. She could almost hear the tabbies behind their fans, regarding her with calculating looks and knowing smiles. They'd say the undue marital haste was due to her springing the trap, making sure of her prey.

They'd titter with malice and point to the unfortunate Lady Suzannah, the unwitting "jilt" of the piece. Cassandra could see it all, and see it clearly. Too well she knew the type of gossip that society relished and fed upon. She had no wish for that. Not for herself, not for the duke, and not for the unknown quantity in this drama, the Lady Suzannah.

It was hard to voice her thoughts. The duke was gazing at her, and her heart plummeted, for she felt he did not understand. He did not understand that she needed him to be clear of all ties, all former commitments, no matter how tenuous. She wanted so much to revel in the joy and love and strength of him. She needed to know for herself—and for the world—that his passion was not transient. It must be based not on pity, but on something tangible and enduring. If he was to overset his family's plans for himself, she wanted him to do it openly, deliberately, and with due care for the lady concerned. She would not have it any other way.

The duke lay down the bonnet and cast it across the desk. His face had shuttered and his voice seemed to Cassandra to change to flint. He bowed politely, and the very action brought tears to her eyes. "Forgive me, but I had not thought you entirely impervious to the notion, my dear!" He turned his back to her and went to the hearth, where he poured a restorative from the tall decanter standing at the ready. He swung around to face her, and she noticed his mouth was set in a grim line.

"What is it that you want? If it is the simple matter of banns being posted and a great church wedding with all its attended haut and pomp, you need only say the word." His voice held a slight edge that was unfamiliar to Cassandra. She could bear to see disappointment in his eyes, but she could not endure contempt. Her heart beat very fast as she extended her hand toward him. It went unnoticed. Gulping the drink down in one deep draught, His Grace afforded her a quixotic if ironic bow, then left the room.

"Frances!" Miss Beaumaris looked near tears as she was helped into the landau by her solicitous brother. He looked as bewildered as she to find that the happy glow that had earlier suffused her face was replaced by a sickly pallor un-fetching to the eye. This was made doubly alarming by the fact that Cassandra was not a vapid miss prone easily to swooning and some of the more cow-hearted diversions oth-erwise fitting to her sex.

That something was amiss was plain. Though tired from his recent ordeal, he nonetheless had sufficient wits about him to wrap the silk redingote tightly around his sibling without so much as an inquiring word. He was no fool and easily divined that his host's sudden departure on estate business must be related to the miserable spectacle that now presented itself to him. He was enormously puzzled, given the most favorable interview he had with the duke earlier on in the day. He sup-pressed a sigh. Such a pity Cassandra could be so hot-headed. No doubt it would be left to him to mend the breach.

His thoughts flitted for a moment to a pair of soothing black eyes and his heart ached for the sight. As soon as he was well he knew that he was destined for another channel crossing. He had promised to return and return he would. Whether the statuesque, intriguing, and altogether delightful nurse of Mont Saint Jean would be interested in his suit he did not know, but he cherished hopes.

If Cassandra could not bring herself to accept St. John's proposal, he had no doubt the new countess of Surrey would be delighted to sponsor her in the future. He set his throbbing head back on the crested cushions and closed his eyes.

TWENTY-ONE

The carriage rumbled along the flagstones and made its ponderous way through the narrow city streets before coming to a halt at Twenty-five Saxon Place. The duke was not in a good humor. He was well aware, by now, that he had been at fault. He had judged Cassandra without taking into account the very qualities he loved in her. Of all people, he knew how little she desired the match for the self-serving reasons others would have done. He knew, with wonder, that riches and consequence were not the lure, and he felt ashamed.

For the first time he had been within striking distance of his heart's desire and he had made a wretched mull of the thing. She loved him for himself and himself alone, and he'd insulted her duly. Not by words, perhaps, but by implication. He felt wretched and he deserved to. That knowledge did not help his temper either.

He settled back on the squabs and consulted the time. It was getting late and he was sadly bored. He realized with a wry grimace that the contretemps with Cassandra had overset him more than he'd first imagined. He was as cross as two sticks as no doubt his groom was well aware. He'd thought nothing of it when the young jackanapes had suggested he travel inside rather than take the whip, but now he had his suspicions.

If the dowager marchioness of Langford was preening herself on his imminent arrival, she would be sadly disappointed.

No matter how lovely her protégé, she was not destined to become a duchess. Well, not *his* duchess at all events! With this determined thought, he poured himself a hot lemon toddy from the flask his staff had so thoughtfully prepared.

If he now found himself embarking on a tedious journey to Shropshire with an extremely distasteful task to perform, he would consider it a just punishment. Cassandra could hardly be expected to accept his suit when there was a loose end that needed to be tied. She was not to know how tediously many young ladies had been picked out for his perusal in the past.

Lady Suzannah was only one of a bevy, but her very existence would be sufficient to make the proud Cassandra run shy. He realized, of course, that this trait was just another one of the intangible reasons he felt about her as he did. She had an indomitable mixture of pride coupled with genuine caring. He smiled and resolved never again to judge too hastily if ever he were forgiven. The thought that he might not be cast him in a cloud once more. He downed the drink slowly and stretched his feet.

Not for the first time, he wished his well-meaning, muddling, meddling relatives to go the devil. If only they had left well enough alone, he would not now be in this coil, staring gloomily out of the ducal landau with nothing but a gray sky and the promise of rain to mirror his bleak mood.

No doubt Aunt Elthea, with her frenetic shopping sprees and her insistent puffing off of his consequence, had firmly aroused unwarranted expectations. He could find it in him to be sorry for the girl, who must have spent many a dull hour standing still for seamstresses, milliners, and other necessary persons on his account. Still, she could make a match of it elsewhere. No doubt the reticules and lace and fans and little scented bottles of unspecified substance would be more than sufficient to snare some other poor lord. The duke was even prepared to put in a good word for her with the patronesses of Almack's should that be required. Anything, in fact, short of being leg-shackled to her for the rest of his days.

With these gloomy thoughts, the servants erupted from far and wide carrying portmanteaus, band boxes, and other indispensable items for the journey. His tiger dismounted and set about strapping the luggage to the equipage, a tedious task that would no doubt take yet more time. The duke tapped on the window, and a footman opened the door for him to dismount. This he did with a nimble step and a slight adjustment to his snowy cravat, which was, as ever, impeccable.

"Miles!" Her ladyship beamed.

In spite of himself, Wyndham felt himself smiling as he put her hand to his lips. "Ma'am!"

She beamed at him. "I knew you would come, my dear! We are all in such a pother over here, I hardly know whether we are coming or going! We've been driving in the park all morning, and my head quite spins with the number of people we were obliged to stop for. You can have no notion! And Lady Martin! Well, she insisted on bringing her pugs, and you know what havoc they can cause! I swear I nearly had a fit of laughing when I saw old Colonel Bucksby turn tail at the sight of our approach. He was cornered the other day, you know and quite knocked flat!"

The duke ventured a polite but bewildered smile. He was by now too used to his dear aunt Elthea's ways to be unduly bemused, but he nonetheless could feel the stirring of a faint headache. She continued, blissfully unaware of his plight, or of the hostlers and passersby who were tarrying in faint curiosity. The spectacle of the ducal carriage would have been sufficient to cause comment, but actual sight of the duke! Well, it was little wonder the crowd stared.

"Do come in, Miles! I have only another carriage load of goods to oversee, and I'm quite sure Mildred can do that perfectly! If you would like to come up to the Canary salon, I'll have tea poured." She hesitated a moment, then corrected herself. "Not tea, burgundy! You look quite fagged to death, Miles!"

Her undutiful great nephew grimaced and had a good mind

to tell her why he looked so wretched. He thought better of it, though, when he saw the array of small tarts and petits fours she had summoned for his delectation. The gilt tray was laden with goodies, and he was instantly cast back to the time when he was a small boy in short coats. She had been the best of aunts. He was always assured of a high treat on the occasion of his visits. And petits fours! She had remembered they were his favorite. He always found it hard to be out of temper with the sunny marchioness, no matter how provoked.

"I take it you got my note, Miles. I do find it so hard to confine myself to two wafers!"

"You need not, aunt. You forget you may have all your letters franked, and by heavens I wish you would! Your scrawl is impossible!" He reached out and put her hand in his. It struck him how frail it had become. She glanced at him with dancing eyes, and he realized that age was not a match for her spirit.

"Have you seen my parrots, child?" It had been a long time since he'd been addressed that way, but he made no demur. Before he knew what he was about, he was being whisked off to one of the room's small alcoves, there to be introduced to two brilliant and quite exotic-looking birds. His aunt must have noted his surprise, because she looked extremely smug as she informed him that they were from the wilds of America and cost a pretty penny to boot. He admired them with no small degree of distrust. Their beaks were suspiciously large, and he had a strong but persistent suspicion that his scatterbrained favorite aunt might not have properly engaged the attractive wicker door.

Before he could investigate further, the door opened and a vision of loveliness appeared before him. Her curly dark hair was spangled in the latest mode, and she was bedecked in a primrose muslin tied high at the waist. This did much to emphasize the round curves of her statuesque body and the deep, dark of her fawnlike eyes. A stunning creature. Quite different from the insipid young misses to whom he was accustomed. At all events, to which he was accustomed to being introduced.

His aunt smiled broadly at the impact her gorgeous young protégé had created. She knew Wyndham well and could see his breath taken away. If he was not actually gaping, then he was akin to it. The vision moved gracefully to his side and made a deep curtsy that lacked the simpering coyness to which he was used. She stood up and spoke first, in a delightfully lilting voice that was modulated and schooled charmingly to the English language, despite the odd inflection that was unmistakably foreign.

"I am glad to meet you at last, monsieur le duc."

The duke made a bow and removed the curly beaver from his head. They made a striking pair, both so dark and so tall. He realized with a sinking heart that his task would not be as easy as he had first thought. Not that he was smitten in any way, but the lady somehow deserved more than a disinterested brush off, or one of the set downs for which he was so famous.

"I am honored."

His great aunt looked wickedly pleased, and he had the impulse to throttle her.

Elthea stepped forward. "Suzannah, dear, meet my naughty great nephew, His Grace the Duke Wyndham. Miles, may I present Lady Suzannah De Bonhuit? Cake, I think! There will still be ample time before we are fit to leave. You did not forget your fur muff and your pink pelisse, my dear? I had the second chambermaid pack them, but you might do well to check. She is a trifle scatty, I'm afraid, but I do have a fondness for her!"

Miles's eyes met Suzannah's, and he could have sworn he saw a twinkle in them! He had a feeling that if it were not for the unpleasant business that lay ahead, they might well have become friends. As it was, he was impatient to be on the move. Once his aunt was firmly ensconced in her country home, he would be making off. He had a lot of catching up to do, and he needed to make his peace with Cassandra.

The Lady Suzannah must without delay be gently apprised of his betrothal. He was relieved to feel that she would not cause an unseemly stir and so jeopardize his chances of making peace with Cassandra. He opened his mouth to suggest a quiet walk in the marchioness's sumptuous rose gardens when he was caught off balance by an epithet seldom heard in a lady's home "Hell and damnation, curdle your liver!"

"What?" The duke startled. The ladies, far from being shocked, looked uncommonly amused.

Lady Suzannah put her hand to her mouth to stifle a sudden smile and pointed in the direction of the cage. "It is zee birds, I sink!"

His great aunt chortled. "Did I not tell you, Miles? They have the most startling vocabulary! Not fit for a lady's ears, perhaps, but then I never have cared a toss for the conventions!" She gazed lovingly at her crimson-winged denizens of virtue. "I can't tell you how entertaining they've been! We had that old witch Eleanor Peabody-Frampton poking her nose in the other day. Normally I'd avoid her like the plague, but she was announced just as Suzannah was being fitted for her riding dress. Well, there we were rooted to the spot when in she walks in that snooty high-bred manner of hers. You know! Anyone would think she was a princess of the blood, rather than a common squire's daughter. But there! I'm rattling on to no purpose!" She stopped for breath and beamed seraphically.

Suzannah finished the story. "She walked in and zere zey were, zee beautiful birds! Zey see her and say . . . well, I will not say what zey say!" Her eyes danced with mischief. "It is shocking! It must be so, no? Ze Peabody person she is not amused. She just mutters somesing . . . we do not know what . . . zen she clutches her small reticule and is gone. Tsha! Like so!" She clicked her fingers in an expressive movement, then admonished Miles to take the cage and "not forget the stand." With a sinking heart he knew that his penance was going to be to sit in a carriage with a pair of women and a precarious cage of bawdy-mouthed birds. His decision was instant. He would ride on the box. To hell with the groom!

The great, ivy-trimmed home of the marchioness of Langford was an imposing edifice surrounded by a park and an oak-lined avenue that was the envy of all her friends. Miles was very glad to see it, as he had spent a miserably cold journey enduring the lip of his jovial, impudent, and rather long-in-the-tooth old servant.

Since he had known the duke from birth and seen him breeched, the groom saw no reason to hold his tongue and made several remarks that caused the duke to inwardly seethe. All of them were pointedly about His Grace's lady friend, her prowess on a saddle, and the inability of gentry folk to know a good thing when it stared at them in the face. The duke was not pleased.

The only thing stopping him pensioning the unfortunate minion at once was the fact that he had the rarest skill with horseflesh that Miles had ever come across. Also, it could not be denied that he harbored a loyalty to the duke and his kin that was as touching as it was possibly misguided. Miles was no proof against the man's toothless grin. As they entered the estate, however, His Grace allowed himself a sigh of relief. All things going well, he could disabuse Lady Suzannah's mind of any misapprehension and be on his way well before noon. With any luck, he'd be at a posting house by nightfall and in his own bed the following day. After that . . . well, after that, only time would tell.

"Run along, you two! The unpacking is well under way and I do not, I believe, need you both underfoot."

Miles winced at this blatant manipulation. He knew his aunt's stratagems well, but was embarrassed for Lady Suzannah. Call herself a chaperone! He'd have words with her one of these days, that was for sure! He glanced at the lady in question and was surprised to see amusement etched on her fine, strong features.

Not a china doll, evidently! He surmised that she must have been expecting something of this nature and found the thought lowering. It was hard, indeed, to play the jilt, however blameless he may be. Still, best to swallow the bitter pill early and set the record straight once and for all.

His aunt cunningly suggested a stroll in the aromatic herb garden. A romantic enough setting, but not one in which he wished to dwell. If it were Cassandra who was staring at him with smoky blue eyes . . . well, that would put a different complexion on the matter entirely. As it was, he declined the herb garden as a suitable point for a rendezvous and selected instead the formal morning room.

He put his hand out for Suzannah, who hesitated slightly before accepting it and prosaically wrapping her muff a bit closer. The house was awesome, but the high ceilings made for a bit of a chill and the fires had not yet been properly lit or stoked. Great Aunt Elthea gave a maddening little wave of her hand as she shooed them off, then promptly forgot them in the excitement of the arrival of a shipment of tapers, lace, and farmyard chickens.

Lady Suzannah looked about her with awe. The morning salon was filled with antique collectibles, china dogs, and a great deal of bewildering brick-a-brac that seemed scattered far and wide with little or no thought for the conventional dictates of decor. She removed her bonnet and gave a decisive and satisfied nod. "It ees good, zis house. Like your cher aunt Elthea, no? A leetle beet crazy."

Miles had to agree. He found himself warming to the lady minute by minute. He cleared his throat to get the worst over, but was halted peremptorily by Suzannah herself.

"Your Grace!"

"Yes, my lady?"

"It ez a difficult position we find ourselves in, *n'est pas?*"

"What do you mean?"

"Well, I mean . . . your aunt, she has ze expectations, no? She sinks zat her favorite nephew is still ze little boy. She say, 'I know what is good for you, yes? I know what is good and I won't hear you say no!' " She smiled and the smile lit up her face. "See, I understand. I, too, am instructed by your aunt. She say, 'Marry my Miles, *ma petit*. He is a very good boy.' " She stopped and dimpled at the duke. "Well, I am not ze good girl! I do not wish to marry you at all! Why? Well, I am very sure I wish to marry someone else!"

Miles released a deep breath and felt as though he could kiss her. "Truly? Your heart will not be broken if I do not make you an offer? I do not know what my aunt has promised of me, but I can well imagine!" He shuddered comically. "Steer well clear of matchmaking relatives, my dear! It quite makes one sink!"

Suzannah laughed. "It will be a shock to ze poor Elthea, but she will recover it very soon, I am pozeetive! She just needs a distraction . . . a monkey maybe?" There was definite laughter in her tone, and Miles felt a good deal of lightening spirits. Really, his aunt became more incorrigible by the year! It had not occurred to him that the lady herself would absolve him from the proxy betrothal that had become so distasteful. Quite a redoubtable lady, too!

The duke became aware of a faint commotion outside, the sound of carriage wheels and horses, orders and fluster. He blithely ignored them. Knowing Aunt Elthea, he had become used to expecting the unexpected. Lady Suzannah felt so, too, for she drew the curtains with a cursory glance and rang for some orangeade. "If we wait for my godmama, we will wait here forever!" Her eyes twinkled "So what do you do, monsieur le duc?"

"Me?" The duke was startled. He was not used to such questions, especially not from a lady. Still, none of the events of the day could be termed what he was used to. He sat down and described to her the House of Lords, his canvassing for the repeal of the corn laws, his work on the estate and care of tenants both in Wyndham and in Roscow. He talked, and as he spoke, he found clarity.

He felt comfortable with this Suzannah, who no longer posed a threat. Comfortable enough to speak of Cassandra, his great love and his torment. She counseled him, and very soon he discovered what he knew to be the truth. With the great feeling that he cherished, love would endure. Cassandra would be made to see reason and forgive his foolish outburst of pride. So thinking, he returned the favor and the question.

He listened in fascination as Suzannah outlined her life, dwelling on how her mother had made a runaway marriage and married for love. How she had followed the drum and learned a great many healing skills along the way. How she had endured the war and watched the loss of life and limb. How she had rejoiced in the peace and consented to reconciliation with her mother's family. How her godmother, Elthea, had invited her to visit and how she had promised to come. How, with the coming of peace had come the fruition of that promise. And last, how with the coming of peace had also come love.

She spoke little on this score, but the duke's notoriously sharp eyes gleaned much. When she mentioned La Hay Sainte, he visibly drew in his breath. The coincidence would be too remarkable to believe, but he had to know.

"What rank was this paragon of yours?" he asked.

She looked surprised but obliged the duke crisply. "He was a captain, Monseigneur. Perhaps he has forgotten me, perhaps he has not." She shrugged her shoulders in typically Gaelic style, but the duke read anxiety in the pale shadows of her eyes and in the tiny lines around her mouth.

"He has a name, then, this very fortunate captain?"

She smiled at the compliment. "He does, Your Grace, but zat I cannot say!"

His Grace, the oh so handsome Duke Wyndham, bowed. "May I ask if he knows you are on English soil?"

She looked abashed. "No, he does not yet know. I do not wish to be ze imposition. If he sees me and does not remember, well . . . tsha!" She clicked her fingers. "I will attend ze balls and become . . . how you say? Ze social butterfly! If he remembers . . . well! We shall see, monsieur le duc, we shall see!"

The duke nodded. Privately, he thought that there could not be many English captains who had survived Ney's cavalry onslaught. From the few words Frances had let slip both on the sloop and at their morning interview, he was relatively confident that the young earl harbored reciprocal feelings. Suzannah was not destined to have a broken heart. Not if he could help it! He grinned wickedly at his hitherto unsuspected matchmaking streak. Well, Frances would make a fine brother. What more could he ask but a sister as fair as Suzannah? It was high time he be setting his plan in motion.

A word to his wizened old groom and the duke was back, claiming a headache. Not all of his great aunt's interesting ministrations could be said to have the necessary healing effect, but they served to have her scurrying from kitchen to cellar in a frenzy of effusive good will. Two good things came of this cunning measure: the good lady was too concerned to ponder the outcome of her matrimonial venture, and the cellar yielded a surprisingly good rum, casketed for years and originating, if the duke guessed it right, from unknown but not entirely lawful channels. Trust his great uncle Henry to have had truck with smugglers! Still, if all the yield was as superlative as this . . . The duke was sleeping before he knew it.

A gentle morning sun was mistily creeping through the ivy-grown shutters. Miles found himself in one of the side chambers in the east wing, confronted with a spectacular view of the frozen lake. The past two days had offered a wonderful respite after the madness of the sea venture. He reflected, with affection, that the dowager marchioness of Langford, though scatty, was a superlative hostess.

He had managed to bag a fair amount of pheasants from her extensive estate and even had a grouse or two to show for his trouble. He now found himself quite virtuously hungry and all for a good gallop on one of his grays.

He breakfasted alone, the Lady Suzannah having taken herself for an early stroll into the village, where, he learned, she intended to purchase gooseberries for jam and a quantity of beeswax for he knew not what. His aunt was not yet down, she undergoing a rigid morning toilet that only her dresser, her maid, and a sprinkling of honored servants were ever privy to. He received a message adjuring him to partake of a monumental feast and set to with relish.

If the day turned out as he planned, he would need his stamina! He thanked the footman for the scalding-hot coffee and set off into the crisp, clear morning. Out on the horizon, windmills were spinning in the breeze, and he felt the sight charming. He wished fervently that Cassandra were there to share it with him.

His horse whinnied, and he steadied it, wondering if he had stumbled on a loose stone. If the stallion needed to be reshod, he would have to walk the four miles into the village. Fortunately, he knew the winding path that twisted its cobbled way through the sunbaked fields. On a day like this, such a chore could almost be regarded as a pleasure. He slid down from the saddle and examined the hoof. The shoe was firm and unyielding. Well, that was a good thing.

He dusted himself off and was satisfied that his boots were gleaming in a way that would have pleased even Vallon. A sound caught his attention. Turning, he saw the cause of his sensitive gray's disquiet.

Not far from a cluster of apple trees, a gas-powered balloon was in sharp descent. It looked precariously as though it might topple, then was righted by the breeze. The duke leaped in sudden, horrified recognition. The twins! He would strangle them if they contrived to come to no harm! He only hoped they would not, as the balloon veered decidedly off course. It was heading for a forest of pines and that, Miles knew, could spell disaster.

He shouted to them, but they were too high to hear. The balloon started dropping, and the duke felt his heart in his mouth. He grabbed hold of the stallion's reins and mounted in a flash. Kicking deftly with his shins, he guided the horse at speed to the fork in the road where the forest began its sinuous path through the wooded countryside.

As he watched, the faces staring out from the wide, teetering basket took on their familiar forms. He saw, to his relief, that his wards were not alone. They were accompanied, puzzlingly, by the earl of Surrey, his sister, and Viscount Lyndale.

The duke approached, and the miscreants alighted with impish delight. "Did you see that, Uncle! Did you? We were flying! We were flying! Oh, isn't it heavenly, Rupert? Did you see?" The Ladies Georgina and Grace were euphoric, and the duke found himself unwittingly smiling, loathe to spoil their bright enjoyment.

"We sent a message down to Cassandra to share in the fun! We wanted her to see the ascent, and she came around immediately with Lord Frances!"

"I hope you don't mind, Your Grace! We knew you were out of town and thought it advisable to at least supervise the event." Frances looked apologetic. "As you may imagine, putting a halt to it was impossible."

"I do imagine!" The duke's tone was dry. "Am I to apprehend you have made this journey all the way from London?" His tone was mockingly incredulous.

Frances smiled appreciatively. "No, sir. A compromise was reached. We traveled by chaise and brought the contraption with us. We are stabled at the Red Sails Inn. Do you know it?"

"No, but I have heard of it. All's well that ends well, then.

What a flight that must have been!" He frowned at Rupert and told him that as a penance he was to look after the scoundrels for the whole course of the day. "For" he said, eyeing Cassandra with a lopsided grin she found wholly endearing, "I find I have better things to do with my time!" He helped her down from the basket and decided that his questions would wait.

A cursory review of the time decided him that Lady Suzannah would be homeward bound. If Frances were to set off by foot to the Langford country seat, he would surely arrive coincidentally with, or some time after, the said lady. Not, by his calculations, before. He begged a trifling favor of the earl and pointed him in the right direction.

Rupert he directed to the frozen lake, which he was certain would interest his young rapscallions. He convinced the contrite young lord not to worry about dismantling the bright sails from the basket, since this could be done much later and with a great deal more precision than the twins were likely to contribute. Rupert nodded his thanks with such a sparkle in his eye that the duke was moved to cuff him fondly.

"Do you know," he said, "I just happen to have been provided with a lunch ample to my needs!" He moved to his gray and produced a light luncheon from the saddlebag. If it was anything like as sumptuous as that with which he had been provided the previous day, his wards would make no complaint. With a grateful wave they set off toward the lake, the young viscount gloomily beset by a million questions to which he had no knowledgeable reply.

He began by telling little falsehoods, but soon his stories had grown to such whiskers that the mirth of the twins could be heard on the other side of the park.

The duke looked down at Cassandra. She was looking very fetching, her hair as free as when he had first laid eyes on her, her cheeks shining from the cold, brisk fresh air. She said nothing, but her eyes were speaking. The duke moved toward her and she clung to him. After a moment, he felt his coat to be wet with sobs, and he held her gently away from him so that he could tenderly patch a tear.

"You received my note?"

She nodded, then rubbed her eyes as they lit with laughter. "Your groom arrived hotfoot from Shropshire! I swear he must have ridden without ceasing all the way! Despite the disapproval of your butler and the various hierarchy of house lackeys, he insisted on presenting it to me in person and with such a flourish I was hard-pressed not to laugh!"

"I'll wager he did not stop to wash, either."

"You would win, then, for indeed, he was in a state of grime the like of which you have not before seen!"

"Oh, I think I have."

The duke looked at her meaningfully, and Cassandra blushed. She was not to be turned from her subject, however. "Who *is* that man?"

His Grace grinned. "The bane of my life! That is the problem with old retainers: you can never get rid of them and they always think they know you best! Old George, I am sorry to say, read me such a lecture on the evils of letting pretty maidens like you slip through my very fingers that I was hard-pressed not to give him his comeuppance!"

Cassandra laughed. "He is quite a character, your George! I left him happily cozening your housekeeper into parting with a fresh-baked partridge pie and a huge leg of smoked game. It will not surprise me to hear he is into your hock, for I heard him wheedling Pickering myself!"

The duke's eyes softened as he placed his arm around her waist and drew her closer. "He may have my whole cellar, for all I care! He deserves it! He brought you back to me."

His mouth was very close to hers, and Cassandra could feel her senses reeling. The duke's tone was as tender as silk, and his firm mouth looked tantalizing. She felt her body stiffen with a strange, unfamiliar but quite delightful sensation and she moved yet closer, her eyes closing almost by themselves.

"Forgive me for being such a toplofty old gudgeon?"

She nodded, her mouth offering a most tempting reply.

The duke moved closer still, and the tension was unbearable yet piquantly exciting. His fingers lightly caressed her bodice, and she felt on fire. He played with her laces, and the thought never once crossed her mind that she should slap him, as she had on that first day. Instead, she wantonly moved closer, her cheeks flushed and yielding.

"I have something for you!"

"What can it be?" His Grace looked surprised, but continued playing with the tips of her emerald ribbons. They were of the softest satin and deliciously frivolous. She ducked out of reach, however, and removed one of the dainty lime gloves she had affected for the trip. She shook it out, but with no evident success. Undaunted, she squinted deep inside and removed her other glove so that her fingers were free to explore.

With a satisfied dimple she found what she was seeking and placed it in the palm of His Grace's elegantly jeweled hand. He turned it over in puzzlement. Then a gratifyingly slow smile spread over his face as comprehension dawned.

"Vixen! Do you say you have kept this all the time?"

She nodded. "In my ribbon drawer. Hidden among a wealth of baubles and childish treasures. You can have no notion of how many times I have looked at it!"

"Has it brought you any of the good luck I promised, my sweet?" There was a gleam in the duke's eye as he pocketed his penny. Cassandra found she could only nod, though for some strange reason, her heart was beating far quicker than it strictly ought to have. The duke cursed under his breath, afflicted in the same curious manner. Then in a sudden unexpected movement, he lifted her chin so that he was looking deep into her dark, midnight eyes. It would fascinate him always how the vivid blue mirrored her every mood.

He murmured something, and for a moment she did not understand. His whisper was tickling her ear far too outrageously to concentrate. Then light dawned. Her lips formed a curvaceous, sultry, "Oh."

The earl waited patiently as his lady love emitted her characteristic, thoroughly beloved gurgle of laughter.

"Yes," she said. "Oh, yes, my dear lord! Cherry ripe themselves *do* cry."

The earl silently thanked the poet Herrick before setting aside all literary concerns and kissing Miss Cassandra Beaumaris so thoroughly that she could quote no more. Miss Beaumaris, it must be reported, did not appear to mind in the least. Rather, she curled her arms about the duke and returned his favor in kind.